Where the Road Takes You

Where the Road Takes You

E.E. "Doc" Murdock

H.O.T. Press
Publishing fine books since 1983

H.O.T. Press
Los Angeles, California
www.hotpresspublishing.com

ISBN: 0-923178-47-3
ISBN-13: 978-0-923178-47-5

Books by E.E. "Doc" Murdock4

Novels

- **The Stealth Genius**
- **Death as Concept**
- **The Storyteller of Cottage H**
- **The Robots of Cottage H**
- **God's Messenger – God's Victim**: A *Bildungsroman* Stockholm Syndrome Novel
- **The Pain Artist:** An American Hikikomori
- **My Vietnam War**
- **A Psalm for Cock Robin**: A Harp and His (Dead) Mother Mystery
- **Crueltown**: A Drew Steele Los Angeles-Las Vegas Mystery
- **The End of the Civil War**: A Drew Steele Civil War Mystery
- **Who Owns Arizona**: A Drew Steele Civil War Mystery

Textbooks/How-To Books

- **How to Write Fiction: Tools and Techniques**
- **Self Management: A Guide to More Effective Study**
- **Computers Today**
- **Computers the Easy Way**
- **Windows the Easy Way**
- **DOS the Easy Way**
- **HyperCard the Easy Way**
- **dBASE the Easy Way**

History/Political Books

- **From Washington & Adams to Trump & Biden:** The Stories behind the Story of Every Presidential Election, With Special Focus on the *Volatile* Presidential Election of 2020
- **From Washington & Adams to Hillary & Trump:** The Stories behind the Story of Every Presidential Election

Acknowledgments

I am indebted to the members of the Ojai Writing Workshop who provided valuable feedback as I worked through the many drafts of this book. I would also like to acknowledge the help of all my students at California State University, Long Beach who taught me so much. And of course, without Zoe, this book would not exist.

Chapter One

Call me John. It's the name they stuck on me after they found me in a dirty back alley where my mother dumped me right after I was born. Or so they say. What is truth when you don't know the truth?

Now that I've told you that, forget it. It happened a long time ago, a little over twenty years ago, in fact. And don't feel sorry for me. I don't. So what if they gave me an ordinary name, John Smith, and then bounced me from one foster home to another until I was sixteen. Why should that matter now? It's in the past.

Despite that not-ordinary start in life, I turned out pretty ordinary. Too ordinary, I think. Look at me: ordinary brown hair, ordinary brown eyes, tall but not too tall, just ordinary tall. And growing up, I pretty much did the normal stuff. Not much to report there. The only thing I did that was sort of not so ordinary was join the high school cross country running team. I did okay at that because I like to run, but who notices a skinny kid running around in a park. It's not as if I was on the football team. The truth is that cross country running was about the only thing I ever found interesting at school. The classes were not very challenging; didn't seem to be leading anywhere. I figured if I wanted to learn stuff, why not spend my time reading in the library. So, I spent a lot of time there, not reading anything in particular, just absorbing.

Now that I'm old enough to be on my own, I sure don't want to keep on doing ordinary things. Problem is, I'm still stuck in Illinois, smack in the middle of the American Midwest, home of the ordinary. And so what if I got good grades in school? I was only getting those good grades in public schools in a central Illinois town. Not exactly genius territory.

Still, one high school teacher did tell me I was so smart I should definitely go to college. But how is that going to happen?

College takes money, and I don't have any. Since I graduated from high school, I've been working random construction jobs, trying to get enough money to go to college. Problem is, the standard pay for young construction day workers like me is a dollar an hour. At a dollar an hour, how could I ever save up enough money to go to college? What little money I earn doesn't last long; by the time I get something to eat, buy a few clothes at the Salvation Army thrift store, and pay the rent on my shabby little rented room in the shabby part of town, there's hardly enough of my earnings left to put gas in my good old 1954 Chrysler New Yorker. It's a big car, so I nicknamed it "Moby" after the name of a whale in a great book I read. It runs good because I carefully rebuilt the engine and made everything perfect.

So, should I go ahead and admit that college will never happen for me? No, maybe I just need a different approach. Maybe try something new. In the past, I was good at trying new things, but that sometimes got me into trouble. Luckily, in this ordinary Midwestern town, they don't throw juvenile trouble-makers in jail; they just put you on probation and tell you to mend your ways—or else. I did mend my ways, which unfortunately, made me, like I said, ordinary.

Well, people said the nineteen sixties were going to be different, but here we are, almost halfway through them, and nothing is changing, at least not for me. After work, I'm doing the usual thing, just sitting in Moby, watching ducks swim around in the pond. It's the same pond in the same park where I spent time as a kid, riding my bike, taking unnecessary chances doing trick jumps, just to do it. Until I broke my arm.

But who cares about a stupid broken arm. That was years ago. The arm healed, and I gave up bikes and bike tricks after I figured out how to rebuild the engines of old cars. My first rebuild was only a ratty old '51 Chevy, but I got it running good, all by myself. The important thing about having a car is that you can get girls for backseat romances. At first, those back seat romances were interesting, even kind of exciting. But that too eventually became pretty much ordinary, like everything else.

I don't have any friends, but if I had any, they'd probably tell me to be more satisfied with what I have. After all, nobody else seems to want anything to change. But I keep thinking, how can they be so . . . satisfied? That's the word, satisfied. Everybody seems so damn satisfied with what they've got. Even those ducks. Look at them. They do the same thing every day, swim around in the same old pond, going nowhere. They've got wings; why don't they fly away somewhere else? If I had wings, I'd fly away to someplace more interesting.

I guess I *could* fly away, in a way, if I really wanted to. I just got paid some actual cash money for shoveling sand into a cement mixer all day for five days straight. My arms and back are aching, but I was lucky to get that job when the cement truck drivers went on strike. So, with money in my pocket and ol' Moby full of gas, I should go somewhere. But where?

Well, Route 66 goes right through this town. It's a big highway that's supposed to go all the way out to the West Coast, so I should at least go for a drive on it. What's the point of having a good-running car if you don't use it to escape sometimes.

But I can't go too far because today is Friday, rent day, and if I don't pay the rent on my crappy room right on time, the landlord will lock me out. But paying the rent on my room will take up most of the new cash I just earned, and I'll be right back to where I started, broke.

Still, if I wanted to, I could at least go for a drive on that Route 66. I wonder how far I could get before I had to turn back.

Chapter Two

The sun is moving farther to the west, and I'm still on Route 66, still driving away from my hometown. But I keep on going. It feels a bit crazy, what I'm doing, just going to be going, as if some part of my brain, the part that keeps my right foot pressing down on the accelerator, is stuck on *go*.

Now, that felt like a weird thing to think, that part of my brain wants to just keep on going. Well, maybe it is weird, but I think I'll keep on doing it, at least for a little while longer.

A highway sign says I'm thirty miles from St. Louis. St. Louis? Uh oh, now I've done it. I've gone too far. I should turn around and hurry back home before the landlord locks me out of my room. My clothes and my books are back there. The only clothes I have with me are the work clothes I have on, and my good old running shoes. Actually, I guess I do happen to have a spare T-shirt in the back seat, and I suppose I *could* buy another pair of pants at a thrift store somewhere. So, I might as well just keep driving. Why not?

It takes me some time to figure out the weird twists and turns to get through St. Louis, but now I'm out of the city, and the highway has turned toward the west, toward the setting sun.

Should I go on? Well, why not? It's already too late to get back in time to pay my room rent, and I've seen what the landlord does when somebody doesn't pay the rent right on time; he throws all your stuff out onto the yard and changes the door lock.

Aw, who cares. My good old Moby is taking me somewhere I've never been before. Why not go on for a while longer to see where this Route 66 takes me.

It's getting dark. I think I must be somewhere in Missouri. The highway has turned into three lanes, and that means drivers can use the middle lane to pass—if you're brave enough to do it. Of course, with the monster Chrysler Hemi engine that's in good old Moby, I've got enough power to pass anybody whenever I feel like it. And why not? Might as well make some time while I'm on this three-lane part of Route 66. I know it's risky trying to pass in the dark using the center lane, but not many other cars are risking it, so it's helping me make good time. Sometimes, I'm able to get Moby up to over a hundred. Finally, no limits, no restrictions.

Whoa, look out!

Geez, that was a close one. Another fast moving car, coming from the other direction, was also passing using the center lane. I wonder if it was another young guy like me in a fast car. Maybe I'd better wait to pass until I can see farther ahead.

Damn, the three-lane highway has ended. Now it's only two lanes, and there's not much of a shoulder. Hard to pass anybody on this busy two-lane road. Where am I now? What comes after Missouri? Kansas? Oklahoma?

The highway diverts me through a small town. Slow speed limit. There are probably cops hanging about to give tickets in these small towns. Hopefully, they won't nab me.

I'm out of that small town and back on the highway, but I'm not getting too far because there's road construction. They're using big floodlights, which must mean they're working on this Route 66 highway twenty-four hours a day. I think they're widening it, probably to make it four lanes. Because of the construction, sometimes there's only one lane open, so we have to take turns to get by. Flagmen—actually, it's usually flagboys, teenagers—tell me when it's my turn to go.

I'm finally out of that road construction area and again roaring through the night. A sign finally tells me I'm in Oklahoma. Oklahoma? I guess that means I'm finally "Out West." So far, Out West, at least the Oklahoma version, is mostly flat, with not as many towns as in Illinois. Who would have thought that once I started driving I'd end up this far from the town I grew up in. Well, at least I'm someplace I've never been before. To tell the truth, I'm driving without any kind of plan, just heading west, passing every car I see.

But that's good, definitely not an ordinary thing to be doing.

I've always dreamed about going Out West. Well, now I'm doing it.

Actually, I'm not exactly sure what defines Out West. I guess I must have thought it's where cowboys ride horses and herd cattle. At least, they used to do that. Who knows what it's like now. I guess if I keep driving, when the sun comes up, I'll find out what it looks like.

I pass a drive-in movie. Not sure what the movie is. Looks like gunfighters shooting at each other. No time to stop and look at anything like that.

I pass a lit-up weird-looking motel that has rooms shaped like wigwams. I wonder what it would be like to sleep in a concrete wigwam.

But I don't need a motel because I don't need sleep. I never have worry about falling asleep driving, because I already did that, and it didn't work out so well. The fact is, I'm lucky to still be alive. One night after a party out by the lake, I knew I'd had too much to drink to make it back home, so I just kept driving, looking for a good place to pull over and get a few hours sleep in the back seat of the old rebuilt Pontiac I was driving. I guess I must have fallen asleep still driving, because I woke up to the sound of crashing metal and found myself not in the car anymore. Then, I was in water. I must have gotten thrown out in midair, landing in the lake. Landing in the water meant I didn't even get hurt, or at least not very much. I was bobbing about in the lake, staring back at the Pontiac's two headlights that were under water, pointing down at the lake bottom. Since, I wasn't dead, there was nothing to do but swim back to shore. I climbed back up to the road and managed to get some passersby to go call a tow truck.

Ever since then, I know I will *never* again fall asleep driving. If I ever do feel even a little bit sleepy while driving, the memory of that near-death experience floods into my mind and creates such a strong feeling of panic, I'm instantly wide awake.

I pass a diner made out of an old-fashioned train car. It has a huge neon sign that says "GOOD EATS." I know I'll have to get something to eat sooner or later, but I don't want to waste what little money I have on restaurant food. Maybe I'll get something to snack on at one of the gas stations. I do have to stop every once in a while to get gas. But that doesn't take long. I don't even turn off my car's engine because once it gets heated up, the six-volt battery isn't near powerful enough to turn over Moby's big old engine fast enough to start. I leave the car running while I gas up and pay. Then, I'm right back on the road.

I'm not sure exactly where I am now, but I do know I'm making good time, and that gives me a feeling of . . . what? Excitement, I guess is the word. Maybe awe is an even better word; what a thing to be driving and driving, not stopping for anything except gas, getting farther and farther from home. But I guess I shouldn't call where I was living home anymore. I guess I don't have any home now.

Well, is that what I wanted? Maybe I unconsciously wanted to start driving and not stop in order to force some kind of change in my life. So, where will my new home be? Wherever I stop, I guess, and who knows where that will be. Actually, I think anywhere I land will be better than where I was. At least it will be different, and therefore, not ordinary.

Seems like it should be getting light soon. Good. At least I'll be able to see what the countryside around here looks like.

The highway diverts me into another small town. Not much is open, but there is an open gas station. Nineteen cents a gallon. Not bad. Might as well fill ol' Moby up.

Back on Route 66, it's starting to get light. It's a pretty good road now, so I can push old Moby really fast. And not too many diversions into small towns anymore, which probably means there aren't many towns out here to divert into. Pretty desolate country, but even that's interesting because it's so different. It's flat, but not like Illinois flat with fields on both sides. And those Illinois fields often contain tall corn. Those "walls" of corn stalks used to drive me crazy: I'd get sick of seeing only the four walls of the shabby room I was living in, so I'd go out for my one escape, driving around the countryside. But the endless corn fields on both sides made it feel like I was still stuck inside of walls. Out here in the West, the country is also really flat, but with only grasses you can see for miles. No more walls!

The road takes me over a little rise, so I can see a long way ahead. In the distance, there's a gigantic hole in the ground. Now what could have created a hole that big? Some kind of sink-hole? Mining maybe?

When I get closer to the supposed big hole, I realize it isn't a hole after all, only the dark shadow of a cloud. Joke's on me. I guess I'm going to have to get used to how different things look out here.

I'm coming to another town. Sign says it's Oklahoma City.

Oklahoma City turns out to be a big, spread-out place. Endless businesses next to the road, motels with bright signs, places to eat promising really good food, gas stations competing for the lowest price. I pass a big trading post with lots of signs advertising Indian stuff. I wonder what kinds of Indian stuff would they have. Looks interesting, but no time to stop for that kind of thing.

Oklahoma City is hardly more than a memory when a sign tells me I'm entering Texas. I'm in Texas! For sure that means I really am now "Out West."

So far, it doesn't look much different than Oklahoma, but there is a scattering of cattle out there.

But no cowboys. Maybe they don't have cowboys any-more. But I'm not disappointed; I wanted to know what new places would be like, and now I'm seeing it.

A sign says I'm entering New Mexico. Looks a lot like Texas.

A sign says Truth or Consequences is to the south. Is that a town? The actual name of a town?

On and on, still not much to see. But I'm able to go really fast and see a lot of the country. That's fun.

Every once in a while, there's a series of little signs on fence posts. As I fly by, the sequences of signs spell out messages:

> Does your husband
> Misbehave
> Grunt and grumble
> Rant and rave
> Shoot the brute some
> Burma-Shave

Some of them have obviously been there for a long time:

> Let's make Hitler
> And Hirohito
> Feel as bad
> as Old Benito
> Buy War Bonds
> Burma-Shave

Next is one that seems like a warning to me personally:

> Hardly a driver
> Is now alive
> Who passed
> On hills
> At 75
> Burma-Shave

I'm not heeding that warning though; can't slow down until I get where I'm going.

Wherever that is.

A sign says I'm entering Arizona. By the time I pass Holbrook and Winslow, my gas gauge says I'm getting close to empty.

Ahead is a gas station that's part of a trading post, marked by two giant arrows stuck into the ground. I pull in and fill Moby up. Then, I park and take a chance to turn off the engine while I go into the trading post to try to find something to eat. Turns out they don't have much to eat, but they are selling Snickers bars, two for a dime. That'll have to do for now. I grab a handful and take them to the cashier who's an old guy with a ragged white beard and penetrating eyes. He takes my money and says, "No wonder you're so skinny if this is what you eat."

I wonder if people Out West here will think I'm too skinny. I say, "Well, I'm a runner. Was a runner, anyway. High school cross country team."

"Oh yeah? Where was that?"

"Illinois."

"Did you drive all the way from Illinois? How many days that take you?"

"Oh, not long. I just drove straight here."

Another customer is waiting, an older woman, but he's ignoring her. "Straight through? No way. You must have at least pulled over for a little sleep occasionally."

"Nope. Just drove."

"All the way from Illinois? Now I get it, Bub. You don't eat, you don't sleep, you just drive."

I answer his questioning look with a shrug.

"So, where ya headin'?"

"Well, I'm not really sure. Just seeing the West."

"Well, you keep on heading west, and you'll end up in LA. You won't like it there."

"I won't?"

"Nope. It's not the West. It's a great big city, and not like the big cities back east neither. Too many cars and too many people in a hurry."

I'm not sure what I'm looking for, but it's not too many cars and people in a hurry, so I say, "Okay, where do *you* think the West is?"

"My advice is go south. Flagstaff is just ahead. When you get there, turn south and go down to Phoenix. It's in the desert. Actually, if I was you, I'd go on through Phoenix to Tempe. Big state college there. Arizona State U. You interested in college?"

"Yes, actually, I am. No money though."

"I get it. Then ASU is the place for you. It's a low-priced college. I went for one year. Quite a while back. You ever do construction work?"

"Sure."

"Then you'll do good in Tempe. The university's growing fast, so that means new off-campus apartments goin' up all over the place. Plenty of construction jobs for young strong guys. Hot down there, though. You mind heat?"

"No, I don't think so."

"Then you'll do fine. Just drink lots of water."

The woman elbows her way past me. I guess she was tired of waiting.

The guy takes her money, and then, sure enough, asks her where she's coming from.

I go back outside, but before I get to my car, I notice a drinking fountain. That guy telling me to drink lots of water reminds me that I haven't been drinking anything since I left Illinois. I go to the drinking fountain and drink as much as I can. Then, I go to my car and grab a couple of old empty pop bottles off of the back seat floor. I fill both of them with water. Then, I walk back over to the gas station and get a map of Arizona.

Back in my car, I eat a Snickers bar while I look at the map. It shows a curvy highway from Flagstaff to Phoenix. That guy said if I head south, it'll be desert. I think I'd like to see a desert.

Now, let's see if old Moby's big engine has cooled off enough to start. The car's engine turns over in a slow grumbling way, but then it starts right up. A good sign. I think it means I probably should take that curvy road to Phoenix and check out the desert. The guy said there was a low-priced state college there. I should check that out, too. When I headed west on the spur of the moment, I wasn't really thinking about my dream of going to college; I just wanted to go somewhere different. But now, Arizona seems like a place I should check out. A cheap college and lots of construction jobs.

A sign says I'm coming to an intersection with another highway. It must be the one that leads to Phoenix. I really would like to go see California, but why not take a little detour to see the desert. If it's not interesting there, I can always drive on to the West Coast.

Chapter Three

I take the turn off Route 66, and soon the narrow and twisty two-lane highway tells me I'd better pay attention. I'm still not getting very sleepy, but I've never driven a mountain road before, and for sure, not at night. My headlights aren't very bright, so I guess I could pull over somewhere and wait for daylight. I might even be able to get a little sleep. One of the good things about Moby is that it has a big back seat. I slept in it when I didn't have a real place to live, and I still keep my sleeping bag back there, just in case.

But why stop? If I'm going, why not just keep on going.

I go around a curve and yikes! deer on the road. Lots of them! And they don't move. They just look up at me, as if they got frozen by my headlights. No way to get stopped in time, so I try to guide Moby through without hitting any of them.

Somehow, I make it through without hitting a single deer. Lucky for them that they just froze when they saw me coming, so I could find a path through them. Better slow down though, until I get out of these mountains.

Finally, the road begins to straighten out, and just as the sky starts to get lighter in the east, I come down out of the mountains into a broad valley. Sure enough, like that guy said, it's a desert. But it's not a sand dunes type desert; it's a desert that has lots of low-lying bushes, along with a variety of odd-looking sticker plants mixed in. I assume those plants must be cactuses. Never seen a real live cactus before. New things to see already! Glad I decided to drive down here to check this area out.

It was cool enough in the mountains that I had to use some heat, but now, when I click the heater off, it feels like it's stuck on. I roll down my window, and a blast of hot air hits me. Wow! Can it really be this hot at dawn? For sure never felt anything like this in Illinois. I guess deserts and heat are an aspect of the West I'm going to learn about. I lean over to also roll down the passenger side window. Might as well get some kind of breeze going through the car, even if it is a hot breeze.

Soon, a sign welcomes me to Phoenix, "The Valley of the Sun." Valley of the sun, eh? If it's this hot at dawn, how hot is it going to get when the sun is high overhead?

I don't have air conditioning in ol' Moby. Never even thought about needing it back in Illinois. If I hang around this area for a while, I guess I won't have to worry about a freezing cold winter, like back in Illinois. But am I really thinking about staying here for a while? Who knows?

A wide street leads me past a warehouse area, and then past a lot of small businesses and motels, and then, it takes me right through the middle of downtown Phoenix. Only a few mul-tistory buildings. Phoenix may be a big city, but it's not at all like Chicago, the one big city I went to in Illinois. The only sort-of tall building on this main street looks kind of old. It has a big sign on top: "Hotel Sahara." I guess that's a fitting name for a hotel in this hot desert climate.

A lot of small stores. A Birch's Drug Store has a big bright Coca Cola sign on the front of it. A Dr. Scholl's shoe store has a sign that says "Feet Hurt?" Kind of surprising there would be such small stores on this downtown street; gives Phoenix a kind of small-town feel.

As I leave the main part of the city, it suddenly gets indus-trial. More warehouses, and then a stinky stockyards.

But then, just as suddenly, it's all desert again. A desert this close to a big city? Now that I think about it, I wonder what made them decide to build a city in the middle of a desert in the first place.

I pass a strange looking castle-like stone house all by itself in the middle of desert land. It's surrounded by lots of cac-tuses, so many it makes me wonder if they were planted there. The place has a weird and interesting feel to it, like an old desert ghost mansion. I wonder who could possibly live there, Doctor

Frankenstein?

A sign says Tempe is just ahead. That's where the guy at the trading post said the university was.

The road takes me over a long bridge, but I can see that there's only a dry riverbed way down below. With this tall of a bridge, they must sometimes get a lot of water in that riverbed.

Coming down off the bridge, I enter the town of Tempe. There's a big white concrete building on my left. The sign says "Hayden Mills," and it has a huge painting of a bag of flour on the wall. The building looks old and out of place right here in the downtown part of the city. And there's a big rocky hill behind it that comes almost to the street. Never seen that kind of a big hill in Illinois, and for sure, not right at the edge of a downtown area. I can tell already this place is not going to be anything like where I came from. Good. Just what I wanted.

Soon, I'm driving past what the sign says is Arizona State University. The buildings I can see look very modern, not at all like what I imagined a university would look like. Must be a new university. It might be exactly the kind of unusual college I'd like to go to, if I can somehow figure out a way to pay for it.

It's early in the day, and I'm still not feeling too sleepy. Might as well stop and check the university out. I find a place to park in the neighborhood and walk to the campus.

Walking through the campus, I come to a building that's identified as the Student Union. I smell food. I guess I'm finally feeling a little hungry. Inside, I find where the smells are coming from—a big cafeteria. Not many students. Too early in the day, I guess. Or maybe because it's summer there may not be as many students on campus. I grab a tray and push it along the chrome rails, but nothing looks good enough to waste what little money I have on. When I get to the cashier without anything on my tray, the young woman looks at me oddly. I just shrug and take the tray back to where I found it.

Wandering around the building, I come across a bulletin board with lots of little scraps of paper stuck to it. Mostly people selling things or looking for rides somewhere, but there is a hand-

written note looking for a student to do outdoor painting. Painting? I can do that. But do I want to take a job here? Is this where
I want to stay? Well, maybe the new not-ordinary me should try
to get this job. If I can get used to the heat, I might as well do
some painting as anything else. Make a few bucks and then
decide where to go next.

Chapter Four

To make sure nobody beats me to the job, I take the note off of the board and look at the address. It's on Lemon Tree Drive. The note doesn't say where Lemon Tree Drive is, but the fact that they put their note on this university bulletin board must mean it's close to this campus.

I hurry back to my car and drive into the first gas station I come to. I pull in, and the young guy that comes out cheerfully asks me how much gas I want. I ask him where Lemon Tree Drive is, and he isn't as cheerful when he points back the way I just came from. He says Lemon Tree Drive is close to the university, only a couple of blocks south of the main street.

It doesn't take me long to find the place listed on the job offer; it's a cluster of six single-story apartments leading away from the street. They're made of concrete blocks, painted yellow. I guess yellow makes sense for apartments on a street named for lemon trees. The buildings are a bit run down. A fresh coat of paint would help, so I bet that's the painting job.

I get out and start looking for the manager's apartment. It turns out to be the one farthest back from the street. I knock on the door, and when a man opens it, I show him the note and say, "I'm here about the painting job. Are you the manager?"

He nods, and as he looks me over, I look him over. He's not very tall, and he's not as thin as I am. Probably in his late thirties. Oddly, for a guy living in this hot desert, his face and arms aren't tanned at all. He must spend all his time indoors.

He says, "You do outside painting before? It's gonna be hot."

I can't tell this guy I haven't really ever done any painting of outside walls, especially not in the heat, so I just say, "Oh, sure. No problem." I think I managed to sound sort of confident.

"Well, I can only pay you a dollar an hour."

"Sure, that's what I'm used to."

He says, "Well, I guess you'll do. When can you start?"

"Uh, anytime. Right now, I guess. That is, if you've got a place for me to live. A vacant apartment maybe?"

He shakes his head. "There are no vacancies. I thought you were a student at the university."

"Oh, right, I am. At least I'm going to be. As soon as the fall semester starts. I just rolled into town and went to campus to get something to eat. That's how I found your notice. I haven't found a place to live yet."

"Well, I don't have an empty apartment."

"That's all right. I can sleep in my car until I find a place." I point at my car back out on the street.

He frowns. "You don't have any money to rent a room or something?"

"No problem. It's got a big back seat."

A very attractive dark-haired woman appears behind him. His wife? She seems quite a bit younger than him. Maybe only a few years older than me.

She says, "Harold, we can't have him sleeping in his car out on the street. Why can't he sleep in the shed?"

He looks back at her. "The storage shed?"

"Well," she says, "it used to be an apartment, didn't it? The bathroom back there still works, doesn't it?"

"Yeah, but Debbie, it's where I store . . . everything."

"Well, let him clean it up. It's better than him sleeping in his car."

The manager turns back to me. "Yeah, I guess you can sleep back there. But only as long as the painting job lasts, okay?"

"Sure. That's fine with me."

She disappears back inside their apartment, and he leads me to a sort of lean-to room with a low slanting ceiling that's attached to the back of their apartment. It's obvious he's been using it as a depository for junk, whatever he doesn't want to throw away. Stuff is stacked all over the place.

He says, "There's a bathroom, but it might be plugged up. Hasn't been used for years. But you can probably get it going. There's a plunger in here . . . somewhere. And there's a cot over there." He points. "You can dig it out while I go to the paint store. There's still plenty of time before dark, so you can get started painting right away. The owner came by yesterday and threw a fit about how run-down the place was looking. He wants it spiffied up right away. And you'll have to do it right, too, 'cause it's my neck on the line. Got it?"

"Sure, no problem. And thank you for letting me sleep back here."

"Well, that was my wife's idea, but I guess you might as well. If you don't mind sleeping in the middle of all this clutter. I'll be back with the paint pretty soon."

He leaves, and I look the shed over. It's a real mess. Obviously, the guy just tosses things in here, without any real storage plan. I can see the open door to the bathroom, but there's no real path to it. I hope he's right that the plumbing still works.

Oh well, I guess beggars can't be choosers. It's actually kind of a miracle that I found this job only a few minutes after I hit this town. What more could I ask, a little money coming in, and a free place to live while I figure out what I'm going to do next. Maybe just driving away from Illinois to let whatever happens happen was a pretty crazy idea, but look how well it's turning out.

I pull my car back next to the shed and start cleaning up the place. I dig my way to a narrow cot by stacking all the junk against the wall. I also clear a path to the bathroom. It's a tiny bathroom, but there is a small window. Not much of a view though, only the back wall of the manager's apartment. The sunlight is pretty bright out there, but I think I can see right into their bathroom. I wonder if they know about that.

I crawl under the sink and turn the water on. Unfortunately, there's a small leak. I don't want to mention that to the manager. He might use it as an excuse to not let me sleep here. I go out to my car and get a pair of pliers. Luckily, it only takes a few twists to stop the leak. I also turn the water to the toilet on, and after a few tries, it seems to flush fine. So far, so good.

The manager comes back with a five-gallon plastic bucket of yellow paint, a couple of paint brushes, and a paint roller on a pole. He expects me to get right to work, saying the owner might come by at any time to see that it's being done.

I say I'm ready to start, even though I'm starting to feel really run down, if not actually sleepy. I guess my non-stop driving is finally starting to hit me. But I'm not going to tell him that. If he noticed how tired I look, he doesn't mention it. Maybe he can't imagine a twenty-year-old boy getting tired.

He goes back into his apartment and leaves me to get started painting on my own. It's damn hot. I noticed a box-like air conditioner is built into the wall of his apartment, and it's humming away, so what does he care if it's hot out here.

I grab the painting stuff and go out to get started. Thinking that the owner of the apartments might show up at any time to check on my progress, I start with the front wall of the apartment that's closest to the street. Besides, right now, that part is in the shade.

I open the paint bucket and pour some of it into the roller pan. I know as soon as I start using the roller, I'm sure to get my T-shirt speckled with yellow paint, so I take it off. My pants are going to get covered too, but they're actually my work pants, so no problem. Amazing to think that yesterday after work I didn't even go home to change my clothes; I just started driving without a thought about it.

No, wait, that wasn't yesterday. It was the day before. Hard to believe all that's happened since I lit out from Illinois.

Oh well, better get started painting. I've never actually painted an outside wall before, so I'd better develop a wall-painting technique.

I soak the roller in the roller tray to get it really full of paint, and then I slop it onto the wall. Next, I roll all that paint out smooth. That works okay. I hope the manager isn't unhappy that I'm dripping some of the yellow paint on the ground. But it's just gravel, so I think later I'll be able to stir up the gravel a bit to hide most of the paint drips. When I get to the windows and doors, I have to slow down and be extra careful because they're white. I use the smallest brush to avoid getting yellow paint on the white areas, so it takes me as much time to go carefully around a window with the small paint brush as it does to paint a whole wall yellow with the roller.

For some reason, the slow detailing process around windows and doors makes me a lot more aware of how hot it is. Needing to focus also makes my sleepy eyes blurry. I hope the manager doesn't think I'm intentionally going slow to get more of my dollar-an-hour pay, but I know if he comes out to watch, he'll see I'm actually painting pretty fast and doing a good job.

The painting is becoming a grind: soak the roller, slop paint onto the wall, roll it out. Then comes the slow detail work around the windows and doors. I'm making pretty good progress as I work my way around the building, and surprisingly, the manager hasn't come out to check on my progress.

People come and go out of the apartments, but they don't pay much attention to me. They're not young people, so probably not students. Odd, since these apartments are close to the university. Maybe the owner doesn't like to rent to students.

"You must be hot."

I turn. It's the manager's pretty wife. She's holding out a tall, frosty-looking glass that reminds me I've been forgetting to drink anything.

I look the young woman over. She's dressed in a yellow dress that's sort of the same color as the paint I'm putting on the walls, a dress so lightweight it looks like it could blow away in the breeze. If there was any breeze.

She says, "Don't you want it?"

"Oh, yes. Sure I do. Thanks." I take the glass from her and gulp down half of it. "I was just remembering a guy who told me to drink a lot, and I haven't been doing it."

"Oh, what guy was that?"

"Oh, just a guy I met on the road. At a gas station."

"You've been on the road?"

"Yeah, I just drove in from Illinois."

"Illinois? Really? I've never been there. Actually, I've never been anywhere. Grew up in Coolidge, and got married. That's it."

At first, she seemed happy and light, but now she seems sad. I wonder why. I say, "Uh, Coolidge. Is that near here?"

"Oh, that's right, you're not from around here. Yeah, Coolidge is not too far." She points over her shoulder with her thumb. "Out in the desert. A flyspeck of a place that has a high-way going through it. But nobody ever stops."

She seems unhappy to have come from that town. I don't know what else to say, so I just say, "I haven't been anywhere in Arizona. Not yet. But I do plan to travel around some."

"Well, don't go south. Nothin' down there. Go that way." She points. "The Superstition Mountains are out there. A famous gold mine that got famous for being lost. At least that's what they say. I haven't been out there either. I haven't been anywhere."

"I hadn't been anywhere either before coming here. I just got in my car and started driving. I ended up here."

She's staring at me oddly. Maybe I shouldn't have said all that. I add, "I'm going to start at the university. In the fall."

Now she's gone silent, and she's staring at the ground. For a young woman that pretty, she sure doesn't smile very much. She must be hot because her flimsy dress is sticking to her, espe-cially to her breasts. It means she doesn't have anything on underneath that dress. I wonder what her husband would think about her coming out to talk to me dressed like that. I take another drink of the lemonade, but I don't finish it; if I finish it, she'll probably go away.

Finally, she looks back toward her apartment and says, "Well, I'd better get back or he'll . . . "

"Oh, right," I say, and gulp down the rest of the lemonade.

She takes the glass and walks away. I watch her go. A pretty young woman who says she hasn't been anywhere. She can't be all that much older than me. Maybe she got married right out of high school.

Well, I can't get hung up thinking about her. Better get back to painting.

By the time it starts to get dark, I'm fading. The lack of sleep and the long drive is finally hitting me. I should knock off the painting and go back to my sleeping shed. On the other hand, maybe the night will be cooler. I could get a lot more done if it would only cool off a little. I keep on painting.

But by the time it's completely dark, I'm soaked with sweat, and the night doesn't feel like it's going to offer much relief from the heat. Either way, I've had it. The manager hasn't come out to check on me, and the owner hasn't shown up either, so why not knock off.

I put the lid back on the paint bucket and put some water from an outside faucet into the roller tray. I put the brushes and the roller in there to soak overnight.

Back at the shed, I get my sleeping bag out of my car. Even though it's night now, I know it's still way too hot to actually get into the sleeping bag, but I'll put it under me so I don't have to lie on the dirty canvas of the cot. I'm not sure there's a light in this shed, or even electricity, so I also grab my flashlight.

Inside the shed's bathroom, I take off all my clothes and rinse myself off. Then, I lie down on the cot, trying not to think about the stifling heat. But I can't ignore it. As tired as I am, it's too hot in this shed to sleep. And it's dusty in here, too. There is a window. I wonder if I can get it open. I get up and try to pull it up, but it's stuck. I have a big screwdriver in my car. Maybe I can pry the window open.

I don't bother to put any clothes on because I'm sure everybody is already asleep inside their air-conditioned apartments, but by the time I get to my car, I have second thoughts about being out here naked. I should of at least put some pants on. What if the manager comes out and sees me like this? On the other hand, what if his wife comes out and sees me like this? But would that be so bad?

Now don't start thinking like that. You were lucky to get this job and a place to sleep. You don't want to screw it up now. I get my big screwdriver out of the trunk and start back in. But I notice my last Snickers bar on the backseat. I could eat it before I go to sleep. But I'm still not hungry. I wonder why.

I grab the candy bar and head back inside. In the morning, I'll have to use the last of my money to get something real to eat.

Using the big screwdriver, I do manage to pry the window up a few inches, but if I was hoping for an evening breeze, I'm out of luck. The air still feels hot and still. Hell with it. I've got to get some sleep. I lie down again, and this time, I can't keep my eyes open.

I feel a sharp pain on my chest. I must have been asleep. I try to push the pain away, but I feel something on my chest. I think it was a bug, a big one. I know I knocked it off of my chest, but I probably didn't kill it.

I turn on my flashlight and shine it around the floor. I don't see anything, but there's so much junk piled all around, a bug like that would have plenty of places to hide.

I shine the flashlight on my chest, and sure enough, there's a little red spot where it bit into me. A bug that would bite a human! Has that bug been here since back when this room was used as an apartment? Could it have been waiting here all this time for someone to chew on? Well, whatever it was, now that it's been smacked, it probably won't come back again. Still, I'll keep my flashlight handy.

I feel the same sharp pain in my chest. I must have finally got back to sleep again when I felt that same pain. This time, I don't smack the bug; I grab it. I've got the bug in my hand. I can feel it squirming to get out. I click on my flashlight and carefully open my hand, but just a little.

In a flash, the bug springs out of my hand and races across the floor. It was a big cockroach, and my grabbing it didn't even seem to cripple it. What a tough little bugger!

This time, I saw where it went; it's hiding under an old cabinet. Unfortunately, I piled a bunch of junk on top of that cabinet, so I won't be able to get at it without pulling all of that stuff off. But do I want to go to all that trouble just to try to find the damn bug? The bug would just run back deeper under all the other junk. If I can get through until morning without getting eaten alive, I'll ask the manager if he has any bug spray.

No, that's not a good idea. If he thinks this shed is overrun with bugs, he might not want me sleeping in here. But wait, you'd think in all this junk there'd be some bug spray in here somewhere. I keep the flashlight turned on and start looking. I look in the bathroom cabinet, but it's completely empty. Next, I look in the cabinet the bug ran under. There is a bunch of canned cleaning stuff in there. And a can of Raid! I shake it. There seems to be a little bit of liquid left in it. I try spraying under the cabinet, and luckily some spray does come out. Not a very smart bug to run right under the very cabinet where the can of Raid was stored. Hopefully, I got him, and hopefully he's a loner. Maybe it's been so long since this room was used his brothers and sisters have all taken off. I keep spraying, behind the cabinet and all around it. If that didn't kill the little rascal, it should of at least told him I'm too dangerous to be biting on.

I get back on the cot, but I keep the flashlight and the can of Raid close by. Maybe now I can finally get some sleep.

I open my eyes. It's getting light outside the window. I wonder what time it is. It must be early morning, but it's still hot. Thankfully, the cockroach never came back. I hope he's gone for good. I had planned to go out and get something real to eat today, but now I think I should get some painting done before it gets even hotter. Later, when the sun gets high in the sky, I can go try to find a grocery store to get something to nibble on.

I noticed a metal cup in the cabinet where I found the bug spray, so I get it and go into the bathroom to get some water out of the sink tap. I drink several cups full. In this heat, I need to drink more, like that guy up by Flagstaff told me. And even though I'm not hungry, I should get some food into my stomach. I tear open the Snickers bar, but it's all melted. Oh well, just treat it like chocolate pudding and lap it up.

As soon as I've eaten it all and licked the paper clean, I rinse my hands and put on my pants. I don't bother to put on my shirt. In this kind of heat, no way I'm going to wear a shirt.

Once I get started painting, I'm feeling a little better than yesterday. It means I must have gotten at least a few hours sleep, despite the cockroach wars. .

"You sure are a hard worker."

I turn. It's the manager's wife again, and this time she's dressed in a white dress that looks just as flimsy as the yellow dress she had on yesterday. Unfortunately, this time, she doesn't have any lemonade for me.

She says, "I was just sitting in there watching TV when I realized you were out here working in the heat. I was going to bring you something to drink, but then, I wondered if you'd had anything to eat. Would you like me to bring you something?"

"Oh, you don't have to bother. I can take a break pretty soon and go get something."

"If you do that, he won't pay you for the time you're gone. He's like that. But if I fix you something, you can eat it here like you're still on the job. You can eat and tell me about Illinois. And get paid for it."

"Well . . . "

"No, don't say anything. That way, I can tell him it was all my idea, and he won't be able to blame you." She hurries away.

As I watch her go, I wonder why she's being so nice to me. She said she wanted to talk about Illinois. She's never been anywhere, so she probably just wants to dream about going to other places.

I go back to painting, and soon she's back with two tuna sandwiches on white bread and another large glass of lemonade. I sit down on the sidewalk in the shade to eat, and she surprises me by sitting right next to me, very close. I hope her husband doesn't come out and see how close she's sitting, especially since she's wearing that flimsy dress, and I don't have a shirt on.

"Okay," she says, "tell me about Illinois."

I'm not sure what she wants to hear. She probably doesn't want to hear how ordinary Illinois is, all flatlands with fields filled with crops like corn. "Well, Illinois is pretty much agricultural, except for Chicago. Chicago is a really big city."

"Lots of people in Chicago? And lots of cars?"

"Oh, sure. In Chicago, they're putting in new freeways all over the place." I take a big gulp of the lemonade, and add, "Hey, you'll like this. One of the downtown freeways goes right through a big building. I think it's the post office."

"No kidding? Right through a building? What do the workers in there think of that?"

I chuckle. "When I drove through it, I wondered the same thing. Can you imagine it? You're in there sorting mail or something and a big truck rumbles by over your head."

She laughs. "I bet a thing like that could make you lose track of what you were doing."

"It sure could."

She's silent for a few moments, then, "Okay, what else?"

"Listen, Debbie, the reason—"

"Don't call me Debbie. My parents named me Debbie, but it makes me sound like a little girl. I want you to call me Deb."

"Okay, Deb. My name's John. What I was saying is that the reason I left Illinois is because I wanted a change, to see something different."

"Oh."

She sounds disappointed. I don't want her to think I'm not interesting just because I came from a not-interesting place, so I say, "Traveling is interesting. All along Route 66, there are funny things designed to get you to pull off the road and buy stuff. There are funny giant statues, and . . . other things. Things are painted to look weird. Like old cars. Even some of the water towers are painted funny."

She's staring off into space as she says, "That's what I want to do. Travel. See things . . . different." She sighs. "But that's probably never going to happen as long as . . . ." She glances back toward her apartment.

Is she thinking about her husband in there, doing whatever he does all day? Is she hinting that she'd like to find someone who would take her traveling? No, better not hook into that line of thinking.

As if she also wants to back off from that topic, she suddenly stands up. "Are you finished with your lemonade? I'd better get back inside before he . . . "

I also stand up and hand back her glass. "Right. I'd better get back to work. But it was really nice of you to bring me something to eat. And nice to talk to you."

She stares at me for a long moment, and then says, "You liked talking to me?"

"Sure. You can come out here and talk to me anytime you want to."

"I can? You don't mind me bothering you?"

"Not at all. You could talk to me while I paint."

"Oh. Well, okay then. I'll bring you some more lemonade. I mean, from time to time."

"That would be great."

She hurries away.

As I watch her go, I try to imagine what her life is like. I think she feels stuck. Married young, stuck at home all day. Maybe she also felt stuck in Coolidge, wherever that is, and got married to a city guy to get away. But now she's here in the city, close to a big university, but still stuck.

As I paint, I try to stay in the shade, but it's impossible. The moving sun seems to chase me around each of the apartment buildings, and eventually it's so high in the sky I have no choice but to paint out in direct sunlight. Not only am I worried about getting sunburned, the sun makes the painting harder because the paint dries out too fast; I can't just slop it on and then smooth it out.

I'm grateful when I see Deb coming with another big glass of lemonade.

She beckons for me to come into the shade.

I put the paint roller into the tray and go to take the lemonade from her. As I take it, she touches my fingers, longer than necessary, I think.

She watches me drink, and then moves closer to me, too close if her husband might happen to come out. But I've never seen him since I started this job, so he must not come out very often. I don't move away.

She watches me gulp down the cold lemonade, and then says, "I don't know how you stand it out here, John. You were right out in the sun."

"Well, I ran out of shade."

"The sun moves, doesn't it? So, why not wait for the shade to come back? You can take breaks, you know."

"Uh, well, I wasn't sure. I mean, what your husband might think."

"Oh, you don't have to worry about him. He won't be coming out. He's got his . . . other business. Stays in his office. He doesn't even know I'm bringing you lemonade. He doesn't care what I do, as long as I keep the house clean, bring him his meals, and wash the dishes." She glances back toward their apartment and does a little laugh.

I wonder what that kind of laugh means. I don't think it's a real laugh.

"Hey, try this." She takes out a small spray bottle out of her pocket and sprays my bare chest. "Cooler, eh?"

As the water evaporates, it does feel a little cooler. I say, "Yep. Good idea."

She says, "I use it all the time, when I have to be out here."

She sprays her own chest several times. The water turns her flimsy dress almost completely transparent. I can see her breasts quite clearly. Does she realize what she's doing?

I lift my eyes away from her chest and catch her staring at me. She's got a slight smile on her face. What does that smile mean? Does she like me looking at her breasts? Or is she making fun of me? I don't have enough experience to know what a look like that might mean from a married woman. Before I can think of anything to say, she hands me the spray bottle and says, "Here, go ahead and spray yourself, and then you can tell me more about Illinois.

I do squirt myself a few times, but when I try to hand the spray bottle back to her, she says, "Now you do me."

I cautiously spray her shoulders, but then she sticks her chest out farther, as if inviting me to do something. Does she want me to touch her there? I know I shouldn't do that, no matter how much I'd like to. After all, we're right out here in the open, between two apartments. And both of the apartments have windows. Anybody could be watching from behind their curtains. I hand the spray bottle back to her and say, "Well, I'd probably better get back to painting."

She nods, still smiling. "Okay. I'll just sit here and watch. Until my dress dries."

I go back to painting, and before long, she gets up and goes back into her own apartment. Is she disappointed in me? What did she expect me to do? Have I blown any chance at getting together with her? That seems like what she wants. Or is it? And is that what I want? She's at least a couple of years older than me, and she is married to my boss, my only source of income right now. Maybe even more important, it's a job that provides me with a place to stay, rent free. Maybe she was testing me, seeing what I would do if she gave me the chance? Maybe I could have asked her to come visit me in the shed tonight.

No, I'd better just stick to my painting. This job is only going to take me a few weeks to finish, and then I'll get paid. And then what? I guess I'll have to find another job and find another place to live. And I still need to go check out the university, find out how much it would cost to take a few classes. Maybe I'll meet other girls and have forgotten all about Deb.

Maybe.

When it gets too dark to paint any longer, I put the roller and brush in the roller tray and cover them with water.

Back in the shed, I'm soaked with sweat, so the first thing

I do is go into the bathroom and get completely naked. I wipe myself down all over with a wet rag. The cold water on my skin feels good, so I don't bother to dry off. I lie down on the cot with the wet rag over my chest. It'll have to be my air conditioning, and maybe it will also keep that damn cockroach off of me.

As I lie there in the darkness, staring up at the low slanting ceiling, I suddenly realize I'm hungry. After Deb brought me those two sandwiches, she didn't bring me anything more to eat all day. Was she disappointed in me?

Well anyhow, I'd better go get something to eat first thing in the morning.

I hear water running from behind the wall. I sure hope there isn't another leak in the bathroom. I hop out of bed and go in there to check. But I forgot to grab my flashlight.

I listen, but the sound of water running isn't coming from here, it seems to be coming from behind the wall. Somebody in the connected manager's apartment must be running water. I go to the little window and see what it is: Deb is taking a shower next door. As I noticed before, I can see into their bathroom window. It's only a few feet from my window, and Deb is facing toward me. I can see the entire top half of her, all the way down to her belly button. Damn, she's even more beautiful when she's naked. When her dress was wet, I got a good idea of what her breasts looked like, but now I can see it all. I've seen naked girls before, but that was in the back seat of my car, at night, without much light. Seeing Deb naked now, in her bright bathroom, is . . . different. I'm getting excited, but I'm not sure I should be spying on a married woman through her bathroom window. But I can't stop looking. She's letting water run over herself, and she's looking out her open window, right toward me. Is it possible she knows I can see her? It's dark here in my bathroom, but with that bright overhead light in her bathroom, maybe she can see my face looking out at her.

She closes her eyes and seems to be saying something.

Maybe if I carefully slide open my little window, I can hear what she's saying.

I push at the window, but it's stuck. I push harder, and finally, it moves a couple of inches. Now, I can hear her.

But she's not talking, she's moaning, still with her eyes closed. And she seems to be doing something with her hands down below what I can see.

Uh oh, I bet I know what she's doing.

Her moaning is getting louder. I think she's reaching her climax, and now there are words mixed in with her moans: "Johnny. Oh, Johnny."

She's moaning my name? Is she imagining I'm with her, making love to her?

Suddenly, her shower curtain is jerked back.

"What the hell are you doing, Debbie?"

It's her husband, and he yelled really loud. He's looking past her, right at me.

I quickly duck back, but it might of been too late. Could he have seen me? Or did he just remember I have a window in here facing their shower window?

I go back to bed and lie there staring up into the darkness. If he saw me, or if he even suspected she might be fantasizing about me, my job here will be done for. But maybe he didn't see me. Maybe he just caught her doing something he doesn't like. I should just go to sleep and not worry about it.

But I'm having trouble getting to sleep. I keep listening for footsteps outside if he comes to beat me up. Or, worse.

When I wake up, it's getting light outside. He didn't come after all. Maybe I dodged a bullet and still have a job. I get up and go into the bathroom to drink some water from the sink tap. But I don't go anywhere near the bathroom window. I put my pants on and get ready to go out to start painting while it's at least a little bit cool. Should I put my shirt on? No, it's too hot, no matter what he might think.

I'm pouring the paint into the roller tray when he shows up.

"No need to do that," he says. "I've decided I don't need you anymore."

Uh oh, he must have seen me at my bathroom window last night. "But I'm not even half done."

He just stares at me. He looks angry.

"Listen, sir, I can finish up he painting in a few days. And I think I'm doing a good job. I'm being very careful around the windows and doors."

"No, you're done. Here's your pay." He hands me a twenty-dollar bill. "Get your stuff and go. Right now!"

"Twenty bucks? Now wait a minute. This job was supposed to last me many days. And despite the heat. I didn't even take time out to go get anything to eat, or . . . anything. If I'd of known you were going to fire me, I could have been scouting around for another job.

"Don't act so innocent, kid. As if you don't know why I'm firing you. Okay, here's another twenty." He hands me the bill. He must have had it ready in case I complained.

"That's it. Only two twenties?"

Now he's looking irritated, but also nervous. Is he afraid of me?

"Listen, kid, forty is more than you deserve. Get your stuff and go. And I don't want you coming by here again. Ever. You got that? She's going to be behind locked doors as far as you're concerned." He turns and walks away.

He may or may not know she's been coming out to talk to me, but he for sure saw something last night in their shower he didn't like. Well, hell, if I wanted to get together with her, I should of done something sooner. I could have at least asked her to come visit me in the shed, just to see what she'd do.

No, that wouldn't have worked. She might have been willing to come to my bed in the middle of the night, but what if they sleep in the same bed, and he's a light sleeper? Maybe people out here in the West have guns, and know how to use them. I could have ended up dead. So, no use fantasizing about that kind of thing now.

I go back to the shed and grab my sleeping bag and the other few things I'd brought in from my car. Interesting that I only needed these few things to move into this shed. But then, I didn't have much more than this in my room back in Illinois, and I just walked away from there without taking any of it with me. Maybe this is what my life is going to be like now, ready to pick up and move on at any time. I kind of like that idea, like being a nomad with nothing to hold me.

I put my stuff in the car and pull out of the driveway. I go slow, in case Deb wants to come out to talk to me. But what would I do if she wants to go with me, wants me to take her traveling?

No, she's not going to do that. She may not like her current life, but she's got a husband who provides her with food and clothes and a place to live. What could I offer her? A kid with forty bucks and an old car. If she does come out, I'd be smart to just wave goodbye and keep on driving. I'm just starting this adventure. Who knows where it's going to take me, but I think wherever it is, I need to do it on my own.

I drive past their apartment, and their door doesn't open. Good. Better that way. Once I'm out on the street, I give old Moby some gas and don't look back.

Chapter Five

Okay, now what? After I drive to the end of Lemon Tree Street, I stop at the main street intersection. Where to go from here? I guess I should just look around a bit, see if there are any possible construction jobs around here. Staying on the main street, I pass restaurants, and I am feeling hungry, but I still can't make myself spend money on restaurant food. When I was a kid in Illinois, I only ate in a restaurant once, when the uncle of a foster home woman invited me out. I can't remember what I ate, but I do remember what happened afterwards: he said we should go to his house. I didn't see any reason to do that, and by then I'd learned to be cautious, so I just got out of his car and walked back home. I'm not sure why he wanted me to go with him to his house, maybe to pay him back in some way for buying me a meal. Who knows.

Turns out, the next town is named Mesa. Kind of a sleepy-looking town, but there is a huge white building, right in the middle of it. A sign out front identifies it as a "Church of Jesus Christ of Latter-day Saints." I wonder what kind of church would have such a big imposing building. Sure doesn't fit in with the street's small commercial buildings. There's a clothing store, a drug store, an appliance dealer, and a movie theater with a lit-up bright front that's advertising "The Sons of Katie Elder," starring John Wayne and Dean Martin. Must be a western. How long since I've been to a movie? A long time, now that I think about it. Not since one of the older orphan boys talked me into going with him to see what he described as a "dirty movie." It turned out to be a boring movie with a lot of talking and one beach scene that showed a bunch of girls wearing only swimming suit bottoms and no tops. Why haven't I been to a single movie since then? Other people go to movies. Well, movies *do* cost money, and I've never had much. But it must be more than that. Maybe it's a group thing; you go to movies with friends, and I've never had any. And now, here I am, on the road, still by myself. Will that change? Not likely if it's just the way I am. But is it the way I am? In school, I was around other boys, but only in sports. I never became friends with any of them outside of playing the sport. I wonder why that was. Looking back, I know I did intentionally avoid getting close to anybody, but why? I remember not being interested in the things they were interested in, but it must have been more than that. I felt different from them, and it wasn't just because I was an orphan. I didn't make friends with any of the other orphan kids either.

Interesting the things I find myself thinking about on this driving adventure. Maybe the new things I'm seeing, and the different people I'm running into are changing me. Actually, I'm ready to let that happen. I guess when I drove away from Illinois, I thought I was just wanting to see some new things, but maybe I was also hoping being somewhere different would change me in some way. Now that I think about it, I suppose it's going to be inevitable that this trip will change me. But in what way? I guess I'll find out.

Once I'm through Mesa, it's desert again. I could find a place to park out here and sleep in my car. That's an option, but the day is just getting started, so I should first look around for other options. After all, I found that painting job and a place to stay simply by looking at a bulletin board. I should at least go back and look at that board again. In fact, maybe I should make the university my headquarters. Might be more opportunities around there, and now that I've got a few bucks in my pocket, I could even take some classes. I wonder how much that would cost. I make a U-turn and head back to Tempe.

As I drive, I again realize how hungry I am. I should find something real to eat besides Snickers bars. I could stop at a market and find something. But I'm still wearing my old T-shirt and my work pants, now covered with splatters of yellow paint. I should first find a thrift store to get some new clothes.

As if my thinking about it created it, I come to a Salvation Army thrift store, and it seems to be open. I pull into the small parking lot and go inside. The store is cluttered with a lot of junk, but I soon find a pair of pants that look okay. I also find a light blue dress shirt, that might be what a university student would wear.

Back in my car, clothes taken care of, it's time to think about getting something to eat. If I go to the university to check that bulletin board again, I should also go back to that cafeteria in the student union and force myself to eat something.

I again park in the neighborhood near the university. Nobody's around in this quiet neighborhood of small houses that, surprisingly in this blistering heat, are still trying to grow grass lawns. They're not having much luck at it.

I slip into my new clothes and head for the student union.

In the cafeteria, sliding my tray along the chrome rails, I remember none of the food in this place looked appetizing the last time I was here, but now, a lot of it looks exactly like what I'd like to eat. I must be really hungry. I put a lot of food on my tray, but before I get to the cashier, I change my mind and put half of it back. Who knows how long the money I have is going to have to last me.

After I finish eating, I go back upstairs to that bulletin board. Mixed in with all the other personal notes, is a handwritten note on a torn-off piece of paper that says a fraternity house is looking for a student who can act as groundskeeper and general fix-it person. It says the job includes a free place to live. Ah ha! Just what I'm looking for.

I take the note off of the bulletin board and ask a passing student where the listed fraternity house is. He points to the south and tells me fraternity row is a short walk off campus.

I go back to my car and drive in the direction he pointed. I soon find a curving street with one-story houses, all in a row. This must be fraternity row.

Surprisingly, despite the heat, they all have somewhat green front lawns, all of them in need of mowing. Not many cars parked on the street. Must not be many fraternity members here in the summer.

I park in front of the fraternity house that's listed in the note. The front door is wide open. Seems odd, but I go right in. Nobody around. I go along a hallway and into what must be their dining room: a bunch of long tables are surrounded by chairs, but still nobody around. The next room is smaller, with chairs roughly arranged in rows. Must be their meeting room.

I go out the nearby door, which leads me into a backyard where there's another building. I look into a window. Beds. This must be where the fraternity members stay.

In the yard behind the main building, there's a drooping volleyball net and two bicycles, both of them lying on their sides as if they were just dropped there.

Finally, I see an actual person, a short pudgy guy with a mop of blonde hair. He's about my age, and he's sitting on the grass in the shade of the main building, working on the chain of a bicycle. It must not be going very well because he's cussing at it. Lying next to him is a huge Saint Bernard dog. The dog seems to be asleep, but he's panting. I bet a big furry dog like that doesn't do all that well in this heat.

I go to the guy and hold out the note. "Excuse me, do you know who put up this note? It was over at the university. On a bulletin board."

He doesn't look up from his task. "What's it say?"

"It says this fraternity house is looking for a groundskeeper and general handyman. It says it includes a free room."

Now, he does look up at me. "You a student?"

"Yeah. I mean, I'll be starting soon. Fall semester."

"Okay. No, I don't know who put the note up, but I did hear they were looking for somebody to kind of take care of the place. The guy who did that left. Got married. What the note may not say is you also have to take care of this damn dog. I'm the only one around today, so I had to take care of him."

"That's okay. I like dogs," I say, hoping I *will* like dogs, even though I've never had one.

"Well then, you're hired. Uh, I mean, I guess I can hire you. I'm about the only one here right now. Summer, you know."

"Hire me? Does that mean I get paid?"

"I doubt it. If the note said you get a free room, that's probably it. So it's okay with me if you wanna go ahead and move in." He nods toward the building. "The rooms are almost all vacant in the summer anyhow. Some might even be vacant once school starts again. Until pledging starts."

"Uh, okay. So I should just pick one?"

"Sure. Grab any room that seems vacant."

"Okay." I turn to go look for a vacant room.

"Hey, don't forget the dog. He'll stay in your room with you."

"Oh. Okay, what's his name?"

"The guy just called him Spud. I don't know why."

At the sound of his name, the dog looks up.

I guess if I'm going to be the one who takes care of this dog, I might as well see if he'll come to me. I hold out my hand and say, "Here, Spud," in what I think might be a good dog-call-ing voice.

It works! The dog gets up and slowly lumbers to my side. I pet him on the top of his big head and say, "Good dog."

The dog seems to appreciate that. He looks up at me, as if he's waiting for my next command, so I say, "Well, Spud, shall we go look for a room?"

I start walking, and sure enough, he comes along with me. Maybe I am good with dogs. No family I ever lived with had a dog. Some of the families I got assigned to had cats. One lady in particular had a lot of cats. All over her "Shoe" (one of the clever kids said she was the old woman who lived in a shoe with so many kids she didn't know what to do, so of course, from then on, her narrow two-story house had to be called "the Shoe").

The first few rooms I look into are cluttered with clothes and stuff, but the next one isn't. It has a window that looks out on the street where my car is parked, and another window on the side that overlooks the back yard. There are two beds. I guess that means I might end up with a roommate. But if I let Spud sleep on the second bed, maybe I won't have to share this room. Anyhow, it seems like a pretty good place to live free for a while. Apparently, they aren't going to pay me, but if I don't have too many duties, I can probably get a construction job somewhere around here. Interesting that, so far, I seem to be pretty lucky at this finding free places to live. Pretty amazing, really, that I just got in my car and started driving, and in this place I ended up, I'm doing fine.

Spud and I go back out to talk to the guy working on his bike. I say, "Number five looks vacant. Okay if Spud and I move in there?"

He looks up. "Sure. What's your name?"

"John."

"Okay, John. My name's Tim, but nobody calls me that. They call me Tin."

"Tin?"

"Yeah. Can't remember when that nickname got started, but it doesn't matter, if I say my name's Tin, people just think I said Tim."

"Okay, but what should *I* call you?"

"Oh hell, just call me Tin. I'm used to it."

"Okay, Tin it is. Well, I guess I'll go get my stuff out of my car."

"You've got a car?"

"Yeah. It's only an old Chrysler, but it runs good."

"Damn, no kidding. Hey listen, John. You wanna make some money with that good running car of yours?"

"Well, I guess so. Doing what?"

"I been tellin' myself I can't go on being a virgin forever. Been thinkin' if I only had a car, I'd go down to Canal Street and get myself laid."

"Canal Street?"

"You don't know about Canal Street?"

"No. This is the first time I've been to Arizona."

"Canal Street isn't in Arizona, it's the name of this back street down in Nogales, the town right across the border down in Mexico. They say they got real cute girls there who'll do it for cheap. If you'll drive me down there, I'll pay you . . . say, uh, twenty bucks."

He wants me to drive him down to Mexico so he can get laid? Well, Mexico might be interesting. And put twenty bucks in my pocket besides. I say, "Okay. Plus gas. But tell me, Tin, is it safe to drive in Mexico?"

"Sure. Some of the guys go down there all the time. To get laid, or to buy stuff cheap in Mexico. Cigs and booze. So, should we go?"

"Now?"

"Why not right now? It's only a couple of hours away. "We'll grab some food from the kitchen and be back later this afternoon."

Well, I started this driving trip to see new things, so why not throw in a trip to Mexico?

Chapter Six

Tin leads me into the fraternity house kitchen where he grabs two apples and two overly-ripe bananas. In my car, he directs me to a nearby gas station. He pays for the gas, and then he explains how to get out of town and onto a highway heading south.

Of course, I expect it'll take us longer than his estimate of "a couple of hours" to get to Mexico, but according to the Arizona map I picked up in Flagstaff, it actually doesn't seem all that far, and the road looks mostly straight. With the speed Moby can maintain on a straight road, maybe it will only take us a few hours.

Tin is in such a hurry to get down to where those Mexican girls are, he keeps on telling me to drive faster. I'm willing to go see what Mexico is like, but I also want to look around on the way. The whole idea of this road trip was to see different things.

The map says the town of Coolidge is along the way to Tucson. That's the place Deb said she grew up in. She called it a flyspeck of a place that the road goes through, but nobody ever stops. Now, I'll get the chance to see what she was talking about.

Before we get to Coolidge, there's a sign that says we're coming to a National Monument called Casa Grande Ruins. When we get to it, I pull into the parking lot. Mine is the only car there, and the fact that we're in the middle of a flat barren desert gives the place a weird lonely feeling.

Tin holds up both hands. "Hey, why we stopping?"

"It's a national monument. Let's check it out."

"Naw, we gotta get on down there to Mexico."

He really is in a hurry to get laid. I say, "I'm pretty sure those girls will still be down there, even if my stopping here delays us for a few minutes."

Turns out, Casa Grande Ruins really is only a ruin. Not much left of it. Not surprising because it looks like it was built out of mud. But somebody—some government agency, I suppose —has put a big new roof over it supported by four sturdy steel pillars. I guess they're trying to try to save what's left of it.

A sign says it was built out of adobe mud by the Hohokam people about seven hundred years ago, but it was later abandoned. Strange that they don't know why the people left. I walk around the whole thing, trying to figure out how they built it. The walls are a lot thicker at the base. That probably helped keep it standing all this time. And it obviously doesn't rain much out here in this desert. Unfortunately, visitors have been carving their initials in the soft walls. Not a very nice thing to do. I'm kind of fascinated by the old ruin, and I take the time to look inside every doorway, but Tin must be getting really impatient watching me explore the ruin, because he starts honking the horn. I'm glad I didn't leave the key in the car; he wants to get down there to those Mexican girls so bad, he might have taken off without me.

Back in the car, Tin is pouting, but he doesn't say anything.

It's only a short drive from the Casa Grande ruin to the small town of Coolidge. As I drive right on through the dusty-looking town, I can see why Deb complained about living here; not much to the place. I have the strange thought that someday it might end up an abandoned ruin like that Casa Grande monument.

A short distance past Coolidge, I see ahead what seems to be another small town. But as I drive past, it doesn't really look like a town; it's just a scattered collection of one-story brick buildings. A sign in front of what must be the main building says it's the Arizona Children's Colony. What kind of children's colony would be built out here in the middle of the desert? I'd better not stop to find out; Tin would get really upset.

The road is straight, so, to get Tin to stop grouching about me stopping, I'll show him what Moby can do. I floor it, and the roar of Moby's engine startles him. The rate we're picking up speed has got him all rigid. Once I get Moby over a hundred, he starts hanging onto the armrest with both hands. I can tell he's really scared, but I bet he won't say a word because this is what he wants, to get down there to those girls fast.

And we are moving really fast on this two-lane road. Even when there are other cars ahead, the road is so straight I can time my approaches and zip past them without hardly having to slow down at all. Now that I've passed a few cars that way, Tin seems to be getting used to it. I think his fear is turning into a kind of thrill. But when he sees us coming up on an old slow-moving farm truck, he tenses up again. I see another car coming toward us in the other lane, but I think if I really push it, I should be able to just get around the old truck. I remember I had to do this a bunch of times on that three-lane highway back in Missouri, so I have a pretty good idea of just how to time it. As we close in on the old truck, Tin says, "What the hell" and groans as if he's hurting inside. I wave off his complaint and say, "No problem. Hang on."

He grabs onto the arm rest again, and says, "Jesus, John, at least keep both your hands on the wheel."

He's hanging onto the armrest so tight it's making his fingers turn white.

I've really got old Moby going now, and we're coming up on the old truck fast. I still think my timing is about right, so I should be able to zip past the old truck with some room to spare before the oncoming car gets to us.

But apparently, the driver of the old truck doesn't understand I can do that, because he dives off the highway, straight out onto the flat desert.

He must have thought I was some kind of suicidal maniac who was going to smash right into the back of him. I can't help but chuckle as we speed on down the highway, but I feel bad that the old guy had to drive off into the desert like that. I see in my rear-view mirror that he's managing to drive back onto the highway, so I guess no harm done.

Tin finally lets loose of the armrest and says, "What the hell was that about?"

I chuckle again. "Hey, you said you were in a hurry."

He shakes his head and turns to look out his window.

A sign says the city of Tucson is just ahead. I know I'd better slow down, or I'll get yet another ticket. I got a lot of speeding tickets back in Illinois, and just paid fines, but out here in Arizona, they might not take kindly to a car with Illinois plates speeding through their town.

Tucson gets Tin talking again, about how beautiful he's heard those Mexican girls are.

Interesting that at first all he cared about was getting laid, but now he wants the girl to be beautiful.

The highway takes us right through downtown Tucson. The streets are wide, with cars parked on both sides. Looks a lot like when I drove through downtown Phoenix. There are a few somewhat tall buildings, and a bunch of small shops: a dry cleaners, a drug store, a furniture store, and even a car repair place, right here in the middle of downtown. There's a Salvation Army store, but I better not stop to look around. Tin would probably throw a fit.

I see a sign advertising an upcoming rodeo called "La Fiesta de los Vaqueros." Interesting that the sign is in Spanish. Another sign in a window says Barry Goldwater's presidential campaign is coming to town. Or maybe he's already been here and gone, leaving only the colorful signs. I haven't been paying much attention to the upcoming presidential election. Actually, I haven't been paying much attention to politics at all since the assassination of President Kennedy, and, of course, I haven't been near a TV since I left Illinois, so I have no idea what's going on now. I suppose others must care a lot about the presidential election. It gives me an oddly satisfied feeling to be on the road and not to have to pay attention to that kind of thing.

Tin says, "Why are you going so slow? Let's get moving."

I don't explain to him that I'm enjoying looking around. This is just what I wanted, going to completely different places, places that give me different feelings. Actually, I've been having those kinds of different feelings ever since I got on the road; I just haven't taken a moment to stop and think about it. From when I started driving on Route 66, just about everything looked and felt different from what I grew up with in Illinois. It's not only that I'm no longer living that same old ordinary existence, but I also like the fact that I did it on my own, without any plan. I just up and did it. And now look where I am, in a dusty desert city with a really big mountain close by. Arizona feels less like Illinois than any place I could have imagined.

So, what is it about traveling that's giving me those kinds of new feelings? I guess I don't really know, but I like it. And I'm ready for more. We're getting close enough to Mexico that I'm starting to wonder what it's going to feel like there. Different, I'm sure. Hopefully, real different.

Once we're through Tucson's downtown area, the houses look mostly all the same—one-story, and most of them built out of painted concrete blocks. Okay, time to speed up. Although he still doesn't say a word, I suspect Tin was starting to get used to how fast I drive. And now that we're moving fast again, Tin stops brooding and goes back to talking about those beautiful young Mexican girls. He says he's sure they'll be really pretty and eager to "do it."

The desert we're passing through is pretty much flat now. Very few bushes or cactuses, and the wind seems to be picking up. It's creating spinning whirlwinds of dust in the distance. I wonder what causes them.

We roar past a big old-looking stone church. It looks too old and run down to still be in use, but there are a couple of cars next to it.

It isn't long before we get to the town of Nogales. It's a small town, and it feels old. Or maybe not exactly old, but tired, worn out. Maybe the dusty desert winds wear down these small desert towns. Or maybe it just feels that way to me because I'm used to the way everything looked back there in Illinois, all green, with everybody competing to have cute grass yards with plenty of flowers. The people here don't seem to care much about green. Instead, they decorate their sandy yards with silly things like little windmills and metal sculptures of cats.

In the downtown area, a lot of the storefront signs are in a mix of English and Spanish. In my high school history class, I learned the Southwest was settled by Spaniards who subjugated the Indians. Then, the Americans took over after the Mexican-American War. Not surprising that the Spanish language would still be used here, especially here in a town that's right next to Mexico. The main street through town leads right to the border. I thought I'd have to stop, but driving across the border from the Arizona part of Nogales into the Mexico side is hardly noticeable. A few uniformed Mexican policemen are standing around, but they hardly glance at us as we pass by.

The town on the Mexican side of the border seems even more run-down than the Arizona side. And kind of . . . haphazard: the streets are paved, but they're narrow and not in very good shape. Cars are parked in a way that seems random, as if there are no rules here.

I pass a Pemex gas station that looks absolutely filthy, as if dirty oil got loose and sprayed all over the place.

I ask Tin, "Okay, do you know where this Canal Street is?"

"Don't have any idea. We'd better ask somebody."

I look at the people passing by on the sidewalk. Just normal looking Mexican people, going about their business. Mixed in are a few that look like they might be tourists, just wandering around. "So, you think we should just stop somebody and ask them where to find the young prostitutes?"

"Hell, Canal Street is famous. I bet everybody knows where it is. Here, pull over. I'll ask this guy."

As soon as I pull over, Tin leans out the window and waves to a guy walking on the sidewalk. "Hey, bud, how do we find Canal Street?"

The guy comes closer and leans down to look in Tin's window. "*¿Qué calle?*"

Tin says, "He's speaking Spanish. We need to find some-body who speaks English."

I say, "Maybe we can figure it out."

I lean across Tim. "Sorry, sir. We don't speak Spanish. Canal Street?"

"*Ah, Calle Canal.* He points ahead. He swerves his hand to the right. "*¿Lo entiendes?*"

I think he's indicating a right turn. I ask, "Are you saying we stay on this street? Then turn right at a canal?" I mimic his right turn gesture."

He nods and says, "*Si, si.*"

"Okay, thanks.

The man says, "*Ustedes chicos se divierten.*"

Tin asks, "What did he say that time?"

"Don't know, but I think he meant we should find a street that turns right, probably next to a canal."

I drive on until I spot a canal that runs under the street we're on. There's a dirt road next to it, so I turn onto it.

"Tin says, "What are you doing? This must be some kind of canal maintenance road. It's all beat up."

"Right, but maybe it's all beat up because a lot of boys like us have been driving in here looking for those girls."

He doesn't seem convinced, but I drive on, even though the road gets worse.

Tin says, "I don't like this. We don't know where we're going."

I point ahead and say, "Let's go a little farther. See where this road goes." Besides, I like this. Why not go for a drive on a rutted dirt road in Mexico?"

Going on, the road gets so bad, I'm looking for a way to turn around when I see activity ahead. Cars are parked on the dirt street, and young men are walking around. This must be it. There are two buildings, one on each side, and both of them have beer signs in the windows. Must be competing bars. Are the girls in the bars?

Tin shouts, "Girls! I see girls! They're on the porch of that place."

He's sitting so far forward, his face is almost up against the windshield.

I pull in front of that building, and sure enough, there are two cute young girls, probably in their early teens, on the porch, sitting in lawn chairs. Although they're outside, they're dressed for the bedroom in flimsy negligees. As I pull up, one of the girls smiles at us and pulls aside her negligee to show us her naked breast.

"Did you see that!" Tin shouts. "She showed me her boob. Come on, let's go!"

Before I can respond, he's out of the car and on the steps leading up to the porch.

But then, he stops and waits while I lock my car. When I catch up to him, he grabs my arm and whispers, "What do I say to her?"

He's asking me what you say to a young Mexican prostitute? Am I now the expert on sexual matters? Well, compared to Tin, a self-described virgin, I guess I am. I say, "I don't think it matters what you say to her, Tin. As long as you have money."

"Oh yeah, money. How much should I give her?"

"I expect that's up to her. Just ask how much, and I bet she'll take care of the rest."

"But what's too much? I mean I don't have very much with me. Maybe you can give me back that twenty I gave you."

"First things first, Tin. Let's go talk to them."

"Oh, okay. But you do the talking. I don't know how to talk to girls."

"You've never talked to a girl?"

"Well, sure, I've talked to girls. But not about . . . you know, sleeping with one."

"Okay, I'll do the talking. Just don't tell them how much money you have on you."

We go up the steps, and I go to the girl who showed us her breast. "My friend here wants to have sex with you."

She's shaking her head. "*No. Tu entras.*" She's pointing toward the door.

I get it. These girls out here are the come-ons. The bait. The business part of this operation must be inside. I say to Tin. "I think she means we have to go inside."

He leans closer to me. "Inside? Do you think it's safe to go in."

"Well, if you want a girl, I expect that's where they are."

He seems doubtful, but he follows me in.

Inside, it's somewhat dark. There are a lot of small round tables. Young men are seated at several of them, drinking beer and talking to scantily-clad young girls. The customers don't look Mexican; they look like us, probably college students from the US.

A young woman hurries over to greet us. "*Hola, Niños.* My *nombre Clara.*"

Unlike the girls out on the porch and the girls at the tables, she's wearing white pants and a white shirt. And she's older than the other girls, probably in her mid-twenties. She has very watchful eyes, constantly looking around the room.

She gestures for us to come with her, so we follow her to an empty table.

When we sit down, she also sits down and says, "*¿Beber?* Beer?"

I say, "Oh, sure. I'd drink a beer. How about you, Tin?"

He leans closer to me and whispers, "We didn't come all the way down there to drink beer. You know what I want."

I turn back to Clara. "What my friend here wants is to have sex with a young girl. Is that possible?"

She smiles. "*Si*. How much *dinero* friend have?"

She's speaking a little English mixed in with her Spanish. I guess *dinero* means money. She's getting right to the point.

I say, "Not too much. How much would he need?"

She's still smiling. "*Cinco dolares*." She holds up five fingers. *Americano*."

Tin scoots his chair closer to her. "Five dollars? You bet. With you?"

"*No, no. Mi amiga*."

She turns to wave at one of the girls who's sitting at a table with boys. The girl jumps up and hurries to us. She's very young, and not bad looking. Probably exactly what Tin was hoping for.

Clara points at Tin. "*Ve con este. Cinco*."

The girl takes Tin by the hand and leads him toward a door at the side of the room. He looks back at me, and he can't stop smiling. I guess he's satisfied with the girl he got.

After they disappear through that door, Clara points at me. "¿Ahor, tú?"

"Me?"

"¿Una señorita?"

"Actually, for now, I think I'll just have that beer."

She raises her hand. I can't see who she's signaling, but another young girl immediately comes out of the same side door the other girl took Tin into. When she comes to our table, Clara says, *Cerveza. Uno*."

The girl disappears back through that same side door, but she's almost instantly back with a bottle of beer in her hand. Did someone back there hand her that already-opened bottle of beer? Is somebody back there watching what's going on in this room? The only employees I've seen so far are young girls, but I can't imagine they are the management of this kind of place.

After the girl brings me the beer, and after she takes my dollar, she again disappears through that side door. I doubt if she'll be bringing me back any change. An expensive bottle of beer.

Clara watches me drink the beer with those watchful eyes of hers. She's very attractive, but not what I would call cute, at least not the kind of cute represented by the other girls. Something about her seems . . . tough?

Two young men come in, and Clara gets up to go greet them, leaving me to wonder what she must think of a twenty-year-old guy who comes into a place like this, but doesn't want a girl. So, why don't I want to go in the back with a girl like Tin did? Well, I chose not to pursue sex with Deb either, but that was different; she was a married woman. So, what is it this time? Am I afraid of disease? Or do I just not like the idea of paying for it?

I'm for sure not holding back waiting for true love either; I don't think I'm likely to find that. I think the real reason is that after the high school sex adventures I had in the backseat of my car means I've had enough of casual sex.

I had my first experience of that kind when I was sixteen, soon after I got my first car. At that time, I was still under state supervision as an orphan, but the family I was assigned to didn't pay much attention to what I did. They got paid a stipend to house me, and that stipend was really all they cared about. They had me living in a room they'd fashioned together out of a storeroom in the back of their garage. It was still pretty much a storeroom when they put me in it, but they did have somebody install a toilet and a sink. The wife was grouchy, but she did bring me out a pretty good meal every evening. I almost never saw her husband, but I knew he existed because he was the one who signed the monthly "underprivileged" ticket for the free lunches I got at the high school cafeteria. The truant officer made sure I attended school, but other than that, nobody cared what I did. I even had spending money because I made good use of the garage I was living in by repairing my schoolmate's cars. In time, I made enough money to buy my own car. It was a near wreck, an old Chevy, but it didn't take me long to get it running good.

It was in the back seat of that old Chevy that I had my first sexual experience. It was with a girl I met at what I used to think of as the "hoodlum dances." They were held every Friday night in the gymnasium of a downtown youth center "to keep the kids off the streets." It was not a place where nice boys were likely to go, and therefore, not a place for nice girls either. For a while, I hardly ever missed a Friday night there. The records played for the dances were chosen by a grouchy old man who wouldn't take any suggestions. He mixed fast-paced rock and roll music with slow songs. On one of my first nights there, I spotted an interesting looking girl who was about my same age, so when the next slow song came on, I asked her to dance. She didn't wait for me to pull her close; she pulled *me* close. Real close. She seemed both eager and nervous at the same time. As the end of the song approached, I whispered into her ear, "Want to go for a ride in my car?"

"You have a car? Your parents' car?"

"Nope, my own."

"Oh boy. Let's go."

It seemed sure that I was about to have my first sexual experience. I drove out to a lonely country road, and we got into the back seat and took our clothes off. She was trembling. I wasn't sure if she was overly excited or overly scared. Here I finally had a totally naked girl in the back seat of my car who was apparently ready for me to start. But it wasn't like I had envisioned it; she was on her back, with her eyes closed, but she didn't seem to be able to stop trembling. I just stared at her naked body for a while, and then decided I didn't want to do anything to this scared girl.

I got dressed, and while she was in the back seat getting dressed, I drove her back to the hoodlum dance. Her girl friends were there waiting outside, pretending to be grown up by smoking cigarettes. She jumped out of my car and ran up to them, shouting, "I think I'm pregnant."

The next time I got a girl to leave the hoodlum dance and go out to that same country road with me, this one was more "experienced." She was eager to get *me* into the back seat, and when we were finished, she said, "Hey, man. That was great. But don't you have any booze?" After that, I had a few more successes with "experienced girls," and one night, after sex, the girl insisted I should get her "an opener necklace." I said okay, even though I had no idea what she was talking about.

Back at the dance, I asked a few of the other boys, and found out what she wanted was a sharpened beer can opener on a chain to wear around her neck. Apparently, it was all the rage among the hoodlum girls. The idea was that such a necklace would mean she was "my girl," and that any other boy who wanted her would have to fight me using that kind of sharpened beer can opener as a weapon. I immediately realized that was why many of the hoodlum boys had scars on their faces, exactly the kind of scars those sharpened beer can openers would leave. In fact, it was almost as if those pointed beer can openers were designed to open up flesh enough to leave that kind of scar. I guess those scars were supposed to prove they were tough. I not only did not get that girl a sharpened beer can opener, I stopped going to the hoodlum dances.

I see Clara coming back. Is she going to try to talk me into going into the back with a girl? Maybe she gets a commission.

She sits down at the table, but she's hardly paying any attention to me; she's carefully watching everything that's going on in the room. Maybe I give her cover, so she can be seen to be with a male, a potential customer, doing her job. But she's not doing her job; she isn't even talking to me.

Curious about her, I ask, "Uh, how long have you been the hostess here, or whatever you call your job?" Not exactly a clever way to start a conversation, but I can't think what else to say.

She doesn't answer my question. Instead, she leans closer to me and asks, "Name?"

"My name? Uh, John."

"¿*Tienes auto?*"

"Auto? My car?"

"*Sí.* Car."

"Sure. It's parked right out front."

"Where you vive?"

Where do I live?" I can't imagine why she would want to know that. Aren't I just another customer? Maybe the fact that I wasn't eager to dash off into the back room with a girl has made her think of me in a different way. I say, "I'm a student at Arizona State University. Up in Tempe. Or at least I will be when the fall semester begins. Assuming I can find a job to make enough money."

She stares at me for a few moments, and then says, "Money? *¿Mucho dinero para* university?"

Does she want to know how much money it takes to go to a university? Why would she want to know that? I say, "Over a hundred, I expect. For tuition"

"Hundred? *Cien.* I can get."

Uh oh, this is getting weird. "You can? You can get me a hundred dollars? To do what?"

She doesn't answer that question. Instead, she points toward the door. "You and *amigo* go."

She wants Tin and me to leave? "Uh, why?"

"Go. Across *calle.*"

She wants us to go across the street.

"Auto. No lock, *¿Comprender?"*

"Uh, okay." She wants me to unlock my car and take Tin across the street. What is she up to? Does she plan to wait for us in my car? Maybe she wants me to drive her someplace. But why would she pay me so much? Maybe she wants me to take her across the border into the United States. Is it that hard to get across the border? It sure wasn't hard getting into this country; we just drove right across.

She gets up and disappears through that same door where the girl took Tin.

Should I do what she said, unlock my car? If she's willing to pay me a hundred dollars, it must be something illegal. It might even be dangerous.

Before I can think it through, Tin comes back and plops down in the chair next to me. He's beaming and says, "That was great, John. Thanks for bringing me down here. That girl knew what she was doing. I was nervous as hell, but she knew how to calm me down. I was scared I wasn't going to hold it long enough to actually do anything, but she knew how to take care of that, too. Slow and easy."

"Sounds good, Tin." I stand up. "Let's go."

"Already? I like this place. I'm ready for that beer now."

"There's another place across the street. Let's go over there."

"Another place? Sure."

He stands up and follows me to the door. As soon as we're outside, he asks me how my girl was.

I just say "Fine" and go to unlock my car.

Tin asks, "What are you doing?"

"Just checking my car door locks. Let's go across the street."

On our way across the rutted dirt street to the other building, Tin can't stop talking about how great the girl was. "I'd like to marry a girl like that. A girl who knows what she's doing."

"Really? That's your main marriage quality?"

"Well, I mean not one that works in a place like that, but one who knows how to do it."

Inside the other place, the room looks a lot like the first one, with small tables scattered around, but it's more crowded. Some of the girls are sitting on the laps of the boys, and they have even less clothes on than the girls across the street. Some of them don't have on any tops at all.

We find an empty table, and we're barely seated when two young girls come over to join us. One of them sits on Tin's lap, and I can tell he likes that a lot.

The other girl tries to sit on my lap, but even when I tell her I'm not interested, she keeps at it, sitting close to me and shoving her hand down into the front of my pants. I gently remove her hand, but I don't think she would have given up except she sees two more boys coming in through the door and goes to greet them.

The other girl keeps at Tin, and I suspect he would have been willing to go into the back with her if he hadn't just finished with the girl in the other place.

There's a stage at the end of the room, and suddenly bright lights come on there. Is there going to be some kind of show?

Sure enough, a naked girl—actually, more of a naked older woman with sagging breasts—comes out onto the stage, followed by a man leading a donkey.

What's this about? A naked woman, and a man with a donkey? I hope this is not what I think it's going to be.

But it is. The woman leans over, bracing herself against a wooden railing, while the man manipulates the donkey into position so it can get at her from behind.

It looks pretty disgusting to me, but the rest of the customers all seem to like it. They're all laughing and cheering. They think this is funny?

Tin is spellbound, watching it all play out.

Before the show is over, I've had enough. I grab Tin's arm and say, "Come on, Tin, let's get out of here."

He obviously doesn't want to leave, and he keeps his eyes on the sex show so I have to just about drag him out the door.

As we walk back across the street to my car, Tin is talking nonstop. "Did you see the size of that thing? And that woman took it all. Amazing."

I don't see Clara waiting in my car. Maybe I didn't give her enough time. Or maybe she changed her mind.

As soon as we're in the car, I reach over the seat to feel if anybody is on the rear seat floor. I feel someone. She is there!

Tin is jabbering on about what a great afternoon it was and how he wants to come back and do it again soon.

I don't mention Clara is in the back seat.

Chapter Seven

When I hit a bump on the rough dirt road, I hear a sound from the back seat.

Tin hears it too and turns around to look. "Hey, John, stop! There's people in your back seat."

"People? You mean a person?"

"No, two people. They're down on the back seat floor."

As soon as I pull over and stop, Clara and a little girl crawl up onto the back seat. Is the little girl Clara's daughter?

Tin looks at me. "You knew about this?"

"Clara asked me to unlock my car door. I didn't know why." I ask, "What's going on, Clara? Is the little girl your daughter?"

Clara puts her arm around the girl's shoulder. "We go. Say, 'How much Maria?'"

"What do you mean? How much for what?"

"*Para* sex."

"They wanted your daughter for sex?

"*Si. Para virgen.*"

The little girl is cowering in the corner, as if she's trying to make herself invisible.

"Let me make sure I understand, Clara. Your bosses wanted to use your daughter for sex, especially because she's a virgin?"

"*Si, si. Pero* I say no. *Absolutamente no.*" She points ahead. "*Borde.* Cross. No can *encontrar.*"

I turn back to Tin, "She thinks if she can get her daughter across the border into Arizona, they won't be able to get at her."

Tin nods. "Well then, I guess we have to do it. I can't believe that place would make a little girl do that."

For a moment, I think about reminding him that it was "that place" that supplied him with a young girl for sex. But I don't say it. I just get moving again and start back to the border crossing.

When we get to the border, there's a line of cars waiting to cross. Seems like it's not as easy to get back into the United States as it was getting into this country.

When we finally get up to the guard booth, the officer asks us where we've been.

I say, "Just here in Nogales."

"Doing what?"

"Just looking around."

"I noticed your license plate is from Illinois. You're a long way from home, son."

"Yes, I'm a student at ASU. Up in Tempe. My friend Tin is also a student there."

"I see. And how about those two in the back seat? Are they students there too?"

I look back at Clara and her daughter. It doesn't look like Clara wants to say anything.

"No, they're just friends. Clara, and her daughter."

"Just your friends, eh? Well, I'd better see some IDs. All of you."

I suspect Clara doesn't have the kind of identification he's looking for, so after Tin and I show our drivers licenses, I say, "Clara is going across to do some shopping. Just for today. Her daughter needs new clothes for school."

The officer says, "New clothes, eh? Well, she can't go across without identification." He points. "Go over there to the turn-around lane. Come back when they have some kind of identification."

I don't want to draw too much attention by arguing, so I do what he says.

Once I'm back in Mexico, I pull over to the side to think what to do.

Tin is glaring at me as if he thinks I'm crazy. "What the hell are you doing, John? It's not our problem. Just let them out so we can go home."

Clara says, "*Si, si. Cruce peatonal.*"

I have no idea what she's saying.

"*Caminar.* Walk."

"You want to try walking across?"

"*Si.*"

Tin says, "Okay, just let them out, and let's get out of this weird country."

I know he's right. There nothing more I can do for them.

But before I can let them out, Clara points and ducks down. "*No, No. ¡Ir!*"

"What's the matter, Clara?"

"*¡Ellos!* Go!"

"Are those the men from where you worked? Are they after you?"

"*Si. Están detrás de María. ¡Apurarse!*"

I quickly drive a few blocks away before pulling over again.

Tin says, "What are you going to do?"

I say, "It was the men from Canal Street. Where she worked. She thinks they're still after her daughter."

"Okay, but what can we do about it?"

Clara pops back up. "Déjanos salir." She pushes against Tin's seat.

She wants out of the car and seems a little panicked because there's no rear-seat door. I touch her shoulder. "Why do you want out, Clara? Where will you go?"

She continues to push against Tin's seat to get out. "*Otra manera.*"

"I don't understand, Clara. Please tell me. Where will you go?"

"*Desierto.*"

"*Desierto?* Desert? You and Maria are going to try to walk across the border into Arizona through the desert?"

"*Si.* Desert. *Otra manera.*"

Tin says, "It's hot as hell today, John. It'd be even hotter out there in the desert."

"I know, Tin, but I think she's desperate. She'll do any-thing to protect her daughter."

He shrugs. "Okay." He opens his door and pulls his seat forward to let them out.

Clara and her daughter quickly climb out and hurry down the street.

"Jesus," says Tin. "If they try to walk through the desert in this heat, they could die out there. Especially that little girl."

The little girl is following her mother, but she keeps on looking back at me. Does she want me to help? But how can I be of any help to them?

Tin says, "Well, there they go. Now can we go home?"

"Listen, Tin, I think I'd better go with them."

"Go with them? To the desert? Are you crazy? What can you do?"

"I don't know. Maybe I can help in some way, especially help that little girl. You go ahead and drive my car back to the fraternity house. I'll meet you there."

"And what if you don't show up? What if you die out there in the desert with them? I keep telling you it's gonna be too damn hot."

"Then I guess you'll have a good old car to drive around."

"Really?"

"No, not really. I was on my high school cross country team, and we raced on some really hot days. I can make it. You go back, and you better take good care of my car. Or else."

I put on my White Sox baseball cap and hop out of the car. As I run to catch up with them, I'm wondering if there really is any way I can help. But I do know I have to try.

Tin said what I'm doing is crazy. Well, maybe that's why I'm doing it.

Chapter Eight

I catch up with them and say, "Okay, Clara, where are we going?"

Clara says, "*¿Qué estás haciendo?*"

I say, "Listen, Clara, if I'm going to go along with you, you've got to help me with the language. You understand some English. I know you do. And I think you speak English a lot better than I understand Spanish. So help me. I don't care if you speak correct English. Just give me one word at a time if you have to."

"Why come?"

"Why did I want to come along with you? The answer is I don't really know. I've been doing a lot of things lately that I don't know why I do them. I just want to do things. New things, things that are different."

She makes a scoffing sound.

"And I like you. Isn't that enough?"

"*Veo.* You want sex."

I shake my head, hard. "No, no. That's not it at all. I just like you and Maria. I want to help."

"No sex Maria."

"No, Clara, I do not want that. Uh, do you know the word adventure? Uh, fun."

"Desert? Fun?"

"Well, maybe not fun exactly. I just want to do things. New things. Comprehend?"

From the look on her face, I think she at least partly understands what I'm trying to say. But I don't think she believes me. I guess her only interaction with boys my age is the boys that come in wanting to have sex with young girls.

With our language difficulties, I probably can't convince her that I'm any different. I'll just have to show her. "Okay, Clara, let's go to the desert. You lead, I'll follow."

She stares at me for a long moment, then says, "*Nosotras necesitamos agua.*"

"In English, Clara."

"*Agua.* Need *agua.*"

"Oh, right. Water. If we're going out into the desert in this heat, we'll need water. All we can carry. Do you know where we can get some?"

She's already walking away. Am I supposed to just follow her?

Maria reaches out her hand. I take it, and then we hurry to catch up with her mother. At least Maria trusts me. I guess the only way I'm going to get her mother to trust me is if I'm helpful to them. I should let Clara take the lead. This is her country. I doubt if she's ever gone into the desert to get across the border, but she may have gotten advice from others who have. I should just follow her and help in any way I can.

When we catch up with Clara, Maria still has ahold of my hand. I wonder why she trusts me when her mother doesn't. Maybe she once had a father, so she trusts men. Or is it the opposite; she never had a father and wishes she had one?

I've never imagined being a father, but I'm willing to be in that role for a while if it helps this little girl be less scared.

Clara leads us down several back streets. She seems to know where she's going. At the edge of town, we come to a dirt road, and she hurries ahead on it.

Maria is having trouble keeping up with her mother, but she doesn't complain. I wonder if she has any idea why we're so urgently doing this.

Soon, we come to a three-strand wire fence. Is that minimal fence the border?

We walk quite a ways next to the wire fence before we come to what seems to be a sort of store. It has goods on shelves, but there's no front wall. It doesn't look like there's any way to close it. Does that mean it stays open the time?

A little dried-up man is sitting in the small amount of shade created by a ragged awning. He's sitting in a straight-back wooden chair, watching us approach. I wonder if he lives in his store.

Clara walks up to him and says, "*Mucha agua.*" She's holding up two fingers.

The man opens a cabinet and brings out two large bottles of water. If he wonders why she needs so much water, he's not saying. Maybe a lot of the people come by his store on their way to sneak across the border. In fact, that may be why his store is here.

Clara seems to only be getting water for her and Maria. She's still not accepting that I really am going to go with them.

Clara says "*Linterna,*" and then "*Sombrero.*" She again holds up two fingers.

The man brings out two flashlights and two straw hats. Again, he seems to have such things ready to go, and he doesn't change his blank expression.

Clara checks the flashlights to make sure they have batteries in them. They do.

That means she must plan to travel at night. In this terrible heat, that would be smart.

She pays what the man asks and starts on down the road again. Well, at least they've got hats now, and both of them are dressed in pants and light shirts. Maybe they'll make it, as long as they don't stay out in the hot sun too long.

Maria follows Clara, but she keeps on looking back at me. I think that means she wants me to go along with them. Time to make a final decision. Should I go with them, or not? I suppose the smart thing, the normal thing, would be to just walk back to town, walk across the border, and get a bus back to Tempe. But am I that kind of person anymore? Apparently not. It's going to get dark soon. Finding a way across the border, in the desert, at night, could be the greatest adventure of my life. So, why not.

And maybe I can be of some help to little Maria, besides.

So, that's it then, I'll go along with them, no matter what Clara wants. That means I'll need some water too. I ask the storekeeper for *agua*.

He shakes his head.

What does that mean? Doesn't he want to sell it to me?

I ask for a flashlight, using the *Linterna* word Clara used.

He again shakes his head and just stares at me.

Well, I have money, and I know he has what I'm asking for, so I'm not going to let this old man stop me. I take out a twenty-dollar bill and wave it at him. *"Agua. Linterna."*

My American twenty-dollar bill gets his attention. He hesitates for only a moment before he takes my money and brings out another big bottle of water and a flashlight.

I do what Clara did and test the flashlight to be sure it has batteries in it. It works.

I'm wearing my baseball cap, so I guess I don't need the type of straw hat Clara bought, but I am feeling a bit hungry. I wonder if this old man has anything to eat. I say, "Candy bars? Snickers?"

He says, *"¿Cuantos?"*

He's asking the quantity. "Uh, five." I hold up five fingers in case he doesn't understand the English word.

The old man doesn't answer, but he does open what looks like a small cooler, and amazingly, takes out five Snickers bars. I guess Snickers candy bars must be universal.

After he hands me the candy bars, he just stares at me. I think he means to keep my twenty-dollar bill. Twenty dollars for a bottle of water, a flashlight, and a few candy bars seems pretty steep, but there's nothing I can do about it. I stuff the candy bars in my pocket, grab the water and the flashlight, and hurry on down the dirt road after Clara and Maria.

But I don't see them. Did they already cross the border? If so, maybe it's yet another indication that Clara doesn't want me with them. Too late for that. Now, I'm with them to the end.

I round a bend in the road and see them ahead in the distance. Clara is moving so fast, and Maria is struggling to keep up.

So, last chance, do I run to catch them, or do I accept her wish to get rid of me?

I look at what I'm carrying in my hands, a big bottle of water and a flashlight. What an adventure they imply.

I start running. I'll catch up to them in no time.

Chapter Nine

When I catch up to them, Maria smiles at me, but Clara doesn't. She faces me and points back the way we came. "*Tu vuelves.*"

She's again telling me to go back. I ask, "Why?"

"Nosotras no te necesitamos."

"Necesitamos? Does that mean necessary? You don't need me along?"

"*¡Ir!*" She continues to point.

"Listen, Clara, I just want to help. Why else do you think I'm, here?"

She again points back the way we came. "*No necesitamos la ayuda de un niño rico de Estados Unidos.*"

"I'm not sure what you said, Clara, I think I heard something about being a rich boy from the United States. Well, I'm not that. I've never been rich. I grew up an orphan. Do you understand that word, orphan?"

She doesn't answer, and after a moment's hesitation, she turns and goes back to walking. Maria follows her, but she keeps looking back at me.

There's nothing to do but follow them. I've come this far, and I'm not turning back. I continue to follow them, but I stay back a ways. I can understand why she might not trust me. In her job, she only met males who came looking to have sex with young girls. She must think we're all like that. And her reference to rich boys means she thinks I can't have any idea of the hard life she's led. Of course, she's right about that; her life must be really hard, harder than anything I've gone through. She probably started out as one of those girls who go into the back room with the males and worked her way up to being the hostess.

But as an orphan, my life wasn't all that easy. I got bounced around from one situation to another, run-down places, often with all of us kids crowded together in one bedroom. Places that were cold in the winter and hot in the summer. And there was constant stealing from each other, and of course, lots of fights. I had to show the bullies early on that I knew how to defend myself, but of course that meant I sometimes had to get beat on by the bigger, older boys. When I finally got into a better situation, living on my own in a little room in the back of a garage, it was tiny, and it always smelled like old oil. I was always worried that the place would catch fire, and I'd be trapped back there in that little room with no window.

Clara keeps on moving fast, and somehow Maria is keeping up. The sun is getting lower in the west, but the air isn't getting much cooler.

All I can do is just follow along a ways behind, keeping them in sight.

I've always been good at keeping quiet and watching. Being a watcher is safer, and it's a good way to figure out why people are the way they are. Now, watching Clara hurry on down the dusty road ahead of me, I wonder if maybe she was an orphan too. She did seem to react when I used the orphan word. Maybe she never knew who her mother was either.

For a while, I did try to find out who my mother was. I figured she might still be around the city somewhere. But nobody could, or would, tell me anything. One social worker lady told me I was better off not asking. She said it was clear my mother didn't want me, and that should be enough for me. Could that have anything to do with why I'm sticking with Clara and Maria? Am I looking for family? I don't think so, but I do feel sorry for little Maria.

Clara continues on the dirt road, always heading away from the afternoon sun. She's moving so fast, Maria is almost running to keep up with her. Where the heck is Clara going? It's as if she wants to get away from Canal Street as fast as she can. But apparently, she isn't ready to head north across the border into the United States just yet. Is she looking for some kind of special place to cross?

Maybe I should think more about what I'm doing. What happens when we do cross the border? Will we get arrested? Even if I am a US citizen, am I breaking some kind of law by helping them?

Let's say we do get across the border without getting arrested. Will that mean I'll then be responsible for them? What about my own life? What about my plan to start college in the fall?

I keep thinking of reasons to turn back.

No, that wouldn't be why you got into your car back there in Illinois and just started driving; if you wanted to end up in new places, doing new things, isn't this it?

Jogging, it doesn't take me long to catch up with Maria and Clara. As I approach them, Maria is looking back at me and smiling. I think she was worried that I'd turned back. Clara is not looking back, but I suspect she knows I'm still close behind.

There's a pretty good dirt road on the other side of the fence. That could be a road used by US border patrol vehicles. Maybe Clara doesn't want to cross over as long as that road is still right over there.

Ahead, the dirt road has ended, but there's a narrow trail that continues on. Clara goes onto it, not slowing down a bit. Maria is somehow still staying with her. That little girl is tougher than she looks.

I wonder why the dirt road ended in this desolate place. Do border-crossers normally get left off here? I can see that the trail ahead is well worn, and there's still that fence on our left. But now, the fence is only sagging wires attached to leaning wooden poles.

Still, Clara doesn't turn toward it. I wonder why not. We could easily get through that loose-wire fence. Clara acts like she knows where she's going, but how could she? Does she know a special route to get across the border?

I hurry to catch up with them and ask Clara, "How much farther before we cross?"

She stops and turns to face me. For some reason, my words seemed to make her angry. She reaches down and pulls up her pant leg to reveal a big knife in a leather sheath strapped to her leg. She pulls it out and uses it to point back the way we came. She yells, "¡*Volver!*"

I don't know that word, but I get it, she's telling me to go back, and she pulled out a knife to try to make me do it. Well, I'm not going back. She won't stab me, especially not in front of her daughter.

"*Nunca tocarás a María.*"

She said something about Maria. "What the hell, Clara? You don't need to protect Maria from me. If you think I'm interested in Maria the way those men back on Canal Street were, you're crazy. I'm not like that. You know I'm not. I let my friend take my car back north so I could help you and Maria. As soon as we get across the border in the US, you'll need the help of a *gringo*."

So far, she hasn't put the knife away. Am I wrong? Will she stab me?

We just stand there, her still holding that big knife, me keeping my eyes locked on it. Once before, in high school, I got threatened with a knife. I had already learned that when in a fight, ignore anything that's said and keep your eyes on the opponent's hands. So when that kid, who I could tell was scared of me, pulled out a knife, I just watched the knife while I talked him out of doing anything. Now, it's time to do the same thing; "Clara, can't you see you're scaring Maria? You don't want to be doing this, not in front of her."

That works. Or at least it causes her to look at Maria who really is scared and seems about to start crying.

Finally, she put the knife away and goes to put her arm around Maria. She whispers something, but Maria shakes her head. I hope Maria is saying she trusts me. Whatever went on between them, it causes Clara to start walking again.

I hope it means that's the last I'll see of that stupid knife.

Clara is moving even faster now, and Maria is still managing to keep up. I follow close behind, determined not to let Clara's attitude keep me being with them in case they really do need help.

I can see Clara is sweating, but she must be in surprisingly good shape to be moving so fast in this heat. Her pace is making me sweat, too.

For some reason, seeing the back of Clara's damp shirt reminds me of that hot day when I was painting those apartments, and Deb came out and made me spray the front of her thin dress with water. Right now, that seems far away, and a long time ago. And there is nothing about Clara to remind me of Deb. Maybe when this is over, I should go back to see Deb. I don't really want to get involved with her, but I could at least tell her she doesn't have to be stuck in a life she hates.

But I probably won't do that. Even though it hasn't been that long since I was sleeping in that shed and watching Deb take a shower through my bathroom window, that moment in my life feels like a long time ago, a life before this life. And despite what a short time it's been since I drove down into Arizona, I feel like I've changed. A lot.

But how can going to a different place and meeting different people change a person that much? If I'm now a different person from the person who drove away from Illinois, who was that person, and who am I now? I guess at some point, I should take time to try to find answers to such questions.

Chapter Ten

As the sun gets lower in the sky behind us, the terrain is getting rougher, more rocky. We often have to work our way down through ravines. But there still are cactuses, casting human-like, or maybe alien-like, shadows. They have a dead look about them, but they are obviously still living plants.

Looking closer under my feet, I see tiny flowers. Lots of different kinds. Despite the heat, I wish Clara wasn't moving so fast; there are a lot of things out here in the desert I'd like to spend more time looking at.

I can feel the hot sun on the back of my neck, so I turn my baseball hat around to try to protect it. But it's probably too late. Clara and Maria are wearing large hats, but I can see they're also getting sunburned in places. And I can see their water bottles are rapidly getting lower. We haven't even crossed the border yet, and they're both drinking a lot. Is thirst going to be our biggest problem?

I catch up with them and take a Snickers bar out of my pocket. "I bought some candy bars back there. What some?"

Clara shakes her head and keeps on hurrying ahead, but Maria seems interested. She looks at her mother who ignores her. Clara is always worried about her daughter, so why isn't she thinking about what it means to bring Maria out into this unforgiving desert with nothing to eat?

I give Maria a Snickers bar, and she eagerly tears into it. She doesn't seem to care that it's getting all over her fingers. The way she's so eagerly eating the candy bar makes me wonder if she's ever had anything like it before. I say, "Good, eh?"

She nods, smiling, and offers the remains of the candy bar back to me.

"No thank you, Maria. I have one of my own." I take another one out of my pocket and take a bite out of it. It's somewhat melted, but it tastes exactly like the Snickers bars I've been eating my whole life. I guess there's no reason to be surprised about that.

Clara leads us on, moving surprisingly fast despite the heat. Maria is staying back with me. I'm not sure where Clara is leading us, but except for the heat, I don't mind what we're doing. I've always liked hiking on trails, seeing nature. Maybe that's why I joined the high school cross country running team, even though I was not usually a joiner. I'd already hiked all the trails near my home town, but I heard the cross country team would get to go on a bus to races in other parts of Illinois. That was enough for me to join up.

The trail dips down into a rocky ravine, and Clara stops. She's looking north. Is this where she wants to cross the border?

I catch up with her. Even if she doesn't like me asking questions, I need to ask her how much longer we're going to be out here. I can see Maria is getting low on water.

But before I can say anything, she says, "*Casi llegamos.*"

"What does that mean, Clara? Is this where we're crossing the border?"

She ignores me, but she's looking at the border fence. Now, it's only two strands of sagging wire.

The sun is going down. Is that what she was waiting for?

Clara says, "*Vamos,*" and starts to move toward the fence.

So, we're finally going to cross into the US. Good.

At the fence, Clara waits and holds the wires apart for Maria to get through.

Once Maria is through, she lets the wires go, so I have to manage for myself.

Okay with me.

On the other side, there's a faint path, heading north. Clara follows it.

Does she know where she's going, or is she just trying to get farther away from the border?

As we go on, the desert doesn't change much. It's still hot and dry. I guess that's what makes it a desert. We're sure not likely to find any water out here.

Before long, it gets dark enough that we have to turn on

our flashlights. We often have to pick our way through cactus fields, and sometimes the lights of our flashlights pick up what seems like tall men ahead, but they always turn out to be the tall cactuses with arm-like appendages.

Clara doesn't slow down. Why is she in such a hurry? Does she think her bosses could still be following us?

Maria seems to be stumbling more. I'm watching her so closely, I accidentally brush my arm against a cactus that has fuzzy-looking balls on short stalks. A couple of the cactus balls stick onto my shirt, and when I try to pick them off, the spines stick into my fingers. Ow! It stings like hell. I manage to find a stick and knock the cactus balls off, but it still stings. I'd better keep a closer eye on where I'm going.

I hurry to catch up with Clara and Maria, but when I get to them, I find them sitting on the ground in the darkness.

Clara whispers, "Off light."

She sounds so urgent, I quickly snap off my flashlight and sit down on the ground with them.

Clara whispers again: "Coyote!"

Did she see an animal?

I hear a voice and see movement. Somebody is out there with a flashlight.

I sit very still, but soon a flashlight is shining in my eyes

"*¿Quién eres?*"

A deep male voice.

Clara and Maria stand up, so I do too.

The light moves toward us.

It's only one flashlight. I wouldn't have expected a Border Patrol agent to be out here alone.

He says, "*¿Dije quien eres?*"

I snap on my flashlight and train it on him.

He's not wearing any kind of uniform, so it's not the Border Patrol. It's a young Hispanic guy, kind of husky.

Behind him are two young women, each of them hugging a young boy. I think the boys are even younger than Maria, and they seem very afraid. Are they afraid of us? And what is this guy doing out here in the desert in the darkness with women and children? Did they also come across the border?

I point my flashlight back at the man and say, "Hello. Do you speak any English?"

He makes a "Huh" kind of sound and says, "*Gringo*? What'n hell *tú aquí*?"

I say, "We're just heading north."

He doesn't respond. He's got his flashlight trained on Maria. Clara is not going to like that.

Clara jumps up and says, "*No la estés mirando. dejarnos solos.*"

The guy smiles and keeps his flashlight on Maria. "*¿Qué tal si vienes conmigo pequeña linda?*"

Clara steps in front of Maria. "*¿Qué quieres con ella?*"

The guy says, "*Sólo unos minutos en los arbustos,*" and points at the nearby thick bushes.

Clara shakes her head. "*¡De ninguna manera! Ella es mi hija.*" She takes a step toward him.

The guy stops smiling and pulls out a pistol.

Damn, a gun! He's got it pointed straight at Clara. He says, *Está bien. Los llevaré a los dos.*"

I should do something. But what? Maybe I can rush him while he's engaged with Clara.

Faced with the pistol, Clara suddenly changes. She smiles and says, "*Bueno. Vamos.*" She reaches for his hand and starts pulling him toward the bushes.

I say, "Now wait a minute. Leave her alone!"

The man points the pistol at me. "*No te muevas, gringo.*"

I have to keep calm. He wouldn't dare shoot a US citizen, would he? I say, "Listen, mister, we're not bothering you. Just let us go on."

He takes a step closer to me, and points his pistol right at my face. *Dije que te alejes de esto, gringo.*

Clara jumps in front of him and puts her hand against his chest. "*No le hagas caso. Vamos.*" She takes his hand and again pulls him toward the bushes.

I know what she's doing. She's going into the bushes with this man, sacrificing herself. To protect me? Not a chance. She's trying to protect her daughter. But will that work? When he's finished with her, won't he still want her daughter?

As they disappear into the bushes, I hear Maria crying. I go to her and put my arm around her shoulders. I whisper, "Let's just wait and see what happens, Maria. Maybe your mother knows what she's doing."

Maria probably didn't understand much of what I said, but she does stop crying. Despite the heat, she's shaking, so I pull her close and keep on trying to tell her it will be all right.

But I'm not at all sure it will be all right. That man has a gun.

The two woman and their kids have backed away into the darkness. Did they run away?

I point my flashlight toward the bushes. Should I go over there to see what's happening?

But before I can decide what to do, Clara comes out of the bushes. Her shirt is torn, but other than that, she seems all right.

I stand up. "Where is the man, Clara? Should we run?"

She ignores me and takes Maria by the hand. She leads her away, moving fast, again heading straight north.

I catch up. "What happened, Clara? Where did that man go?"

She's still ignoring me.

Using my flashlight, I see a red stain on Clara's sleeve. Did she use her knife on that man? If so, what happened to the man's gun?

I catch up to them. "Clara, talk to me."

She continues to ignore me, so I grab her arm. "Clara, what happened? Did you kill him?"

She shakes loose my grip. "*Un* coyote. *No hagas preguntas. Caminar.*"

I don't know what she said, but I can tell she doesn't want me asking questions. If she did stab that man, what did she do with the gun? I can see she doesn't have it on her, so that must mean she threw it away, or hid it. And it probably means she really did kill that man, or hurt him so bad he can't follow us anymore. Maybe she stabbed him when he was all caught up in raping her. Whatever, it's no use me asking her any questions.

As I walk, I think about what just happened. This woman is really dangerous. When she threatened me with that big knife, I guess I didn't really take it all that seriously. Maybe I just wasn't willing to accept that I'd gotten myself into such a dangerous situation. Maybe my desire to go with new situations to learn from them led me into not wanting to believe I could be in any real danger.

If so, it at least tells me something about myself. But for now, there's nothing to do but keep on going until we get to some kind of civilization. But I sure do need to think about what it tells me about myself.

At least now Clara should understand that I really do want to help them. But she probably won't ever think of me as a friend. Maybe she's become so hardened by the life she's led that she doesn't believe in friends, especially not male friends. But hopefully, she won't think she needs to threaten me with that knife anymore.

She's still walking fast, her flashlight dancing ahead. It feels like she's got someplace in particular she wants to get to. I wonder where that place is. Wherever it is, I guess it's where I'm going too.

Chapter Eleven

We've been walking for hours, and although it is getting a tiny bit cooler, it's still really hot. It reminds me of when I drove down out of the mountains and into the desert near Phoenix. I thought my heater must be stuck on. but it wasn't. That seems like a long time ago. A crazy lot of things have happened to me since then. I went to Tempe, met Deb, and then soon met a guy named Tin at a frat house who wanted to go down to Mexico to have sex with a young girl. Now, here I am, walking through the night in a blistering hot desert. Assuming I survive this episode, what's next?

I hear the sound of cars. Have we finally made it to civilization?

It's a highway, busy with cars!

Clara has stopped She's hiding in a shallow ravine next to the highway.

I go to her and say, "We made it. I can flag down a ride for us."

She holds up both hands and says, "*No.*"

"Why not, Clara? We could get somebody to take us to a city. We're getting low on water. We don't want to die of thirst out here, do we?"

She shakes her head and says, "*No* Tucson. She spots a break in the traffic and jumps up. She grabs Maria's hand, and before I can do anything, she and Maria run across the highway. All I can do is run after them, and soon we're back in the desert, still heading north.

Why was Clara afraid to go to Tucson? Is she afraid the men from Canal street are waiting for her there?

We're gradually going more uphill, and it's getting more rocky. I'm getting low on water, and I can see Maria is completely out. I need to save some for her. I wonder if Clara has any left.

Clara stops. Is she looking for some kind of route marker?

I quickly catch up with her and ask, "Do you know where we are?"

"*Sólo busco la mejor manera.*"

"What?"

"*¿Mejor?* Best."

"The best way? You want to keep going straight north? What about water? Do you still have water?"

She shows me her empty water bottle.

So, she hasn't been conserving water. And yet, she refuses turning west to go to civilization. I hand my water bottle to her, and point to Maria. "For her, too."

"*¿Me estás dando tu agua?*"

"I know you said something about water. *Agua.* Yes, Clara, I've been saving *agua.* I again point at Maria. For her."

She looks me in the eyes for a long moment, and then says, "*Gracias,* John."

She actually thanked me! And she even remembered my name. Is she finally going to admit I might be of some help to her and Maria.

There's a hill to our right. I point and say, "Should I hike up higher to see what's ahead?"

She does a wave that I think may mean go ahead.

"Okay," I say. "Don't go anywhere. I'll be right back."

I hike up the hill, and because there's a moon coming up, I can usually avoid using my flashlight. Small birds are flitting through the bushes ahead of me. I think they're doves because of the unusual sound they make when they take off. There were also doves in Illinois. The man of the house in one of the homes I was housed in was very much into hunting. When dove-hunting season came about—in the fall, as I remember—he took me out hunting with him. It was about the only time he ever interacted with me. I had the feeling he wanted somebody to see him hunting, maybe to witness his hunting skill. After a long drive in his pickup truck, still before dawn, we pulled over behind a line of similar pickup trucks that were parked next to the road. He got his shotgun out of the back, and we hiked to a large meadow in the middle of some woods. There, with other hunters, we waited. As soon as the sun just barely started to peek over the horizons, the shooting started. It sounded like some kind of war, dozens of shotguns gone off all at the same time. I stayed well back, wondering how they managed to keep from shooting each other. By about noon, it was all over. The man I was with somehow had managed to get one single dove. As we drove back home, I was wondering, with all the shooting going on, how he knew which gun had killed that one little dove.

At the top of the hill, there are tire tracks. A sign of civilization! I follow them for a short distance and find what seems to be a miracle, four plastic milk bottles. Some kind person must have left water out here for thirsty hikers. But for what hikers? There's not likely to be anybody out here except people sneaking across the border. Somebody must be willing to help such people. I pick up the first bottle, but it's almost empty. I see why: there's a hole in it. Looks like somebody shot it. I tip it up and drink the tiny amount of water that's left in it. The other bottles have also been shot, and are completely empty. Who would do such a thing? They didn't just dump out the water, but shot the bottles. As a warning? I look around. Could somebody be watching me right now? I feel very alone out here, but I'd better always listen for vehicles.

I look back down the hill. Clara ignored my advice and is going on. No matter; I'm pretty sure I can catch up with them. I'm still wearing the good old running shoes I wore on the high school cross country team, and I feel like I'm still in somewhat good shape.

Now, I see people moving behind them. It must be those two women and their kids. Why haven't they turned west to find civilization? Do they think Clara will lead them to safety? They must be totally lost and think Clara is their only hope, but they're staying quite a ways back.

But does Clara really have any idea where she's going? If she doesn't turn west soon, she and Maria could die of thirst. I wonder if that happens often out here, people who sneaked across the border later found dead in the desert. Maybe that's why the border fence is not maintained; the desert itself is as good as a fence.

I'm about to start back down when I see something in the distance, a faint glimmer in the moonlight. But now it's gone. I wait, but whatever it was, I can't see it anymore. Whatever it was, it's gone now. I might as well go back down and hurry to catch up with Clara and Maria.

But there it is again. A very slight movement, in exactly the same place. It seems to flicker, and then it's gone. What the heck could it be?

Now, for the first time since we crossed the border, I feel a bit of breeze. In this heat, I'm grateful for it.

But wait! That thought about a breeze starting up tells me what I might be seeing out there in the distance: it could be a windmill! It could be a very brief reflection of moonlight on the blades of a turning windmill. And that could mean water. Farmers in Illinois used windmills to pump water. And even if this windmill isn't for pumping water, it might be part of a ranch where we could get some help. Would people at a ranch out here in the middle of this desert be willing to help us? They might assume we're illegal immigrants and call the police.

Well, I'm not an immigrant. I'm a US citizen, and I have my driver's license to prove it. I could say I was just out hiking and got lost. Ask them for some water.

I hurry back down off the hill and run to catch up with Clara and Maria. But before I can catch up with them, I come to the two women and their children. As soon as they see me, they run off into the darkness. I call to them: "I won't hurt you. I might know where you can get some water. *Agua.*"

They don't come back. I wish I had enough Spanish to tell them I don't mean them any harm, but I need to hurry and catch up with Clara and Maria to tell them about the water. Once we head for the windmill, those people will probably follow, so they'll be able to get some water too.

When I catch up with Clara and Maria, they're still moving, but it's obvious they've slowed dramatically. They must be getting seriously dehydrated. They'll be glad to hear what I found out.

As soon as I catch my breath, I tell them, "I think I spotted a windmill. We may be able to get water there. *Agua.*"

Clara says, "*¿Dónde?*"

I point. "Off that way."

"*No. Nosotras vamos al norte.*" She starts walking again, still going north.

I catch up and grab her arm. "Clara, there could be water there. Without water, we won't make it."

She shakes off my grip and continues walking north.

Okay, if she wants to die out here, I don't. And I don't want Maria to die either. I say, "Well, I'm going to go get some water. And I'm taking Maria with me." I grab Maria's arm and try to pull her with me.

Clara immediately pulls out her big knife and yells, "*¡No la toques!*"

That damn knife again. Well, this time, I'm going to stand up to her. I'm not going to let her threats stop us from getting water. "I don't care about your stupid knife, Clara. We're going to get water. *Agua.*" I again start to move away, and I keep ahold of Maria's arm.

Clara raises the knife, but Maria jumps in front of me. "*Mamá. Necesito agua.*"

Clara hesitates.

I say, "She's right. We need *Agua*. We have to go. You might be able to make it without water, but Maria won't."

Maria and I start moving again, and this time, Clara follows.

As I hurry toward where I think the windmill is, Maria drops back to join her mother. But thankfully, every time I look back, they're still following me.

Finally, I see it in the distance; it *is* a windmill. I point and yell, There it is!"

When we get to it, I point my flashlight up at it. It's not a very tall windmill, and it looks pretty old. But I'm sure what I saw was it turning. There's a deep metal trough next to it that's mostly full of water. A rusty pipe leads from the windmill to the trough. It means the windmill *does* produce water. There are no hoof prints in the hard-packed earth around the trough, so why is it out here? Maybe they just don't put cattle out here in the heat of the summer.

I glance back at Clara and see that she's scooping water out of the metal tank with both hands and holding it for Maria. I yell, "No! Wait for the windmill to turn." I point upward.

Clara hesitates, and luckily, just then, a slight breeze starts up causing the windmill to turn which soon sends a gush of water out of the pipe. Clara hurries to it and puts her mouth under it. She calls Maria over to also drink her fill.

When they're done drinking, I say, "Let's fill our water bottles."

But the breeze stops, and the water stops coming out of the pipe.

We wait, but the wind doesn't start up again. Is the wind stopped for the night? If so, I'll be the only one that didn't get to drink. Will I have to eventually drink water out of that trough? I use my flashlight to look down into it. The water looks fairly clean, but that doesn't mean there couldn't be some kind of bad microscopic bugs in it. We should wait for the breeze to come back.

But Clara starts moving away. I think she wants to get back to her northbound direction.

I yell, "Clara, before you go, leave me your bottles. I'll wait for the windmill to start up again, and I'll fill them."

She hesitates, and then hands me both of their empty bottles. Then, she hurries away, followed closely by Maria who turns to look back at me. She does a timid little wave. I wave back and mimic a running motion to show her I'll catch up. But will I? What if the windmill has stopped pumping for the night? There's nothing I can do but wait.

I hear a sound and turn on my flashlight. It's the two women and their children. They followed Clara and Maria. I give them a friendly wave to show them it's all right to approach.

They creep closer, keeping their eyes on the water trough. They may have been carrying even less water than we were. I point at the water and say, "Don't drink the water out of the tank. It may not be safe."

But my words do no good; they run to the water, and even though I hold up both hands and say, "No!" I can't stop them. They're scooping handfuls of water out of the tank, drinking as fast as they can. They must be desperately thirsty. I can only hope the water in the tank is safe.

After they have drunk all they can, they start backing away, keeping their eyes on me.

I say, "You don't need to be afraid. I won't hurt you."

My words don't do a bit of good. In fact, they have the opposite effect: they turn and run off into the darkness. I wish they'd stop following us north and turn west toward Tucson.

Suddenly, a light breeze comes and the windmill starts turning. I quickly put my mouth under the pipe and drink as much as I can. Then, I fill the first bottle. Now, the windmill is barely turning, and the water is coming out very slowly. But I manage to get two bottles filled before the windmill stops turning. Okay, two bottles will have to do. I leave the extra bottle for the next hikers and start running after Clara and Maria. My flashlight seems to be getting a little dim, so I turn it off. I can mostly see the trail in the moonlight.

It feels good to be running despite the heat and the burden of carrying two heavy bottles of water. But running without using my flashlight, I keep on stepping on rocks and dips in the trail. Somehow, I'm managing to keep moving without falling.

But now I step on something soft. What the heck? I turn and click on my flashlight. Damn! It's a snake, a coiled snake. It must have been sleeping, but now it's awake and rattling its tail. A rattlesnake! How about that? My first rattlesnake, and I stepped right on it. I'm lucky it didn't bite me. If I'm going to continue running, I'd better be more careful where my feet are landing. I wish my flashlight wasn't dying.

Oh well, nothing I can do about rattlesnakes. I'll either step on another one, or I won't. If I keep moving fast, maybe they won't have time to bite me before I've gone past them. Whatever, it's their desert, not mine. Actually, I wish I had more time to study him. Even from that brief look, he really was an amazingly interesting creature.

I keep on running. It gets easier because the trail is getting wider and smoother. Is it an old road? At least it means there's less danger of running into a cactus, or rattlesnakes. I click on my flashlight and see Clara and Maria's footprints, still going straight north. Where does she think she's going?

Well, wherever she's going, I guess I am too.

Chapter Twelve

I finally catch up with them. If Clara is happy to see me, she doesn't show it, even when I give her a bottle of water. Maria, on the other hand, smiles and runs to give me a hug. I share my bottle of water with her, and after she drinks, we follow her mother, hand in hand.

I see lights ahead. Another highway. This time the highway seems to be heading toward the northwest. Maybe now Clara will be willing to let me try to flag down a ride. I point to the highway and say, "Autos. Going north."

She seems unsure. *¿Qué pasa con la patrulla fronteriza?*

"English, Clara."

"Border *policía*."

"No, the border police won't be looking for illegal crossers this far north."

She doesn't answer, but I can tell she's thinking about it. After walking all this way in the heat, even she must be getting tired.

I say, "You and Maria stay here. I'll go out and flag down a car."

I'm not sure she understands what I said, so I point to the north and say, "Auto. I'll get us a ride."

I start moving, and she doesn't try to stop me, so I go out to the far edge of the highway and stick out my thumb. The cars go whizzing by. Maybe it's still too dark for them to see me until they're already past. Or maybe they're afraid to pick somebody up out here in the middle of the night.

But now a white four-door sedan is slowing to get a look at me.

I give them a friendly wave.

They stop, and I run to the driver's side just as the young man is rolling down his window. A young woman, probably his wife, is in the passenger seat. I say, "Hi, I'm a student up at ASU, in Tempe. We were out hiking in the desert and my car got stuck in the sand.

The guy still looks friendly enough, but he says, "We?"

"Yeah. My girlfriend and me. They're coming." I turn to wave. I can only hope they *will* come.

"So, you need a ride to get a tow truck?" asks the guy.

"Naw, I'm not sure any tow truck would want to go out into the desert. Besides I can't afford that. I'll just go back to the frat house. The guys there will help me."

"Okay. If that's what you want. We're going to Phoenix. We can drop you off in Tempe."

"Great. Thanks a lot."

Despite all my waving, Clara doesn't come. I yell, "These people will take us. Hurry!

I wish she'd hurry up before these people get worried and drive away. If Clara doesn't come, I'll go back and drag them both out of that ditch, for Maria's sake.

Finally, I see their heads pop up, and they come running.

We get into the back seat, and Clara is smart enough to only say "Hello" in English, and nothing more.

The woman is staring at Maria. Maybe she doesn't believe my story about us hiking in the desert. But it doesn't matter what she thinks, because her husband pulls back out onto the highway and is picking up speed.

I say, "This is really great of you."

Neither of them answer me.

Maria leans her head against my shoulder, and is immediately asleep. The poor kid must be really exhausted.

I say, "We won't be any bother. In fact, maybe we'll just take a nap. We were stuck out there all night."

As they drive on through the darkness, the young couple is discussing something about how to deal with her in-laws in Phoenix.

Good. Maybe they'll forget all about us and won't ask any questions.

I lean back and close my eyes and pretend to sleep.

Clara also has her eyes closed. Is she also pretending to sleep? Or has the heat and the endless desert hiking finally gotten to her?

As the miles go by, the couple seems to be having some kind of disagreement about what they're going to do when they get to Phoenix. I try not to pay any attention and just think about what I should do when we get to Tempe. I sure hope Tin is there, and he hasn't wrecked my car.

It doesn't seem to take long at all until I realize we're on the main street of Tempe. I must have fallen asleep after all.

When I see the university, I point and say, "Thanks. You can let us out here."

The guy pulls over. As we get out, I thank them, but I don't think they heard me because they're still arguing.

As we watch them drive away, Clara says, "*Aquí no es donde necesito ir.*"

I recognize the word *donde*. "Where are we? This is the ASU university, Clara. In Tempe. This is where my car is. Auto. Let's go get it, and then we can get something to eat. Food? *¿Si?* Maria must be hungry."

"No *comer. Nosotras vamos.* Mesa." She starts to walk away.

Does she think we're in Mesa? I grab her arm. "Clara, Mesa is far away." I point toward the east. "Come with me. My auto, remember? If it's Mesa you want to go to, I'll take you there. You're tired. Maria is tired. You can't walk there. Let's go get my auto." I start toward the street that leads to the frat house, hoping she'll follow. I keep walking, and when I look back, I can see that Maria seems to want to come with me. She's pulling on her mother's arm. Finally, that gets Clara moving in my direction. Good. Now that we're safely in the US, Clara should let me take the lead. I don't think we've become friends, but by now she must know I really do want to help her and Maria.

Chapter Thirteen

When we get to the frat house, I don't see my car anywhere. Damn. I hope Tin didn't wreck it on the way back from Mexico. Hopefully, he's just using it to run his own errands. I guess all we can do is wait to see if he shows up. I lead them around back of the house, and see a young guy in the backyard struggling to set up a volleyball net.

As soon as he spots me, he yells, "Hey, help me. The Signa Chis came over in the night and knocked our net down."

I guess I should help him. After all, I guess I was "hired" to help out around this house. And maybe he knows where Tin is.

I tell Clara and Maria to wait for a minute while I go to help the guy.

Spud sees me and jumps to his feet to run to me. Amazing after meeting me only that one time, the big pooch seems to know I'm the one who'll take care of him. I pat him on his big head, and as I go to help the guy with the volleyball net, he comes right along after me.

The guy says, "Hey, Spud knows you."

"Yeah, I got hired to look after him, along with other stuff."

"Oh, so you're the guy. Tin told me he hired a new groundskeeper, and he said you drove him down to Mexico to get him laid. He said he had a really great time down there. Said I should do it, too. He said you took off on some kind of adventure, and he had to drive your car back here."

I hold one end of the volleyball net up while he drives the other pole into the ground. "Oh, so he did make it back here without crashing my car. Where is he?"

"He took off this morning. To do some errands, he said." He comes to my end of the volleyball net and drives that pole into the ground also. It looks like it might stand up for a while.

He glances at Clara and Maria, and says, I see you brought a couple of chicks."

I say, "Just a friend and her daughter. I promised to drive them to Mesa."

"Okay. Course, no girls allowed in the rooms. Not that guys don't break that rule all the time. Tin should be back soon." He turns away and heads for the main house.

I show Clara and Maria to my room, and Spud again surprises me by hopping up onto the spare bed. Then, Maria also surprises me by lying down next to him and hugging him. She's probably never had a dog. And for sure not a dog as big and fluffy as Spud. To a child's eyes, he must look like a big fluffy toy.

I point at the other bed. "Rest, Clara. My auto will be back soon. Then we go. Mesa." I again point toward the west.

She looks suspicious, but after hesitating for a moment, she does lie down. As much as she doesn't want to admit it, she must be exhausted. Maybe they can both get a little sleep while we wait for Tin to get back with my car.

I wouldn't mind getting a little sleep myself, but I don't think Clara would appreciate my lying on the bed next to her, and she definitely would not want me lying down next to Maria.

There's no chair in this room, so I just stand by the window that overlooks the street. I should be able to see when Tin gets back with my car.

Soon, Clara and Maria both seem to be sound asleep. Clara is sleeping on her back, slightly snoring. Maria is sleeping with one arm draped around Spud who also seems to be fast asleep. It's an interesting moment, watching two humans and a big dog, all of them asleep. I feel like I'm standing guard over them.

Watching Clara and Maria sleep, I think I'm going to miss them when I leave them wherever they want me to take them. I guess that will mean my Mexico and desert adventure is over, and it's time for me to move on to whatever my life is going to be from here on. I've got a place to stay, but I need to start figuring out how I'm going to take some classes at the university.

Out the window, I see my car approaching, and it looks undamaged. Great!

I go out, being careful not to wake Clara and Maria. I'll deal with Tin, and then take them wherever it is they want to go.

Out on the street, Tin has parked my car haphazardly with the right side wheels up on the curb. But it's not a very high curb, so probably no damage done. But it might be an indication of how he's been driving. I hope he's not drunk.

He doesn't see me approach, so he's a bit surprised when I jerk open the driver's door.

He says, "So you made it."

"Never mind about that. You know, I didn't give you permission to use my car to do your own errands."

"Oh, sorry. I needed to go see my parents in Phoenix, and when you didn't come back by this morning, I decided this would be a good time to do it."

I step back to look my car over. It seems all right. I say, "Well there better not be any damage."

"No, none at all. I was real careful. And my parents gave me my monthly check, so I filled it up. Okay?"

"Well, okay, but now I need it. We've been waiting for you."

"We?"

"Yeah. Clara and her daughter. They want to go to Mesa."

"Really? They're still with you?"

"They are. I'll go get them."

He walks along with me, and at first seems to be lost in thought. But then he stops me and whispers, "What was it like out there in the desert? Real hot I bet."

"It was. We waited until night, but it was still hot, and we almost ran out of water."

"Geez. I can't imagine it. Tell me the truth, John, why'd you do it? I mean, did you get to do it with her?"

Is he fantasizing being out in the desert with a cute girl? "No, Tin. I just wanted to help them, especially the little girl. Now I'm going to take them over to Mesa"

He shrugs and goes into the frat house.

In my room, Clara and Maria and Spud are still asleep. What a picture seeing them all so seemingly happily snoozing away. I almost hate to wake them up.

I touch Clara's shoulder, and she's instantly awake. She sits up, blinking a few times and looking around as if confused about where she is. But then she looks angry. *¿Qué está sucediendo?*

"My auto is back, Clara. If you're ready, I can take you to Mesa now. Mesa. Comprehend?"

She says, "*Bueno*" and jumps out of the bed to go wake Maria up.

Maria rubs her eyes and says, "*Mamá, tengo hambre.*"

Clara says, "*No hay tiempo para eso. Nosotras vamos.*" She takes Maria's hand and pulls her out the door.

I follow, and Spud wants to come along, too. I let him follow out into the yard, but point my finger at him and say, "No, Spud. You stay."

He still tries to follow Maria, so I have to tell him again: "No!"

He finally turns back and goes to lie down in the shade of the building.

Out on the street, Clara and Maria are already getting into the front seat of my car.

I get into the driver's seat, and turn to face Clara. "Aren't you hungry? I am. I could stop to get something."

"No *hambre*. Go."

"What about Maria? She just said the word *hambre*,"

"*¡No! Anda tu.*"

I know there's no point in trying to convince her, so I try to start Moby up. The starter grinds slowly, and the engine doesn't want to start up. Damn, how far did Tin drive it?

I whisper encouragement to good old Moby and try again.

This time it starts. Good. I head for the Mesa. I'm glad to hear the engine sounds fine, and sure enough, the gas gauge indicates the tank is full.

Clara is sitting forward, looking at everything we pass. I wonder what she thinks of all the buildings, all the stores. Maria is sitting quietly between us. She seems somber, sort of sad. I know she'll go along with whatever her mother wants, but I wonder if maybe she wishes they could stay with me. I bet she especially wishes she could stay with Spud.

But maybe that's not what she's thinking at all. In the time I've been around her, she's always quiet and patient, never giggly or excited like I'd expect a girl her age to be. I wonder if I was at all like her when I was that age. To survive in all those different orphanage situations, I learned to be quiet and watchful, always expecting trouble. The trouble often came from the other kids, the tough ones, but it sometimes also came from the adults that were in charge. Sometimes, trouble even came from unexpected places, like a change in state regulations about how orphans were to be cared for. That got me dropped into some bad places run by people who only saw me as a way to make money. Still, it was another change in regulations that got me living in a better situation. The state—meaning the politicians—decided it would be "healthier" for orphans to be placed individually in loving homes. Unfortunately, they diverted only a small amount of money to that end, so what actually happened was that only families desperate for cash would agree to take in a single orphan. I always felt lucky to have ended up in my own room, even if it was in a tiny room behind their smelly garage. But the older couple that got paid to take care of me were okay; they mostly just left me alone, which was fine with me.

I pass the Mesa city limits sign, and wait for Clara to tell me where she wants to go. She's still leaning forward, looking. I think she's looking at every street sign.

Finally, she points at a street sign and says, "*Allá. Gira aquí.*" She points to the north, so I turn left.

I'm driving past one-story houses made out of light-colored concrete blocks. Each of them has a small front yard of raked sand, which seems appropriate in this desert climate. Many of them have doodads stuck into the ground, very-pink plastic flamingos, colorful fake mushrooms, too-green fake cactuses, sometimes mixed in with small real cactuses.

The neighborhood of houses ends, and I'm driving through tall orange trees on both sides. Must be a commercial orange orchard. Interesting that orange trees could grow so tall in what is essentially a desert. Of course, they would get a lot of sun here, but the bushiness of the trees indicates there must be a plentiful supply of water.

I come to a break in the trees, and there's a large building, probably some kind of warehouse. Several young people are sitting in the shade of it, next to a line of large bins that are full of oranges. There's another small building between the trees, also with more people sitting next to it, including quite a few kids.

Clara says, "¡Deténgase aquí!"

I pull over. I want to ask her what this place is, but before I can ask, she jumps out of the car and pulls Maria after her. A young girl seems to recognize them and runs to hug Clara. They're both excitedly speaking Spanish.

Clara comes back to the car, leaving the girl standing there holding Maria's hand. She opens the passenger door and says, "*Esta bien*. You go." She counts out five twenty-dollar bills, and hands them to me.

So, she really did plan to pay me to bring them into the US, and even though I wasn't able to drive them across the border, she is still willing to pay me. Maybe she did actually appreciate me helping them get through the desert, finding water, or at least driving them here.

As soon as I take the money, she says, "*Adiós*" and starts to close the car door. I lean across to hold the door open. "What are you and Maria going to do here? Will you be all right?"

"We pick *Naranjas. Adiós* now."

"But will Maria be all right? Will she get to go to school?"

She hesitates, and then says, "Maria *bueno*. You go now. *Adiós.* "She forces the door closed.

Despite all we went through together out there in the desert, she doesn't say anything more, not even a "Nice to have known you." I guess where she came from, money for service is the rule. I think she understood what I was suggesting about Maria going to school, but didn't want to talk about that. This place is probably a haven for illegal immigrants, a place where they can make money picking oranges, and it looks like the kids participate, too. But they are in this country illegally, so they may be in danger of the law coming here. I hope they'll be all right.

As I turn my car around, Maria waves goodbye to me. She seems sad.

But she will be with her mother, and with so many kids here, she'll make friends, and it seems likely they'll have to give them some sort of schooling. If so, it will probably be the first formal schooling Maria has ever had.

As I drive back to Tempe, now without Clara and Maria, despite my confrontations with Clara out there in the desert, I know I'll miss them. Maybe I should drive out here from time to time to check in on them. Clara probably wouldn't like that, but I think Maria would.

Chapter Fourteen

Back at the frat house, nobody is around. I go to my room and lie on the bed. Am I finally going to get some sleep?

But no, despite what I've put my body through out there in the desert, I don't feel at all sleepy. So, what should I do? Well, now that I have some extra money in my pocket, I can again start thinking about taking some classes at the university. So, I might as well hike over to the campus and look around. Maybe I'll get some idea of what kind of classes I'd like to take.

At the campus, as I noticed before, all of the buildings look very modern. But after I wander down a long straight sidewalk with tall palm trees on both sides, I see an old-looking red brick building ahead. There's a big round fountain in front of it, and despite the heat, there's a handful of students gathered there. I hear yelling. I move closer. A tall young woman with black hair is standing up on the concrete lip of the wall that surrounds the fountain's pool. She's dressed in loose-fitting black pants and a black sweatshirt with the word "DOWN" on it. Must be some kind of statement.

She's yelling through a bullhorn about the Korean War, saying it was a huge mistake, and the United States might be about to make the same mistake again. Where did she get the idea that this country is about to get involved in another war? My high school history teacher thought the Korean War had been necessary because of the Cold War and the need to stop the Communists, but he also said that despite the loss of many lives, that war ended up right where it started. Doesn't that mean this country would not be as likely to get involved in any more wars like that?

She spots me and points. "Hey you, tall skinny guy. Aren't you afraid of getting drafted so they can train you to become a killer?"

Uh oh. Time to move on and continue my walking tour of this campus.

Nearby, on another wide sidewalk, I find the psychology building. Maybe I could take some psychology classes, learn about human behavior, maybe even learn more about myself

I go in, and find I can look up and see the sky. Never saw a building in Illinois that was open to the sky in the middle. Must be an Arizona thing. I can see through open classroom doors that classes are in session. I stay close and listen for a few minutes. The teacher is talking about the need to make psychology more scientific. Interesting.

I go out a wide doorway on the other side of the building. The next building is labeled "Life Sciences." I go inside, and in the main hallway, there are glass boxes embedded in the walls. I look into one, and I'm surprised to see a curled-up snake in there. Is he dead? There's a water dish in there, so maybe not. Maybe he's just sleeping.

A little sign next to the glass box says it's a Mohave Rattlesnake. I wonder if the one I stepped on out there in the desert was of that type. It was night out there, and I was moving fast, so hard to tell,

Cool idea to put rattlesnakes right out here in the hallway where everybody can see them. It must mean they must teach classes here about these kinds of inhabitants of the desert. I could take some of those classes. I wonder if any of the students ever had the experience I had of stepping right on one of these interesting critters. On down the hallway, there are more glass cases with more rattlesnakes. One snake, labeled a Sidewinder *is* moving, and he seems to be looking out through the glass, right at me. Would he like to bite me? He has a bulge in his middle. Does that mean he just ate something? I wonder what they feed them? Mice, maybe?

When I leave the life science building, I can still hear that young woman yelling over at the fountain. I wonder why she decided to yell specifically at me. Maybe just because she thought I looked to be about draft age. I guess I am, but I never did register for the draft before I left Illinois. The fact is, with me moving from foster home to foster home, I guess they had no way of contacting me. And with no war going on, I haven't even thought about the chance of getting drafted.

My wandering through the campus brings me back to the Student Union building. Right across the street is the university library. I should go in there and try to find some books on learn-ing Spanish.

But right now, I'm finally feeling hungry. I'd better go in to the Student Union cafeteria and force myself to eat something real, something besides Snickers bars. I haven't had a chance to weigh myself for a long time, but I'm pretty sure that by now I'm getting even skinnier.

In the cafeteria, I slowly push my tray along the chrome rails, determined to find something to eat, anything. I spot some small round cake-like things. They're labeled "Bagel." I grab one of them. After I pay for the bagel, I manage to find a small table where I can sit close to some students. I'd like to hear what they talk about.

They're not talking about their classes; they're mostly having conversations about dating or movies or parties. None of them, not even the males, are talking about any chance for a new war. So what was that young woman at the fountain yelling about?

Uh oh, just as I have that thought, that same young woman comes in and seems to be heading straight for me. She doesn't have a tray with food.

"What ya eatin?"

Her voice is firm. A confident person. I say, "Oh, just a snack."

"Is that all you eat? Snacks? No wonder you're so skinny."

"Could be. You want some of this thing. It's called a bagel."

"I know what a bagel is. Don't you?"

"I just haven't run into one before, but it tastes pretty good. Like sweet bread with garlic in it."

"You haven't run into a bagel before? Where have you been living, under a rock?"

"Well, I'm from Illinois."

"Oh right, like I said, under a rock. Give me a piece of it."

I tear off half of the bagel and hand it to her. She stuffs all of it into her mouth, and without waiting to swallow it, says, "Name's Cat. What's yours?"

"John."

"John. What an ordinary name. You should change it. My real name's Barbara, but I hate it, so I changed it to Cat."

"Do you like cats?"

"Not especially. So, are you gonna do what I said, get yourself drafted, and let 'em turn you into a killer?"

"So, you think the US might get involved in another Korea?"

"For sure. They didn't learn a damn thing over there, and with their stupid cold war going on, they're sure to bumble into another one. Don't you watch TV? They go on and on about we need to stop the Communists before they take over the world."

"No, I've been on the road."

"For years?"

"Actually, I didn't have a TV even before I went on the road."

"No TV? Well, with all the crap that's on TV these days, that's probably a good thing."

I'm not sure how to respond to a person who's so sure about things, so I just say, "Is that right?"

She makes a kind of snorting sound and grabs what's left of my bagel. "Well, I gotta go. Got a class." She stands up.

"A class in the summer?"

"Yeah, but I'm only takin' the one class. I'm lucky my people off there in California can afford to send me to college, so why not stick around in the summer? I took this class for fun."

"I'll be starting here in the fall term. Maybe I'll see you around."

"Just starting? Well, you'll probably like it. It's not a bad college, and it gets cooler in the winter. A little."

She does an odd kind of stiff salute and turns away. But then, after only a few steps, she comes back. "Hey, if you got nothin' to do right now, why don't you come to class with me?"

She wants me to come along to her class? "Uh, won't the professor mind?"

"Naw, he's not a real professor. Guest lecturer. Some sort of famous writer. From Scotland. Goes by Callum. I don't know if that's a first name or a last name. Ever heard of him?"

"No."

"Me neither. I guess he wrote a lot of detective novels that got popular in Europe. Anyhow, he's famous enough that ASU hired him to teach a few writing workshops. We're meeting off campus. At one of the student's houses."

"I'm still not sure he'd want me just dropping in."

"I told you he won't mind. What, you got somethin' else so important to do?"

"No. Actually, I just came here to walk around this campus. I'm trying to decide what to study."

"Well then, come along to my class. Maybe you'll decide to study creative writing."

"I don't even know what creative writing is."

"It's writing that makes things up. Fiction. I'm a history major, but I'm taking this one summer writing workshop, like I said, for fun. Come on. Quit stalling. Let's go."

She wants me to go to her class with her. Well, why not. "Okay, if you're sure he won't mind." I get up and fall in beside her.

She says, "The teacher's okay. He's the one that insisted the class should meet at the house of a student. Said the sterile walls of a classroom stifle creativity. It's not too long a walk."

"Actually, I have a car."

"You do? Well, why didn't you say so? Let's go."

We walk to the frat house, and I tell her she can wait in my car while I go inside for a minute. I hurry into the backyard to check on Spud, and as usual, he's asleep in the shade of the building. It looks like he still has plenty of food and water, so I guess he's all right.

Back in my car, Cat directs me through a nearby neighborhood to a small house with a dead lawn. I park, and she leads me into the house, walking right in through the front door without knocking. A half dozen students are in the living room, some of them sitting on couches and chairs, but most of them sitting on the floor. That's where Cat sits, so I join her there.

A grungy-looking guy in jeans and a plain-black T-shirt is sitting in a straight-back chair reading from some papers. He's maybe in his late thirties, but it's hard to tell for sure because he's got a thick, scraggly black beard.

He looks up and says, "Welcome, Cat, even though you're late. And welcome to whoever that guy is with you. I was just saying tonight we're going to be studying dialogue, specifically the use of dialogue by the playwright August Strindberg, who is, even though none of you probably know his work, a master of dialogue. Now, I'll be playing one of the parts. So, who's going to play the other part?"

Nobody raises their hand.

"Okay, let's let the new guy do it." He points at me.

I try to wave him off, but he says, "No, no, you can't back out of it. Besides, you look like the type that could do dialogue in a British accent. Where you from?"

"Illinois."

"Well, then you probably can't do a British accent, but so what? Strindberg himself was Swedish, but I always thought his characters seemed British. Well, let's see how his play sounds Midwestern. Even though I don't know what Midwestern sounds like, I can tell already you don't have a drawl. Thank goodness for that. I hate drawls. What's your name, new guy?"

"John."

"Okay, John. How about a last name? I refer to new students by their last names. To intimidate them."

I hesitate and then say, "John will do." I don't know why I don't want him to know my last name. Maybe because I don't especially like his demanding attitude, but probably also because I've never really identified with my name. After all, it's just a made up name they attached to me because they didn't know my mother's name.

"Okay, John No-name, get up here and sit opposite me."

Do I want to do this? After all, I'm not really a member of this class. He's waving his hand impatiently to call me forward. Cat isn't offering any help, and this particular teacher doesn't seem to be the type to take no for an answer. Well, I didn't want to just continue being just ordinary. so why not. I get up off the floor and go to sit in the chair he indicated. He hands me a piece of paper with lines of type on it, each line labeled either X or Y.

"Your part is labeled X. Sometimes, Strindberg didn't bother to come up with real names for his characters. He thought names locked in a character, and he liked to surprise readers. I'm playing the part of Y. Ready?"

"I guess so."

"Okay, you start."

I read X's first line: "This heat is horrible. I guess we are going to have a thunderstorm."

"No, no, don't just read it. Act it."

"But I don't know the character."

"So? Make it up. In this dialogue exercise, you get to decide what your character's like based on how he talks. Now, do it again."

All I know about Mister X is that he's complaining about the weather. Okay, I'll make him a complainer. I say, "Damn, this heat is horrible. Guess we're gonna have another thunderstorm."

"Good, good." He points at me as he turns to the class. "Did you see that? He ad-libbed. He's getting into the character. The way dialogue is performed says a lot about a character." He turns back to me. "Ever do any acting?"

I shake my head. "No."

"Well, maybe you outta think about it. You might be a natural. Now, let's go on. Your character complained about the weather. Mine says 'What makes you think so?"

I quickly read ahead and see that my character has a long response. I try to read it in a complaining voice: "Well, the bells have a kind of dry ring to them. And the flies are sticky. Don't you feel nervous?"

"A ... uh, a little."

Callum is getting into his part. He read that short line as if he's confused.

I read, "Well, for that matter, you always look as if you are expecting thunderstorms."

Callum stretches, and then says, "Not me. Besides, you're the one who's afraid of being found out."

That was an interesting line, especially the way Callum delivered it, as if he's challenging Mr. X, or accusing him of something. Even though I don't know what the play is about, it's got me wondering where it's going.

"Well, John No-name, are you going to read the next line or not?"

I was reading ahead to figure out where this is going. I think my next line is supposed to be kind of challenging, so I'll read it that way. "Don't you think an intelligent fellow like myself might fix matters so that he was never found out? I'm alone most of the time, with nobody watching, so it wouldn't be all that strange if I put something in my own pockets now and then."

"Yes, but then you'd have to dispose of the stuff."

"Aw, I'd just melt it down. Maybe turn it into coins."

Callum does a clap.

I guess that means he likes the way I'm reading it.

He reads, "And if you got caught, you could make a brilliant speech proving that this gold was *res nullius*, or nobody's, as it had been deposited at a time when property rights did not yet exist."

"Right. Or I could say the theft had been prompted not by

greed but by a mania for collecting, or by scientific aspirations."

"Or, vanity or ambition might excuse what could not be excused by need?"

My last line on the page changes the subject back to the weather, almost as if the script left something out. Maybe Callum rewrote this dialogue to make a point. Whatever. I'll just read the line as it is: "How close the air is! I guess the storm is coming all right."

Callum turns to the class. "So, you see what Strindberg is doing. He thinks of dialogue by a supporting-cast character as *step one*. Then, his protagonist can respond to that with some dialogue or some thought that reveals a little bit more about him. Think of that as *step two*, completing a *two-step* process. Dialogue can also tell the reader more about the story, as if the reader is listening in on the conversation. I call that the *eavesdropping technique*. Most importantly, always remember that every word of dialogue you give your protagonist characterizes him."

Callum suddenly gets up and goes to sit on the floor next to Cat. He lowers his voice as he talks to her, but not so low that we all can't hear him.

"Cat, I've been watching you since this class started. I bet you want to get out of here with me, don't you?"

She looks startled. "Do I?"

"Yes, you do. Let's go." He points at me. "John No-name. You got a car?

"Uh, yes."

"Well, let's go then."

As Callum leads Cat and me through the students to the front door, they all seem a bit startled at his behavior, but not as startled as I might have suspected. Maybe he's done this kind of thing before. Maybe he hits on all the girls in his classes.

Before we go out the door, he turns back to the class. "I've got to talk to Cat about something. For our next class, go to the library and read up on Strindberg."

Cat leads Callum down the front sidewalk toward my car.

Well, this is pretty interesting. Looks like I'm going to

end up driving a university professor who wants to spend time with a young woman I just met.

Callum opens the front passenger door for Cat, and then turns back to me. "Hey, John No-name, got any money?"

"Some."

Well then, you're buying. I know this cool bar." He gets into the car next to Cat.

Interesting. He wants me to pay. All I've got to my name is the small amount of money I made painting that apartment building, and what I made from the trip to Mexico. Isn't he supposed to be a famous writer? Don't famous writers make a lot of money? And doesn't he get paid by the university to teach? But I don't think I'll say anything. This is all too interesting to spoil it now. Here I am, hanging out with a famous writer and university professor, and he's acting like we're old pals.

I get in, and Callum tells me to get going. I drive, and he directs me to what looks like an ordinary house in the same neighborhood. Is this the cool bar he was talking about? It sure doesn't look like any bar I've ever seen.

Callum quickly gets out and reaches back to take Cat's hand. He helps her out, and then bows to her. What's he doing? Playing a part in some kind of play?

And Cat is playing along with his formality, thanking him in a soft-speaking kind of way that I have a feeling is not her normal manner. He keeps ahold of her arm all the way to the house's front door.

I follow. This Callum guy is acting kind of drunk even though, as far as I know, he hasn't had a drink. Did he do some drinking before the class started? And why is Cat going along with it? Does she like him as a potential boyfriend, or is she just playing along because he's the professor?

Inside, the place still doesn't look or smell at all like a bar. The large front room has only a comfortable-looking sofa and two overstuffed chairs. But nobody is sitting. The place is somewhat crowded with what I assume are university students, all standing and chatting in small groups. To my eye, many of them look to be my age, or even younger. Isn't the drinking age in Arizona supposed to be twenty-one?

At the far end of the room, there's a sheet of thick plywood resting on sawhorses to make a table. Behind it is a large refrigerator and some shelves loaded with bottles of booze. The guy that seems to be in charge there also looks like a student.

Callum parks himself on the sofa and pulls Cat down next to him. He seems to be explaining something to her in a really intense sort of way. I'm not sure what I'm supposed to do, so I just stand by.

Callum points at me and says, "Get me a boilermaker. And I bet Cat would like a glass of white wine, right?"

Cat just shrugs.

"Boilermaker?" I say. "Is that a drink?"

He waves me off. "The barman will know."

As I head for where the booze is, I'm thinking about sequences: a college girl eats my bagel, takes me to her class, the professor picks me to play a part in his dialogue lesson, and then takes me out for drinks in a living room bar. Well, why not go along with this? It's getting too interesting to back out now.

As it turns out, the barman does indeed know what a boilermaker is—a glass of beer with whiskey in it.

Should I get something for myself? No, better to just stick with being the observer. One thing for sure, my first exposure to a university class is not anything like what I thought higher education would be like.

I pay, and after I bring them the drinks and start to move away, Callum says, "Hey, John No-name, where do you think you're going? You're going to leave me alone here with this tough woman?"

That gets a laugh from Cat: "So, I'm a tough woman?"

Callum says, "Of course you are. I know the type. You'll play along until you get me where you want me, and then you'll pounce and turn me into a sniveling beggar."

"I will?"

"You sure will. I've been through it before. You'll draw

me in like a black widow spider, and then, when you've got me, wham! Isn't that right, John?"

I smile to show him I get the joke, and say, "Is this another dialogue lesson?"

"Pretty sharp, Mister John No-name. I think I'm going to like you." He reaches out to slap my hand.

After the hand slap, he turns back to Cat and tries to snuggle up to her neck.

She pushes him off and says, "Stop it Callum? People are staring."

He does a friendly wave, supposedly to everybody in the room. "Of course they're staring. Everybody stares at me. I'm a celebrity. Right?"

I look around the room and don't really see anybody watching him, but it was a good question. Does this university professor think he can get away with smooching a student in public? Or does he just not care?

He continues to try to get close to Cat, acting more drunk than I think he can really be.

Finally, she pushes him off more firmly and turns to me. "I'm ready to go home, John."

Before I can agree, Callum, no longer acting drunk, stands up and says, "Sure, we'll take you home. Let's go."

Cat and I follow him out the door, and he again opens the car door for her, again bowing to her. They get into the front seat, and by the time I go around to get into the driver's side, Callum is already acting drunk again and trying to snuggle up to Cat's neck.

Cat tells me where to go, and then she just stares straight ahead, pretty much ignoring what Callum is doing.

I wonder what she thinks of it. Does she like being treated this way by a university professor? Still, she doesn't seem to be trying to give him *too* much encouragement.

Cat's place turns out to be a two-story apartment house with a swimming pool. As soon as I pull up in front, she pushes her way past Callum and gets out.

Callum watches her go, and then he seems glum. "Okay,

John No-name, that's that. Now take me to the nearest liquor store."

So now, it's going to be a liquor store? Where is this evening going? Well, only one way to find out. I say, "Okay," and start driving.

He directs me to a liquor store, and says, "Go in and get me two mini-bottles of Scotch whiskey."

"They won't sell it to me, Callum. I'm not twenty-one yet."

"What? You haven't got yourself a fake ID yet? What're they teaching you kids these days?" He shakes his head. "Okay, I'll come in with you. But you have to pay. I don't have a damn penny to my name."

I'm not sure that's true, but I've come this far with him, so why not see how all this plays out.

Inside the liquor store, he finds the kind of min-bottles he wants. They're kind of expensive, and I see larger bottles right next to them that aren't all that much more, so I say, "Why don't I buy you a bigger bottle? It'd be a lot cheaper in the long run."

He grabs my arm and pulls me toward him. "Jesus, John," he says between clenched teeth, "you trying to kill me? Just give me enough money for these two mini-bottles."

I give him the money, and after he pays for them, he hurries outside and downs the first mini-bottle before we even get to my car.

I get it. He's smart enough not to trust himself with a bigger bottle. I remember a teacher in my high school, the metal shop teacher, who was an alcoholic, and we all knew it. He could barely get through each class before he had to run outside and go behind the band building to hit his pocket flask. Before I finished my four years at that school, he was gone. Word was that he was driving drunk and caused a bad wreck.

But that teacher was a grumpy drunk. Callum, cheers right up as soon as he downs his second mini-bottle. He says, "Well, all right, John, old buddy. Ready to hit the town?"

I expect he needs me along to do the paying. Do I really want to "hit the town" with this character? If I go along with him tonight, what will that mean from now on? Am I going to end up as pals with a university professor?

I knew this situation was getting interesting, but now it's turning out to be more than interesting.

He next place he takes us to is another bar, this one more like what I would expect a bar to look like: it's a one-room place with a long bar and bar stools, plus one small table next to the front window.

A bunch of young guys that must be students are drinking at the bar. I guess they don't check IDs here either. But then, why would they? This close to the campus, the only customers they're likely to get would be students.

I again decide against drinking and sit at the table by the window. Callum goes straight to the bar and starts making friends. Soon, it seems like he's become pals with them. Thankfully, his new friends are more than willing to pay for his drinks.

After a while, Callum throws his arm around the shoulders of a long-haired guy, and they head for the restroom. What's he getting into now?

When they come back, Callum seems much more . . . lively? He waves his arms and yells that they should do a sing-a-long. Before long, he's got them all singing a loud, if not on-key, version of the Beatles song "I Want to Hold Your Hand." Next, they try to sing "Love Me Do," but they aren't doing such a good job with that one.

I guess Callum must have heard those Beatles songs in Scotland, or maybe he's been in this country long enough to hear them on the radio here. Either way, he does seem to know the words, at least some of them.

Fine with me. Let them sing. As long as those guys are buying him drinks, I can just stay sitting where I am to watch the traffic out on the street. There are quite a few drag races starting at the nearby traffic light. Back in Illinois, I made money from kids wanting their cars to go faster in such street races. Amazing how long ago and far away that all seems now.

Uh oh, the bartender is telling the guys that it's time to close the place down, but Callum isn't going for it. He demands one more song, and his new pals are ready to sing along with him.

The bartender comes to me and begs me to drag my friend out.

I tell the man I'll try.

When the song ends, Callum yells, "Which one should we do next?"

While his new friends discuss song titles, I use the opportunity to grab Callum's arm and tell him the place is closing.

Surprisingly, he seems ready to leave. As I lead him staggering to the door, he tries to turn back to wave goodbye to his new friends, but I keep him moving.

Outside, Callum is so unsteady I barely manage to get him into the passenger seat of my car. By the time I get back around to the driver's side, his head is leaning against the side window, and he's snoring. Despite the amount of booze he'd poured into himself, he somehow kept going strong until this moment.

Okay, now that he's conked out, what do I do with him? I don't know where he lives. I shake him to try to ask him directions, but it's no use, he's out cold. Now what? I'm ready to wind down myself, and poor Spud will be still outside, wondering where I am.

I drive to the fraternity house, and by the time I get there, Callum is leaning against my shoulder, still out like a light.

I get out slowly, letting him gradually slide down until he's lying on the seat. He looks pretty comfortable. I might as well let him sleep it off in my car.

I close the car door as quietly as I can, and then look in the window at him. Isn't this something, a university professor sound asleep in my car, the car I drove here to Arizona, all the way from Illinois. Once you start driving, who knows where you'll end up, and who knows what new situations you can get yourself into.

Chapter Fifteen

I wake up with sunlight coming through the blinds. Uh oh, I slept too long, leaving a university professor asleep in my car out on the street. I get up and hurry out to see if he's still there. He isn't. Did he wake up and wonder where he was? Luckily this fraternity row is close to the campus, so hopefully, he found his way over there.

But what if he got so blotto last night he's still hung over and wandering around lost? I should go check on him. I wonder if Cat knows where he lives.

I drive to the apartment building where I dropped Cat off last night. But I don't know which apartment she lives in. I'm about to start knocking on doors when I hear voices coming from the swimming pool area, and I recognize Cat's voice. She's talking in the same loud protest voice she was using at the fountain when she was warning males about getting drafted.

I go to the pool area and look through the metal fence that surrounds it. She's talking to a young guy, probably a student. Is she giving him the same warning about war and maybe getting drafted that she gave me? She's still dressed in her same loose-fitting black pants as last night, but now she's wearing a too-large dark green sweatshirt that has the word "CHANGE" on it. I wonder where she finds those one-word sweatshirts, and what do they mean to her? I should ask her.

Or, maybe I shouldn't.

I don't want to go in there and interrupt her, so I just wait outside the fence and listen. From what I can hear, it sounds like she's saying a new war is about to start, and the guy had better get ready to escape to Canada. Canada? Why would she be talking to him about Canada?

She spots me and points. "There's another one. I'd better go tell him."

She hurries out through the gate and comes to me. "Well, it's happened, John, just like I knew it would. Another war."

"Another war? Really? Where?"

"Yep. This one's gonna be in another Asian country. Vietnam."

"Really? Why would they want another war?"

"Because they always need a war going. They'll say the same things they said about Korea, that we have to stop the Communists from taking over all of Asia."

'Okay, Cat, tell me what's going on."

"You haven't heard? It's all over the TV. Gulf of Tonkin. They're saying one of our warships was attacked there. Near the coast of Vietnam?"

"Really? A US ship attacked?"

"Yes, really. But I don't believe a word of it. No little country like that would attack a US warship."

"You said it was on TV, but you don't believe it?"

"Hell, you can't believe half of what they say on TV. I'm telling you, they just need an excuse to start their next war, and they just found it."

Could she be right? Is another war really coming? And so soon after Korea?

"You look like you don't believe me, John. I'm telling you there really is gonna be another war. Yet another war of invasion, just like Korea. You'll get drafted and sent over there to get killed."

She's so fired up, she's almost yelling. I guess whatever she saw on TV confirms what she's been predicting all along.

"Well?" she says.

"You're saying there'll be another war, in a place called Vietnam."

"You'd better believe it, and you'd better start making plans."

"What plans, Cat?"

"About how to get out of it, of course. We were already

talking about maybe setting up a draft counseling center. Now we'll have to do it for sure. And quick!"

She's getting more and more agitated. "It's hard to believe, Cat. Another war so soon after Korea."

"Oh, that's right. You're the guy who's been living under a rock. You probably never even thought about another war or getting drafted yourself."

"You're right, I didn't. And I don't think I've even heard about a place called Vietnam."

"If you'd studied post-war world events, you'd know about Vietnam. Our ally, the French, have been in that little Asian country for a long time, brutalizing the Vietnamese people. It figures we'd get involved over there, sooner or later."

Is this what history majors do, try to predict where the next war is going to spring up?

She pulls at my sleeve. "Listen to me, John. Way back in the fifties, when you were still in grade school back there in corn country, the Vietnamese people were already starting to resist being taken over by the French. They put together a barefoot army to attack the French military bases. Now that they're starting to have some success, it's for sure time for the US to go over there to help the French."

"You know, Cat, if this Vietnam place is in Asia, won't most people here think it's pretty far away, both in distance and in US interests?"

"Of course it is. They always want it to be far away."

"Who is *they*, Cat?"

"*They* are the ones who are actually running this country, the puppet masters behind the curtain. The money interests. The ones who make money from war."

She's really getting into it now, like she's been practicing this speech for a long time. Is this the way she and her history-major friends talk to each other? I say, "I don't know, Cat, another war so soon after Korea."

"It's already been going on. They just didn't want the public to know about it."

"Already going on?"

"Yes. I found out they're using what they call advisors, US troops fighting on the side of the South Vietnamese. Only they don't want the people to know we've got soldiers over there. That's why they call them advisors."

"Okay, Cat, how could you know that?"

She looks away. "Personal knowledge."

"Personal knowledge. What does that mean?"

"Well, I'm not supposed to talk about it, but now, with this Gulf of Tonkin thing, maybe they won't be able to keep it a secret anymore. One of my best friends, back in California, has a boyfriend in the military. He got sent over there supposedly to *advise* the South Vietnamese. But that's not the way it turned out. He says he's been fighting the North Vietnamese, right next to the South Vietnamese soldiers. So, it was only a matter of time before the US found an excuse to get more involved officially."

"How many of these supposed advisors does she say are there?"

"Thousands. Tens of thousands."

"Really? And nobody knows about it?"

"That's the way they wanted it. So, with this new war starting up, are you going to join us or not?"

"Join you? To do what?"

"To expose them, of course, before it's too late. We'll have to change the focus of our rallies at the fountain. We've gotta let all the boys your age know what's coming before you all get drafted and sent over there to get killed for God and country,"

"But how can I help? I'm not a public speaker."

"Oh yes you are. I saw how well you did that acting job yesterday when Callum got you to play a part in his demo play."

"Oh, that."

"Yes, that. I'm heading to the fountain later to meet my history-major friends. We've gotta get the word out. Will you be there?"

"Listen, Cat, this is all new to me. You and your history major friends have obviously been studying this situation.

Shouldn't I at least start by going to the library to read up on Vietnam?"

"Well, that would be a start. Go and do your reading. You'll see I'm right. Then meet us at the fountain. I'll be waiting for you."

"Okay, but I also want to go check on Callum to make sure he's all right. He got so blotto last night at a bar after we left you, I'm worried about him."

"Aw, you don't have to worry about Callum. Getting blotto is just what he does. He can take care of himself. But go check in on him if you want to. He lives over in the married student housing."

"He's married?"

"No, he's not, and he's not a student either. But those apartments are cheap, and he has a way of worming his way into things."

She abruptly turns and hurries back into her apartment.

I think I'd better go to the library to read up on Vietnam, and then go check on Callum. And what if she's right? What if there really is going to be another war? When they stopped sending soldiers to Korea, they didn't cancel the draft, so I guess I *could* get drafted. Odd that I never thought much about that. And none of the males I knew in high school ever talked about it either. Maybe Cat is right, I guess I have sort of been living under a rock. Okay, now it's time to go to the library to try to learn how much of what she said is true about a possible new war in this place called Vietnam. And if it is a possibility, what will it mean for me and every other male of my age.

Chapter Sixteen

Looking around inside the big library building, it reminds me of how much time I used to spend in my high school library. I always thought the learning I got there was more useful than what the teachers were teaching in my classes.

I find my way to the history section, but I find only one book specifically about Vietnam. Whoever orders books for this library must not think the country of Vietnam is very important. So, if Vietnam is so unimportant, why would the United States want to get into a war in such a place? Well, maybe this book will help me understand.

I find a secluded place to sit and open the book. It says the area that is now known as Vietnam has been populated by many different ethnic groups throughout history. It says the different groups have mostly gotten along with one another, but the biggest determinant of culture and economics has always been their much larger neighbor, China. The book has a colorful map, showing a very large, red-colored, China to the north of the dramatically smaller, green-colored, Vietnam that's shaped like a narrow hook. The map makes it easy to see why the little country of Vietnam would be dominated by its huge neighbor, China.

From my high school history class, I have at least a vague notion of where China is, but I'm sure I've never heard of this Vietnam country, and I bet almost nobody else has either. From the map, the country does have one thing going for it, a long coastline. Is that why the US might have sent warships there? To protect the supposed military "advisors" Cat says are there?

I put down the book to try to think it through. Cat thinks this little country that nobody has ever heard of is going to be the site of the next US war. Could that really be possible? I guess this country did fight a war in Korea, also a small country. But that was because the northern part of Korea was allied with Communist China, which invaded the southern part. US politicians are always quick to take on communists, wherever they are in the world. Could something similar be what's going on in Vietnam?

I keep on reading, and sure enough, it says Vietnam *was* split in two after the second World War, just like Korea. And sure enough, it says the northern part is now allied with Communist China. It says the French long claimed Vietnam as part of their empire, and they've been fighting against the Communists to keep it. The next thing the book says is very surprising, at least to me. It says all the way back to President Eisenhower, the US was worried that if Vietnam fell under Communist rule, other countries in the area might also fall, "like dominoes." And, the book goes on to say soon after John Kennedy was elected president, he authorized sending a large number of special forces troops there as advisors. So Cat is right, the US does have so-called advisors over there, and according to this book, they've been there for a long time. The difference, according to Cat, is that they are not really just advising. They are fighting.

Well, maybe I *should* become a history major. I sure didn't learn much about the world in high school. My high school history teacher was the football coach, and he didn't take us past World War Two. From what I'm reading here, it's starting to look like those post-war decisions to split countries in half isn't leading to any kind of a long-lasting peace.

I put aside the book. So, information about the US being involved in Vietnam is right here in this library. And yet, nobody was talking about it until now. I think I'm going to need to learn a lot more about this place called Vietnam. Maybe we all are.

Chapter Seventeen

After I leave the library, I think about going to the fountain to see if the TV news about the Gulf of Tonkin thing will have managed to attract more students to Cat's anti-war protest. But I should first go to try to find out if Callum is all right. I wonder what he might have to say about all the war talk. Maybe he might even want to go with me to the fountain to see Cat's anti-war protest.

I ask an older-looking student if he knows where married student housing is. He points and says the married student apartments are off campus, but only a block away. "You'll see clothes hanging from the balconies."

Following his directions, I find a row of one-story concrete block buildings that look a lot like the row of apartments I was painting when I first hit this town. And of course, that triggers a quick memory of Deb. I wonder if she's still there. Part of me wishes she would have left her husband by now, but I doubt if she has.

The doors on the apartments don't have any identification on them other than a number, so I just knock on the first one.

A guy in shorts and no shirt opens the door. "Ya?"

"I'm looking for Callum. Do you know which apartment he's in?"

"Don't know." He starts to close the door.

"He's a teacher. From Scotland."

"Oh, that guy. End unit." He points and then closes the door.

I knock on the door of the end unit.

No answer.

I hope Callum made it back here last night. If so, he might be still asleep. I knock again, harder this time.

I hear a muffled, "Yeah?" from inside.

So, he is here. I say, "It's John."

"Who?"

"From last night. We went drinking."

The door bursts open, and he's standing there totally naked. He's got a tiny bent cigarette in his hand, probably marijuana.

The sight of him looking so out of it, and yet so much like what I might have expected, gives me a chuckle.

If he noticed my reaction, he doesn't show it. He holds the little cigarette to me and says, "Want a hit?"

"Uh, Callum, it's not lit."

He looks at it. "Oh yeah. Come on in. I'll find a match."

I follow him in and close the door.

He searches through assorted trash on a low table that's in front of a ragged red couch. He finally finds a pack of matches and lights the little cigarette.

He holds it out to me.

I say, "No thanks" and point to his little TV that's sitting on the floor. "Have you been seeing what's on the TV?"

He takes a big draw on the cigarette before answering. "No, what happened?" he croaks, while holding his breath. "World coming to an end, is it?"

"Well, Cat thinks it could be almost that bad. She says a US warship was confronted off the coast of a place called Vietnam."

He lets his breath out, but no smoke comes out. "Oh, yeah. I know Vietnam. Far East. Not very big. Did your country decide to start another war there?" He sucks in another big intake of smoke from the little cigarette.

"Well, that's what Cat thinks. I was just reading about Vietnam in the library. It was divided after the war, like Korea."

"A new war? Well why not?" He lets out a short sharp laugh, and some smoke finally comes out of his mouth.

"Your big fat country likes to go off rampaging around the world, especially in any place close to Russia. Or China. Gotta get them Commies, right? In Scotland, we don't give a shit about stuff like that. All we care about is our clan." He sucks in more smoke.

"Really?"

"No, not really. I don't have a clue what Scottish people care about. Why do you think I hang around this country? So, what's Cat gonna to do about it?"

"She's leading an anti-war protest. At the fountain."

He smiles. "Protesting, eh? Well, let me throw some clothes on. I'd better go take a look at that."

While he goes into the other room to dress, I kneel down and turn on his TV. It doesn't work.

He comes back dressed in shorts and a T-shirt that says "Due Tomorrow." It has a picture of a dinosaur on it. I think I might have an idea of what that T-shirt means, but I ask him anyhow. "Your T-shirt means?"

"Beats me. Let's go."

He leaves without locking his door. He's a slow walker because he's constantly getting distracted. For some reason, he seems to want to look at everything, flowers and plants, but also the design of cracks on concrete walls, even cracks in the sidewalk.

When we finally get to the fountain, Cat is in her usual place up on the concrete lip of the fountain, yelling through her bullhorn about the coming "Vietnam War." This time, there is a larger group of students there listening to her. Cat is again warning all the males that they'd better start figuring out how to avoid getting drafted and sent off to this new war. She's also talking about their plan to set up a draft counseling center.

Callum and I watch her for several minutes. She's going on and on about "the war," as if it had already started. If she notices Callum and me, she's not letting on.

Finally, Callum turns away with what I think is a wry smile. He takes me by the arm and whispers, "Well, that was interesting. Smart girl. She really got me inspired. To go get a drink, that is. Let's go."

I say, "I guess her message is not for you."

He does his little sarcastic chuckle that I'm getting used to and says, "That's for sure. I'm not a citizen of this crazy country. But you are. Have you thought about what she's saying, about getting drafted?"

"Everybody gets drafted."

"Only boys."

"Well, yeah, that's what I meant."

"You just didn't think about it. You thought, *of course* females don't have to go into the military. But why is that? If the Army doesn't want parents to see the bad image of their little girls gettin' their heads blown off, why couldn't females at least be doing the behind-the-lines support stuff? Somebody has to type official papers, don't they? Do they teach some of the boy soldiers how to type?"

"I guess they must."

"It's just the way things are, John. The way everything is. Nobody notices. Everybody's sound asleep." He waves his hand in the air, and then uses his thumb to point to himself. "Ah hell, there I go again. Wasting good breath. I'm gonna go get that drink now. You comin' or not?"

"I'd better stay here and support Cat."

"You mean support her in bed, don't you? Don't waste your time. I know, I've been trying to get her in the sack all summer. And I asked some of the male students about her. They said nobody has even set foot inside her place."

"No, I didn't mean that, Callum. I mean like I said, to support her in what she's trying to do."

"Okay, Mister John No-name, you stay here and support her. Me, I'm gonna go have some fun."

I watch him shuffle away, still going slow, still stopping to look closely at most everything he sees.

I turn back to listen to Cat. She seems to be losing her audience. I can see why. She's just repeating the same thing over and over, that all the males are going to get drafted and die in this new war.

Finally, when only a few students are still hanging around, and even those few have gathered into small groups and seem more interested in talking among themselves, Cat sits down on the edge of the fountain and looks up at the sky.

I go to her and say, "I enjoyed listening to you, Cat."

She slowly turns toward me, looking glassy-eyed. "Oh, it's you, John. Well, it's started, just like I said it would. The Congress passed what they're calling the Gulf of Tonkin resolution, and Johnson's already ordered bombing."

"Really? Already?"

"Of course. They're all blaming it on the so-called Gulf of Tonkin incident, the supposed attack on a great big US ship by a little Vietnamese patrol boat. Who would believe that such a thing ever happened?"

"Is there going to be a US invasion? Like in Korea?"

"Undoubtedly."

"So, what are you going to do? More protests?"

"Sure. All we can do is protest. History shows protest works. But when I just now suggested we should do bigger protests, the students didn't seem much interested."

"Maybe some of them went away to see what they're saying about it on TV."

"As if the TV people are brave enough to tell the truth."

"So, the TV is not a source of truth?"

"The government makes them keep quiet about it. But it'll come out, eventually. Hey, didn't I see Callum with you just now? Where'd he go?"

"To get a drink, he said."

"Of course, no matter what time of day it is, he needs his booze. I don't know how he's still alive."

"You think he's an alcoholic."

"For sure. And long term, I'd say. At least he's smart enough not to drive anymore. Said his car got totaled. Something about an argument with a truck."

"He said you were smart."

"Really? I didn't think he thought anybody was smart except him."

"Well, he thinks *you're* smart."

"Well, nobody else does. Even the boys your age only listen for a while, then, it's back to their usual nonsense, girls and sports and whatever. But you're smarter than that, John. You gotta believe me. This country is ready for another war over there in Asia, and this one's gonna be bad."

"I do believe you. I went to the library and read about Vietnam. It seems to be a lot like Korea, divided after the war. The book I read said the US has been involved in Vietnam since Eisenhower. To fight communism."

"Of course. That's what I've been trying to tell you. They don't want the Commies to have so much influence in Asia, even if it means war to stop them. It's what the next presidential election is going to be about. Johnson, who's already secretly involved in Vietnam, versus warmonger Goldwater."

"You know, Cat, I've hardly been aware that a presidential election is coming up, but I do know Goldwater is running."

"Goldwater!" She shakes her head. "He's been trying to convince everybody he's Winston Churchill. But he doesn't have a chance. Johnson is painting him as dangerous. That's a laugh, right? Coming from Johnson."

I'm not sure how to respond. I guess I should just be honest, even if she'll think less of me. "Actually, Cat, I'm not as up on that kind of stuff as you are."

"Oh, right, the living under a rock thing. Well, an under-rock liver that's male had better wake up before you're right in the middle of it."

"You're right, Cat. I don't know much about politics or any of that stuff. You could teach me."

"Are you serious? You want *me* to teach *you*? Or are you just saying that to make me feel better?"

"Sure, I'm serious. I came here to go to college. To learn stuff."

"Okay, well, the TV said Goldwater's gonna give a big speech today. It'll probably be in response to the Gulf of Tonkin thing. We should watch it together."

"Sure. Where?"

"At my place. Let's go."

"All right. But first, I should walk back over to the place where I'm staying. It'll just take a few minutes."

"Why?"

"Well, I'm staying at a fraternity house. I kinda take care of the place. And the dog. His name is Spud."

"You're a damn frat house caretaker? And dog guy?"

"Yeah. I rolled into this town with no money. I've been lucky to find places to stay."

"Oh, right. Sorry. I didn't mean anything by it. I sometimes forget that not all university students were born with a silver spoon in their mouth, like me."

"I don't think of you like that."

"Well, don't. It hasn't been a bed of roses for me either. I got orphaned at age five. Car wreck killed both of my parents. Got taken in by my grandparents. They were all right, but it's not the same."

"Me too."

She glances at me with a sharp look. "You too what?"

"I'm an orphan, too."

"No kiddin'? Since how old?"

"Since forever. I never knew my mother."

"Aw, shit. Here I am acting like I got troubles. You got here with nothin'. And found a place to stay right off the bat. Smart. You're the real deal. Next to you, I'm nothin'."

"Now, don't say that, Cat. You're very smart. You know about things. People listen to you."

"Damn it, John. You don't have to lie to me. Nobody gives a damn about anything I say. In fact, my friends back home in California keep telling me I'm crazy to be studying history. They keep asking me what kind of job a history degree prepares you for. And they're right. I am probably wasting my life away."

All of a sudden, she seems to have changed from a confident young woman to a depressed and unsure person. But what can I say to make her feel better if she thinks I'm lying to her?

"So, now you aren't saying a word. Well, forget it. I'm going home. You go take care of your dog."

She abruptly turns and hurries away.

I take a chance and run to catch her arm. "Listen, Cat, I'm telling you the truth. I really do respect your knowledge."

"You respect my knowledge, but not me. Of course, how could anybody respect me. What have I ever done to deserve respect?"

"Hey, stop that, Cat. Remember me? The kid from Illinois. From under a rock, right? I want to learn. That's why I'm here on this campus. You can teach me a lot."

"Oh yeah? Teach you what?"

"Teach me about history. And politics. Things I know nothing about. I want to hear Goldwater's speech and have you tell me what it's all about. Okay?"

She's looking down at the ground. Remembering Callum's words, I wonder if maybe she doesn't really want me inside her apartment.

Finally, she says, "Well, okay. Meet me at my place. Goldwater's gonna be on TV pretty soon."

I watch her walk away, and then I hurry to the frat house to check on Spud. He's still in the backyard sleeping in the shade of the building. Amazing how much he can sleep. Must be the heat, and he's got that big fur coat on.

I check his food bowl, but he hardly seems to have eaten any of it. It looks like he's been drinking water, so I figure he's okay.

Now to go to Cat's apartment to learn more about Goldwater. And her.

Chapter Eighteen

When I get to Cat's apartment, she's waiting out front for me. She says, "I just realized I don't have a thing to eat. Let's go get something and bring it back."

"Okay, there's a Bayless Market nearby."

"No way. I don't eat their packaged crap. I know a Mexican market. It's not far."

She directs me to a little market that has a lot of fruits and vegetables out front in wooden bins. I park and start to get out, but she says, "No, I'm buyin'. You wait here."

She isn't long before she comes back out with a full paper bag. There's a long narrow loaf of bread sticking out of the top, and I can smell that it's freshly baked. That smell triggers a memory that must be from one of the homes I was housed in as a kid, but I can't quite remember which one. I wonder if that fresh-baked bread was one of the reasons Cat wanted to come to this little store instead of going to the Bayless supermarket.

"Okay," she says. "Let's go home and see what old man Goldwater has to say."

Old Goldwater? I wonder how old he actually is. How old are politicians, generally? That thought makes me realize how little I know about Goldwater, or about the whole upcoming presidential election. But then, I never did pay much attention to politics, and none of the other guys that worked on construction sites with me did either, or, if they did, they never mentioned it to me. I wonder if another war gets started, those guys will start to worry about getting drafted. Or maybe they'd be ready to sign up.

Once we're inside her apartment, she arranges the food on a low table in front of the TV.

Goldwater is already on the TV speaking. He pounds his fist on the lectern. "To insist on strength, let me impress on you, is not being in favor of war."

Cat points at the screen and says, "Ha! Didn't I tell you? That means he really *is* a warmonger."

She's so focused on the TV screen and talking so loud, I think I'd better just keep quiet and let her vent.

Goldwater is almost shouting now: "They called another great man, Winston Churchill, an extremist."

Cat laughs and says, "Oh sure you're a great man like Churchill, Goldy. What you really are is a damn right-wing extremist warmonger."

Goldwater points at the camera and says, "But I ask the question, do you men want your wives to be *extremely* faithful to you or just *moderately* faithful. My wife knows what I prefer."

Cat grins and points at him. "That's funny, Goldy. You're a real card." She turns to me. "He thinks because he owns a big department store out in Scottsdale he's smart. Did you ever notice these guys think being rich means they're smart."

Goldwater then starts talking about the "recent Gulf of Tonkin incident." He says it proves China is our greatest threat.

So, he thinks China is the real enemy. He must not think defeating a little country like Vietnam would be much of a problem.

Cat turn to me. "Why aren't you saying anything? You're always watching, never commenting."

"I wanted to let you be the commentator. But I do agree with you. Goldwater seems to be willing to say whatever it takes to win, and he seems to think the news coming out about Vietnam will help his chances of beating Johnson. But wouldn't he do better by opposing a new war in that area of the world? Aren't people tired of those so-called *little* Asian wars that turn out to be not so little?"

Cat waves off that idea, "Naw, *we* might think people wouldn't want to see any more boys getting killed in another Korea, but they don't think that way." Her mouth is full of bread and cheese, but she can't wait to get the words out, so she covers her mouth and says, "People love wars. You know, wave the flag and cheer rah rah for our side. Besides, war gives 'em somethin' exciting to watch on TV."

Could she be right? Does the majority not care about American boys getting killed? Would they vote for another war?

Goldwater goes on: "Remember, the Communists took over China while our eyes were riveted on the Berlin blockade. Now, ladies and gentlemen, actually Communism remains a global, not an isolated, threat."

"That's it!" says Cat. "That's what they always say, the Commie threat. I can see it happening already, John. We might as well get ready for another war."

"Do you really think so?"

"Guaranteed. If I was you, I'd be lookin' for how to get into Canada."

"Canada?"

"Yep. Up there, they don't believe in killing off all their young men. I've been researching it. Landed immigrant. That's what they call it up there if you show up and want permanent residence."

"It's that easy?"

"Right. All you have to do is ask for it. At least I think that's how it works. We're gonna learn more about it. Like I said, we're gonna open a draft counseling center to teach our male students about the ways to get out of the draft. We'll open it right on campus. Or, if they won't let us do that, somewhere near campus. Are you with us?"

"I guess so."

"You guess so? Are you kidding? This is your life we're talking about here, John. You wanna get drafted and go over to some damn little country to get yourself killed?"

Now she's upset with *me*. The way she sees it, I'm either one hundred percent with her, or I'm in favor of war. "I'm not saying you're wrong, Cat. It's just that I haven't had time to think it all through."

"Right, right. I know. Why would you believe me? Why would anybody believe me?"

Now she's getting depressed again. I keep saying the wrong thing. "We don't have to go through that again, Cat. I already told you I do believe you. I do think you're really smart."

She's staring at me, and she doesn't look happy. Did I say the wrong thing again?

"Oh, John, you're so damn nice. You actually think I'm full of crap, but you don't want to say so 'cause you're hoping to get me into bed."

"That's just not true, Cat. In fact, I think I'd better leave now." I stand up, but then I hesitate. I'd hate to walk out and leave things as they are between us, so I say, "Okay, I'm going. But you're wrong about me. I do respect you. I respect your intelligence. I respect your knowledge. Thank you for inviting me here to listen to Goldwater. I enjoyed it. And I learned a lot. From you. I wasn't trying to get you into bed. I was just—"

She reaches out toward me. "Actually, you *can* go to bed with me, John. That is, if you want to. But just to sleep. I'm kind of down right now, and with all that's happening, it'd be nice to have somebody with me tonight."

Well, this is quite a turnaround. She can change moods on a dime. "Sure, Cat, I'd like that."

She leads me to the bedroom and starts taking off all her clothes. I do the same thing, and as soon as we get into her bed, she pulls me close.

I hold my breath. What comes next? This doesn't feel anything like the quickie back seat romances I had when I was a teenager.

Soon, she's sound asleep and breathing softly.

Feeling her naked body pressed so close against me, I'm not sure I'm going to be able to fall asleep. I just stare up at the ceiling, trying not to move. Where is this going? To something like us being together? If so, why did she choose me, a loner to be with? She said I was more of an observer than a participant. She's right about that. And I'm for sure not a member of her group of history majors. But I do like her, and I really would like to spend more time with her. Does it mean, in this new life of mine, in this new place, that I'm not going to be that loner any-more? For right now, I for sure do want to go along with what-ever this is. No need to make any hard and fast decisions right now. Things will go the way they will.

Chapter Nineteen

The morning light is shining through the drapes. I guess I did get some sleep, quite a bit of sleep, actually. I guess I needed to catch up.

I turn my head to look at Cat. This sure is different from anything I've ever experienced before. I'm sleeping next to a beautiful and intelligent young woman that I like very much, in a big comfortable bed. Nothing like the thin narrow mattress I slept on back in Illinois. And also pretty dramatically different from that old cot in a crowded storeroom I slept on while I painted Deb's apartment house, sharing it with a pesky, hungry cockroach. The bed at the frat house isn't so bad, but it's nothing like this.

That thought makes me wonder what Spud thought about having to be outside all night. And he might be hungry. I probably should go check on him.

I quietly get up, but then, I look back at Cat. She's still sleeping soundly, and it doesn't look like she's going to wake up anytime soon. I wonder if she'd want me to be here when she wakes up. And will she want me back in this bed in the future? Well, for now, I should just let her sleep and come back later.

Driving to the frat house, I can't stop thinking about what happened with Cat. I just keep going over it. How did I end up in a comfortable bed with a really nice and really smart young woman that I just met? I guess I really don't know about such things. And why is that? Why have I never had a serious relationship? It wasn't just that I was an orphan; most of the other orphans were pretty social. Didn't I like people? No, I think it was because early on, I became an observer. For my own protection. And making friends is not observing them.

But was self protection the only reason? At some point, when I was very young, I must have actively made the choice to become an observer instead of a participant. What triggered that? Did I not trust people? Or is being an observer, and a loner, just the type of person I am? I need to think more about that.

Chapter Twenty

At the frat house, Spud is still sleeping in his spot next to the building. I rouse him and coax him into my room. If he was happier to now be lying on a soft bed rather than outside on the grass, he doesn't show it; he simply goes right back to sleep. Man, that dog likes to sleep.

I lie on my bed, but I'm not sleepy. I got plenty of sleep at Cat's. And what about my relationship with Cat? What comes next? Should I just ask her? Or should I wait to see what she wants?

I think that's the correct answer; knowing her, it's the only possible path forward. She's quite changeable, so like it or not, I'll just have to wait to see what she wants to do.

"Hey, John, are you awake?"

It's Tin. What does he want now?

"Oh, you are. Listen, I told my friend Mark about our trip down to Canal Street, and now he wants to go, too. How about it?"

He's excited. I should have known he'd want to go down to Canal Street again. And I should have known he'd tell his friends about it. I sit up. "Jeez, Tin, again? The last time we went down there, I could have ended up dying out in the desert."

"Yeah, but that's not gonna happen again. Hey, it's early. We could zoom down there and be back by this afternoon. Why not?"

Do I really want to go down there anymore? I think I've probably already got enough money for my first semester's tuition. On the other hand, what about the semesters after that?

Tin says, "Hey. listen. I'll tell Mark to pay you extra. His family has lots of money. Let's go get him."

"Doesn't he live here in the frat house?"

"Oh, he's a full member of the fraternity, but he's got his own fancy apartment. It's just down the street. We can pick him up on the way."

"Well . . . ."

"Aw, why not? It'll be fun. And it'll get you more money for your tuition and books and stuff. The fall semester's comin' right up."

"Well, okay."

We take Spud back out to his spot in the shade next to the building and go out to my car. Tin directs me a few blocks to a two-story apartment building. He jumps out and brings back Mark, who turns out to be a tall blonde fellow dressed sharp in a white shirt, khakis, and a beige sport coat. I don't think he's going to fit in with the usual T-shirt and shorts guys that hang at Canal Street, but I guess it's up to him.

As they hop into the front seat, Tin introduces him as "My friend Mark."

Mark reaches his hand across Tin and says, "Hey, man, I hear you've got an in with those Mexican girls. Let's roll."

I shake his hand, and Tin tells him to fork over sixty bucks.

They must have already agreed on that because Mark doesn't flinch. He opens a leather wallet that's obviously stuffed with money and takes out three twenties.

I point at his wallet. "You might want to leave some of that money here, Mark."

He seems surprised. "Why? Is it dangerous down there?"

"I haven't run into any thieves down there so far, but I assume you're going to be taking your pants off, aren't you?"

He laughs. "Good point. Well, when I do take 'em off, I'd better keep my eyes on 'em."

"Suit yourself. Ready?"

They both nod enthusiastically. They are definitely ready.

At the gas station, I fill old Moby up, but before starting out, I look at my Arizona map. This time, I think I'll take a different route. The map shows that instead of going through Coolidge,

I can go west of there through a town called Casa Grande. Interesting that it has the same name as the old Hohokam Indian ruins near Coolidge.

I don't tell Tin I'm going to explore a new route, and they're so busy with their excited talk about the girls of Canal Street, I'm sure they won't notice what route I take.

Mark is asking Tin a lot of questions. I wonder if he's a virgin, like Tin was.

The city of Casa Grande turns out to be not all that much bigger than Coolidge. The houses are of the Arizona-typical white-painted concrete block, and almost all of them have sandy front yards with no grass.

I see a sign proudly proclaiming that the town is the spring training location for the San Francisco Giants baseball team. That's interesting, a big city team doing their off-season practicing in a small town in the Arizona desert. The spring weather *is* probably a lot better here, and that's probably all a baseball team would care about.

Once we're through that town, the desert is again the familiar low bushes and cactus plants. I guess the desert is always going to remind me of my long desert trek with Clara and Maria, but it feels like my memory of that experience has changed, now somehow becoming a good memory of overcoming a difficult challenge in an interesting environment.

We pass through some hills. A sign says it's the future home of Picacho Peak State Park. Despite the heat, the variety of interesting cactuses, some of them flowering, makes it seem like a place I'd like to explore. And that thought makes me realize the Arizona desert we're passing through is becoming familiar to me, almost like the Illinois corn fields used to be.

By the time we get to Tucson, Tin and Mark have finally winded down their jabbering, and Mark asks "Aren't we there yet? Tin said it was a short drive."

I just say, "We'll be there soon."

Despite the building heat of the day, Tucson's main street is a lot busier than the last time, probably because it's the weekend. People from surrounding areas must come to the big city of Tucson to do their weekend shopping.

The slow driving through town seems to make Mark even more agitated, but Tin is more patient, telling Mark it won't be long now.

When we're finally through Tucson, I speed up, and we soon go past a sign that says we're coming to Tubac Presidio State Park, Arizona's oldest state park. It looks like a collection of old buildings. I'd like to check out that place, too. Sometime in the future.

When we get to Nogales, Arizona, it's also surprisingly busy. There are red, white, and blue decorations on all of the light poles. I spot a large colorful poster in a store window that shows me the reason for the decorations: Goldwater is coming to town for a campaign event. The only thing I know about Goldwater is what I saw of him on Cat's TV. I wonder if he's going to be the next US president.

As soon as we cross into Mexico, the boys get quiet. Mark is leaning forward, looking out the front window at everything. He doesn't say a word until I turn onto the rough Canal Street road, but then, he says. "Is it really down this old dirt road?"

I say, "Yeah. Here in Mexico, they don't seem to want to make prostitution illegal, but they obviously do want it hidden away."

After that, Mark is quiet, still looking forward. What is he looking for? The girls? Or is he having second doubts because of the possible theft of his money I warned him about? I still don't like the idea of him carrying so much money into a place like Canal Street, but as long as he keeps it hidden away, I guess there's no reason they won't just see us as ordinary college boys.

When I get to the end of the road, the first thing I notice is not many cars and not many young *gringos* hanging about on the street. And when I pull up in front of the same building as before, I'm surprised to see there are no girls out on the front porch.

Mark says, "Hey, Tin, you told me there'd be half-naked girls out front."

Tin says, "Must be too early for them."

They both jump out of the car, but Tin says, "Wait. Let John go in front. He knows what to say."

Mark shrugs, and they follow me inside where, despite the early hour, there are a few customers, young men about our same age, sitting at the tables talking to the scantily-dressed girls and drinking beer. I wonder if any of these girls are the ones that are usually sitting out front.

As we wait by the door, a young woman I don't recognize hurries toward us. She must be the new greeter. I wonder how different this one will be from Clara. She sure is dressed different; unlike Clara's no-nonsense pants and shirt, this one is wearing a tight, formal-looking white dress. And the expression on her face seems stern instead of friendly. I wonder why.

She says, *Hola, chicos,* and gestures for us to follow her to an empty table. Once we're seated, she says, "*Beber?*"

I recognize the word for beer. So far, she hasn't said a word of English. Would they choose a replacement for Clara that doesn't speak English? I say, "No, beer. My friends want to go in the back with a girl."

She looks right at me and says, "*¿Crees que todavía hay chicas aquí? ¿No se fueron todas a recoger naranjas?*

Uh oh, I'm not sure what she said, but I'm sure I heard the Spanish words for "girls," and "oranges." Does she know I helped Clara and Maria get to that orange orchard in the US? How could she know that? I'd better just play dumb. "Like I said, my friends just want a *chica.*"

She's still staring at me, not at Tin and Mark. But she is pointing at them. "Have money?"

So she can speak some English when it comes to getting the money. "Sure," I say. "The usual five bucks. Each."

She shakes her head and holds up both hands, fingers spread. "*Diez.*"

Mark reaches for his wallet, but I catch his arm. "No, that's too much. You know I'm a regular here. I bring my friends, don't I? *Cinco* dollars. American."

She shakes her head and continues to stare at me.

What is she up to? Maybe they don't want me here anymore. Fine with me. I wasn't sure I wanted to be involved with this kind of thing anymore anyhow. For sure, this had better be my last trip down here. But if I walk out now, Mark and Tin will be really disappointed. And I'm curious. Maybe if I'm not coming back here anymore, I can use Mark's money to learn more about the girls here. I turn to Mark. "Give me a twenty."

He's quick to take out a twenty-dollar bill and hand it to me. I hold it out toward the greeter and hold up three fingers. "For all three of us."

She hesitates, but then she takes the money and stands up. She leads us through the same side door Tin went into the last time. Inside is a hallway with doors on both sides.

She tells us to wait, and she's soon back, leading three young girls. They look amazingly alike, all of them probably in their early teens, all dressed in flimsy nightgowns. They seem very happy to see us. Do they really enjoy their life of providing sex to *gringo* boys?

Mark steps forward, ready to grab onto the girl he wants, but I tell him to hold on. I ask the girls, "Do any of you speak English?"

One of the girls, maybe a little older than the others, raises her hand slightly and says, "I do. Little."

I take her by the hand and tell Tin and Mark I'll meet them in the car when they're done.

The girl leads me down the hallway and into a room that's barely bigger than the bed in it. She closes the door and starts to take off her nightgown, but I tell her not to do that.

She seems confused. "No?"

"No. Please, just sit here with me."

She seems unsure, but she does sit on the bed next to me.

"How old are you, miss?"

Now she seems shy. "We not . . . say."

"Okay. Can I ask you how you ended up in this place?"

"Not say."

"Okay, I understand. Just tell me your name."

"Jenny."

"Jenny? Is that your real name?"

"Now she seems confused again. "Real?"

"Okay, never mind about that. Did you know Clara? She used to work here."

That brightens her up. "Clara? All know Clara. She nice."

"Listen, Jenny. I'm a friend of Clara's. I helped her go to the United States."

"Oh, *si*. We hear. Clara go *Estados Unidos*"

"Yes, she wanted to go there, so I helped her. Would you like to go to the United States?"

She frowns. "*Estados Unidos*? What I do *allá*?"

"Okay, let me ask you this, do you like it here?"

"Oh, *si*. I take off now?" She again starts to take off her nightgown, and this time she gets it down to her waist.

She really is a very nice looking young woman. No, not a young woman, a young girl. To have sex with a girl this young back in *Estados Unidos* could land me in jail. But that's not what I want; I just want to talk to her. I gently lift the top of her nightgown back up again. "No, Jenny. That's not what I want. I only want to talk with you. Wouldn't you like to talk? We could talk more about Clara."

She frowns again. "Say Clara wrong.."

"*Calles?* Streets? Is that where you were before you came here? The streets?"

Now she's looking very sad. "*Si. Vida* hard. Me from country. Pigs feed. Not bad. Go school. But get older. Brothers want."

"When you got older, your brothers used you? For sex?"

"*Si*, all nights. Run away. Come city. No good. *Calles* cold. No food."

"And that's where they found you?"

"*Si*. Bring me here. Meet girls. Meet nice *gringos*. Get own room. Warm. Much money. *Comprar* clothes. Birthday parties. Fun."

Now I'm getting it. They recruit these young attractive girls from the streets and give them a life that's a lot better than the life they were living. They get their own room, get to meet *Gringo* boys from the United States, have some fun and make a little money doing it. It sounds like these girls even get to keep some of the money they're making. "So, you wouldn't want to leave, even if I could tell you how?"

She shakes her head, hard. "No leave. Good here. No good in *Estados Unidos.*"

She seems pretty sure she's better off here than in the US. But how long will they give her such a comfortable life if she doesn't do exactly what they tell her to do? And what happens when she gets older and isn't in such demand by those nice *gringo* boys?

The door suddenly bursts open. A large man is in the doorway, scowling at me. "*¿Qué infierno, gringo?*"

I should have known they'd be watching. I say, "We're just talking."

"*¿Hablar* talk, *gringo?*"

"Talk? Yes. Nothing wrong with talking, is there?"

He turns to the girl and yells, "*¡Dejar!*"

The girl hurries out of the room, closing the door behind herself.

I say, "Hey listen, I can talk to a girl if I want to. It's my money."

He takes a step closer to me and holds up one big hand. "*¡Ahórratelo, gringo! ¿Piensas llevar a la chica al otro lado de la frontera?*"

I get the words for the girl and border. They really do seem to know I was the one who helped Clara get across the border.

Quickly, I say, "I don't know what you're talking about, sir. I think it's time for me to leave." I stand up and move toward the door.

He puts his big hand against my chest and pushes me

back.

"Hey, don't push me. I'm a US citizen."

He does the kind of sarcastic laugh that's not really a laugh and says, "US? Want *Consular de Estados Unidos* help you?"

Was that his only worry when I reminded him I was a US citizen, that I might want to see the US Consul? Okay, maybe I can use that. "Yes, I am going to talk to the US Consul. I'm going to leave right now, and you'd better not try to stop me. My father is a friend of Barry Goldwater. *Amigo* Barry Goldwater."

He does his fake laugh again. "*Amigo* Barry Goldwater? *No amigo*."

"Yes, and Goldwater is coming here today."

"*Senior* Barry Goldwater come? No, he no come."

"Yes, he is coming. This very day. Senator Goldwater is coming to the town of Nogales, Arizona for a campaign event. Right across the border. And your town officials from here in Mexico are going across the border to greet him, including the US Consulate. I need to be over there right now to join my father and be with them when they arrive. So, I'm leaving."

I'm not sure the man believes me, but this time, when I move toward the door, he doesn't stop me.

As I go out, I say, "And my friends are leaving with me."

I run down the hallway, pounding on every door. "Mark! Tin! We've gotta go, right now. Hurry!"

Tin comes out first, pulling up his pants. "What the hell? I was gonna go again."

"No time. They want us out of here. Now! And where's Mark?"

Tin points at the next door.

I push that door open and see Mark is still entirely naked, lying on a bed next to a naked girl. They seem to be talking.

I yell at him, "Let's go, Mark."

He sits up "What? No! I haven't started yet."

I rush into the room and grab him by the arm. "They want us out of here. Right now!"

I pick up his clothes and start pulling him out of the room. The girl sits up on the bed, looking surprised.

Mark resists me. "No way. I didn't even get started."

"Listen, Mark, it's not safe here. We have to go."

Tin steps forward from behind me. "Not safe?"

"That's right, Tin, help me get him out of here."

Tin grabs Mark's other arm, and we hurry him down the hallway and out into the main room. The other *gringo* customers show their surprise to see us dragging a naked guy across the room, but all they do is laugh.

Tin and I manage to get Mark to my car and into the front seat. He's still complaining as he struggles to get into his pants.

I drive away fast, hitting the bumps in the rough dirt road too fast, but this time I don't care. I feel like I was really lucky to get out of there without getting beat up, or worse. For sure, now I know I won't be going back here again, ever.

Tin is laughing at Mark as he struggles to get fully dressed.

Mark won't stop glaring at me. "Christ, John, what the hell was all that about? I was just getting to know that girl."

I don't answer until I'm off the dirt road and safely zooming down a street toward the border crossing. "Some guy came into my room and started threatening me. We were lucky to get out of there."

Mark says, "We? I know why the guy might have been after you. Tin told me how you helped some girls escape that place. But why would they hurt me?"

"Because you were with me. Sorry. I thought my helping those girls across the border was over and done with, but I guess they're not about to forgive and forget when they lose one of their top girls. Her name was Clara. She'd worked her way up to being a hostess, but they wanted to start using her young daughter, so I helped them get away. Across the desert."

Mark nods. "Yeah, Tin told me some about that. But why you? Why did she ask you to help her?"

"I'm not sure, Mark. Maybe just because she was desperate and found out I had a car."

Well, damn it, John, you cost me time with that girl."

"Yeah, sorry, Mark And sorry we had to drag you out of there naked, but I really did think we were in danger."

"Well, damn it, I didn't get to do nothin'.""

Tin laughs again. "You should have gotten to it faster, Mark. I got right to it, and I had a great time with my girl. Man, that girl knew what she was doing."

Mark scowls. "Oh, dry up."

I say, "I understand, Mark. I'll give you your money back."

Tin shakes his head. "You don't need to do that. You did your job driving us down there and getting us girls. It was his own fault that he was too slow."

"Was not," says Mark.

"Was too," says Tin.

Mark goes quiet and stares out the window.

Once we're across the border and rolling through Nogales, Arizona, Tin gets cheerful and talkative, describing every detail of his sexual adventure. Mark is trying to ignore him.

I'm mainly just happy to be out of Mexico, but I am enjoying looking at all the town decorations that are ready for Goldwater's big campaign event later today. He'll never know his campaign event was what saved me from who knows what down there on Canal Street.

Chapter Twenty-One

By the time we get back to Tempe, Mark has cheered up and is talking about how great it was to talk to a girl for that long when neither of them had any clothes on.

I stay out of that conversation. I know that will have been my last trip down there, and it'll be fine with me if they pass the word around that it would be dangerous to go down there with me.

When we get back to the frat house, Tin and Mark immediately take off down the street, heading, they say, to go get something to eat.

I watch them go. Tin's arm is draped across Mark's shoulder as he makes jokes. The only part I can hear is him saying is you have to strike while the iron is hot.

I should also go get something to eat. But first, I'd better check on Spud.

Amazingly, he's still sleeping. He still has food and water, so I might as well walk over to the university cafeteria.

But as I start down the street, Cat comes running out of the front door of the frat house. What was she doing in there? And why does she look so pissed off.

Before she even gets to me, she demands, "Where have you been?"

"I uh—"

"And don't bother making up some lie. I know exactly where you've been. I came here looking for you to tell you one of my friends with money has agreed to pay the rent on a hole-in-the-wall office downtown so we can open our draft-counseling office, and one of the frat boys here told me you'd gone down to Mexico. He said you took a couple of the other frat guys down there. I asked him why they would want to go down there, but he didn't want to say. I kept at him, until finally he said, 'You know, girls.' I asked him what girls. but he didn't want to talk to me anymore. Okay, John, what was it he didn't want to tell me? I've heard there are Mexican girls down there who provide sex for money. Is that what it was? You went down there to find Mexican whores?"

"Aw, listen, Cat, these guys are still young. They don't have any experience with girls so—"

"So you provide them with that experience. Do you get paid for being the pimp?"

"Come on, Cat. They saw I had a car and asked me to drive them down there."

"So, while you were there, why not dip in a bit yourself? I can't believe I let you sleep in the same bed with me. It makes me feel dirty."

She seems so angry, I'm not sure there is anything I can say to defend myself.

She turns and walks away, shaking her head.

What should I do now? My trying to explain myself didn't work. Should I just let her go and hope she'll eventually calm down?

As I watch her walk away, I think I detect some hesitation. If she was really as mad as she's letting on, she'd be walking a lot faster to get way away from me. Does that mean she actually does want me to explain? I could try. But maybe I should quit trying to explain and just give her a chance to ask me more questions, if she wants to.

I hurry to catch up to her, but I don't say anything. Instead, I just walk next to her.

We don't go much farther before she stops and says, "Well, are you going to explain yourself, or not?"

"I was telling you the truth, Cat. I always tell you the truth. When one of the fraternity guys found out I had a car, he asked me to drive him down there. He said he was a virgin and he'd heard there were young girls down there in Mexico who would have sex with him."

"So, you helped him."

"I drove him down there."

"I assume he paid for that first-time sex down there. How much do those girls charge?"

She stops walking while she waits for my answer. What is she up to? "Why would you want to know something like that, Cat?"

"Just curious about how this form of commerce works. You know, how much we rich Americans are contributing to the Mexican economy."

"They charged five dollars. American."

"So, you can barely pay for a college education, but you can spring for five bucks when you want to get laid."

"Cat! Why are you wanting to think the worst of me? I didn't have sex with any of those girls. I just drove the guys down there."

"A likely story."

"Cat, I'm going to ask you again, why are you wanting to think the worst of me?"

She looks down at the ground. "Aw, I don't know, John. After we slept together last night, I guess I was thinking we had something special going. And you know . . ."

I reach out to touch her arm. "I thought the same thing, Cat. So, let's not spoil it by thinking the worst of each other. Tell you want, I haven't eaten anything all day, so why don't we go over to the school cafeteria, and I'll tell you all about what happened down there. It's actually a pretty interesting story."

"Okay, but I'm damn tired of the stuff they've got in that cafeteria. How about if I treat us to some better food at a place I know."

"Okay, but I've got money too. Isn't the male supposed to pay?"

"Usually, but not when you can't even afford five bucks for a Mexican whore."

"Very funny, Cat. Just for that, I am going to let you pay."

We walk back to my car, and then Cat guides me to what she says is her favorite restaurant. Turns out, it's a plastic-booth kind of place that serves breakfast all day.

As soon as we slide into a booth by the front window, a young woman comes to take our order. Cat knows her, and tells her she should take my order first because "he's the male." I nod and smile to show her I get the joke and order from the menu what they call a "pancake sandwich, two pancakes with a fried egg in between.

Cat tells the waitress she wants her usual.

As soon as the waitress leaves, Cat tells me her "usual" is French fries and a chocolate milk shake. Because she's "watching her weight."

I ask her how chocolate milkshakes help her lose weight.

She says, "Simple. Once you drink a whole milkshake, especially chocolate, you aren't hungry for hours."

"I guess that makes sense."

"As skinny as you are, I suppose you also have a secret way to keep the weight off."

"I also have a simple method, I forget to eat."

She does a dutiful chuckle.

When the food arrives, I launch into the story of how Tim came to me to ask for a ride down to Mexico, to "lose his virginity" and how that led to my trek in the terrible heat across the desert into the United States with Clara and Maria.

She stops me to ask, "You accompanied them across the desert? Why would you do that?"

"Well, it was something interesting to do, and besides, I was worried about the little girl. Her mother didn't want me anywhere near her, but I tagged along anyhow for the little girl's sake. And it was a good thing I did, because we ran out of water, and I had to go find a rancher's windmill that pumped water out when the wind blew."

"Jesus, John, that little girl might have died out there if you hadn't found that water."

"That's what I was thinking. Well, anyhow, we eventually got out of that desert and came back here."

"And where are they now? Around here?"

"Clara knew some people over in Mesa that worked picking oranges. That's where they went."

"Clara is that close? Do you ever go over there to see her?"

I notice that she said "her" rather than "them," but I decide to ignore that and just say, "No. I'm pretty sure they're okay now. But I do hope Maria will get to go to some kind of school over there, eventually. And I worry about what they'll do when orange-picking season is over."

"We should go over there and check on them."

"Yeah, I suppose we could do that."

"Would I like Clara?"

"Uh, maybe. She can be tough. She knows what she wants. Most importantly, her life revolves around her daughter."

"The only reason? Don't all those poor girls want to escape?"

"No, they don't. I'm glad you asked me that. I talked to one of the girls, and she said—"

"Wait, I thought you didn't go in with any of those girls."

"One of the guys I took down there has a lot of money, and he paid for all of us to go in, so I used the time to ask the girl about her life. She told me they find the girls on the streets, either orphans or runaways from terrible home situations. She said they make sure their life of, uh, servicing *Gringo* boys is a lot better life than the terrible lives they were living. They have fun parties for the girls, and they give them money for shopping."

"So that's how they control them."

"Right."

"But what happens when they get older and aren't in demand anymore?"

"I had that same thought. But right now, they're still kids and only see the life that's right in front of them."

"I hate to think about what's going to happen to them."

"Yeah, probably not good."

After my story is finished, we eat our food in silence. I expect she's thinking about what kind of life those girls are in for. Maybe she wants to go down there and rescue them, even though I just told her they don't want to be rescued.

Finally, Cat says, "Well, will you be going back down there anymore?"

"No, I won't. Even if I wanted to, after I helped Clara and her daughter escape, the management doesn't want to see me in their place of business anymore."

She says, "Good. Glad to hear it." She looks away. "Well, I've got to get to the fountain. We want to tell the audience about getting our draft counseling center open. They want me to be in charge."

"You should be in charge."

"So you say, John, but I've never been in charge of anything. All I've done is get up in front of a few people to yell at them."

"I'm sure you'll be great at being in charge. Just use your . . . energy."

"Energy, eh. In other words, just keep on getting pissed off and yelling at everybody."

I smile and reach out to touch her hand. "If that's what it takes."

"Ha! I guess I'll see, won't I?

We leave the cafe, and I drive her back to the campus. She gets out, but before she closes the door, she leans back in and says, "I guess you'll be picking me up later, right?"

I say, "I am?"

"Sure. Have you forgotten what day this is? Callum's class. It's his last class of the summer."

"I'm not sure I want another night of drunken wandering with Callum."

"Then don't do that part, but you have to come to class with me. I'm not sure I can deal with him anymore."

"Oh, okay. See you then."

As I drive away, I'm not sure I'm any better at dealing with Callum than she is, but for different reasons. He told me he wanted to get her into bed. That's understandable, but what does he want with me? Someone to party with, or just someone to drive him around and pay the tab.

No, there's more to Callum than that. He's smart, and he comes on strong in social situations, but there's something more going on with him, down deep. As if he's got something to prove. Maybe to himself.

Chapter Twenty-Two

I drive back to the frat house to check on Spud. He's finally managed to wake up, and he's waiting for me out at the curb. I guess he missed me.

I don't even make it to my room before I'm intercepted by Tin who has a list of things for me to do, "Just a few little chores around the house," he says. Maybe getting this free room isn't going to be so free after all.

The first thing he says needs to be done is to mow the lawn. He shows me an old push lawn mower, but it's so worn and rusty, I can barely move it. Looking at the state of the mower, it's surprising the grass isn't even higher.

There's a can of motor oil next to the lawn mower. Feels about half full. I use it to soak the moving parts of the old mower, and I'm soon able to at least get the old thing to move, and I'm eventually able to do a fair job of mowing the lawn.

By the time I get all the rest of the chores done, it's time to go pick up Cat for her writing class with Callum.

She's waiting for me out by the street, and I can see she's irritated. I wonder why.

But as we drive away, she's not saying what has her upset. Is it still the fact that I drove the guys down to the girls in Mexico?

"You know John, I don't think it's right for a male professor to hit on female students."

"I assume you're thinking about Callum."

She doesn't answer, so I say, "So, why don't you tell him?"

She takes a quick look at me, and then turns away. "You know why."

"I do?"

"Sure. A lot of the professors like to check girls out to see how far they'll go. And some girls learn it's a way to get a good grade."

"So, they're both playing the game?"

"Don't be naive, John. It's a kind of blackmail. If the girl doesn't go along with it, they might get a bad grade."

I see her point. In the high school I went to, there was a PE teacher who always chose an attractive girl when he wanted to demonstrate the proper way to hit a volleyball. He'd lift them up by the waist, supposedly to show the proper hitting posture. I don't think it ever went any further than that, but maybe it did and we just never knew about it.

Cat stares at me, frowning. "You don't have anything to say about it?"

"I was just trying to remember if I ever saw anything like that in high school. Like you said, I'm the one who's been living under a rock back there in Illinois."

"Don't try to use that one. It doesn't take college experience to know what's right and what isn't. Besides, by now I'm onto you. You watch people to learn about them. You don't try to prove you're smart, but you are. Damn smart."

"Nice of you to say that, Cat."

"Stop that!" She shakes her finger at me. "Don't play dumb. Are we going to have real conversations or not?"

Interesting. She's being complimentary while she insults me. But I get it. She's telling me if I want to keep spending time with her, I'm going to have to respond honestly, and more in depth. She's demanding it, so I guess if I'm going to spend time with her, I'll have to figure out how to respond in that way. "Yes, Cat, I do want to have real conversations with you. But I'm out of my element here. Don't make fun of my under-a-rock metaphor. I grew up an orphan in an ordinary Midwestern town. Went to ordinary Midwestern public schools. What would I know about how it is to be a college student? For all I knew, your relationship with Callum might have been established long ago."

She starts to respond, but I hold up my hand to interrupt

her: "You said you were going to teach me things, Cat. So, teach me."

That stops her. She's staring at me. "So, you deny being smart?'

"I never said that, but until I got here in Arizona, what did I have to compare it with? Is it smart being able to rebuild a car engine?"

"Pull over to the side."

"Pull over?"

"Yes, let's have this out."

Now, she seems angry again. Or maybe it's not anger, just her style of intensity, a way to get serious. I pull over to the curb and wait for her to go on. She's staring at me, wearing a sort of bemused smile.

"Okay, mister ordinary Midwest, let's start with what you just said. How can a kid figure out how to rebuild a car engine without being really smart?"

"It's not that big a deal, Cat. Lots of young guys work in auto shops."

"Right, they learn from others, in a car repair place. But I didn't get the idea you learned in that kind of environment."

"No, I didn't have that opportunity, but I wanted to do it, so I'd get my hands on a wreck to practice on. There were plenty of them around, abandoned, free or nearly free. I just started tearing a car engine down to figure out how to get it running again."

"As if that was easy."

"Well, it wasn't all that hard once you figure it out."

"You're telling me figuring out something as complex as a car engine is easy."

"Well, relatively easy, Cat. You take the engine apart to see what's broken. You get a replacement for the broken part, and then you put it all back together."

"No, that is not easy, *John*. And don't go adding my name to the end of every sentence to make sure I'm believing you. I do believe you, *John*. We don't have a problem with that. My problem is with you hiding your intelligence. It's understandable if you want to hide it from the world, but don't hide it from me. Now tell me, how did you really learn how to rebuild an engine, all by yourself."

"Well, you learn as you go along." I pause, and then smiling, add, "*Cat.* You just grab a wrench and start doing things. Pretty soon, the parts and pieces start to add up, so you learn to keep track of it all. I don't suppose it's the usual way, but I laid parts out on labeled pieces of paper. Later, I used those notes to put it all back together."

"As easy as that, eh?"

"Well, when I was first learning about engines, I was doing it just for that, for learning. I was working on an old wrecked car, so I didn't have anybody waiting for me to get it done. I could take my time as I was learning."

"And you didn't run into anything you couldn't solve all by yourself?"

" I did worry that I might need some specialized tools. All I had was basic hammers and wrenches and stuff."

"Specialized like what?"

"Like a torque wrench, for example."

"What's that?"

"Are you sure you want to know?"

"Sure. You're teaching me, right?"

"Okay. When you put an engine back together, there are some things you should tighten to a specific tightness. For that, you need a torque wrench."

"And you didn't have one."

"Right. I just tightened down the bolts until they felt tight."

"Did that work?"

"Not really. In the first engine I rebuilt, I was scared I might break something, so I didn't tighten the head bolts tight enough."

"Did the engine blow up?"

"No, it just leaked oil around the gaskets. All I had to do was tighten them down some more until the leaks stopped. But the exciting part was that my first rebuilt car did run. When it started and seemed to be running fine, I felt like I'd done something miraculous."

"Sounds pretty miraculous to me, because you did it by yourself, without teachers or books. Sounds like genius stuff to me."

"Aw, Cat, I think anybody could work on car engines. All they'd have to do is stick with it until they learn it."

"Yeah, stick-to-itiveness. Thomas Edison said genius is a little bit of inspiration and a lot of perspiration. I mean, really, how many have that amazing combination of skills? Only geniuses"

"Well, I did tend to stick to things. I eventually got more tools and pretty soon, I was in the business of working on cars for other kids. I even learned some tricks to make their cars go faster, and the word got around about that, so I ended up working on the cars for a lot of the guys in my high school."

"You just proved my point. I got straight As in school, but not because I was all that smart. I just read the books and studied for the tests. You learned new things on your own. You're all about learning. That's what geniuses do."

Am I really all that smart? Maybe she's just saying that because she likes me. Or does she need me to be smart in order to measure up to be her boyfriend? Time to change the subject. "Well, don't you think we'd better get to your class?"

She's smiling and nodding. "Okay, mister smart guy. Let's go, but know I'm onto you."

She doesn't say anything else as I drive to the neighborhood where Callum's class is held, but I do wonder what she's thinking. She wants me to be very smart, probably to measure up to her own intelligence. She said she got top grades in school, but she tried to play that down. Why? Does she think she got those top grades by just studying harder than others. But is that really possible, to get the highest grades without being the smartest? Still, thinking back, the kids in my schools that got reputations for being smart, got those reputations because they got the top grades. And they were the ones most often called on in class by the teachers. Did I think I was smarter than them? I guess I did, but only with regard to things outside of class. I was pretty sure those smart kids would struggle in the world I lived in. It really did take a lot of learning, with constant heightened awareness, to figure out a functional route, actually, a functional behavioral and psychological route, through the everyday challenges of being an orphan, with its ever-changing sets of rules and requirements.

Once we arrive at the house and go in, the room is set up pretty much the same as the last time—students sitting around waiting while Callum looks over his notes.

As we search for an open place to sit on the floor, Callum looks up. "Well, here you are at last, Cat. And with mister John No-name. Just for being late, John, you have to be my victim again."

I ignore him and sit on the floor next to Cat. I wonder what he'll do if I refuse to participate.

Callum says, "Well, Cat, is it all right if we get started now?"

She holds out both hands, palms up, her way of telling him to go right ahead.

Callum says, "Okay, now that we have Cat's permission, where did we leave off last time?"

Nobody answers, so he points at me. "John no-name will know."

I say, "You were having us learn about dialogue by studying Strindberg."

"I was? Damn, that sounds like a good lesson. Maybe I'm not such a bad teacher after all. Okay, should we do more of that?"

Nobody answers.

"Okay, if you don't want to do Strindberg, we can do something else. Last time, I heard some of you whispering, 'Why doesn't he teach us about an author we've heard of?'"

Some of the students are shaking their heads.

"Now, now, don't deny it. You are all desperate to learn about the use of dialogue in stories, not in plays. And you want a famous author. Okay, if you insist, how about the most famous story maker ever, Charles Dickens. And since you are all demanding a story you've heard of, we can do his best story, *Oliver Twist*. It works somewhat for a dialog lesson because when Dickens does a conversation between two people, he identifies the speaker every time, almost as if he was laying out lines in a play. Today's readers wouldn't put up with that kind of endless repeating of the speaker's names. Now, they assume alternating lines of quoted material in a story refer to alternating speakers, what I call ping-pong dialogue."

He holds up the papers he'd been reading. "I just happen to have a few pages of that story."

He points at me. "Come on back up here, John."

I might as well. I can tell he won't start the lesson until I get up there. After what evolved between us the last time, he thinks I'll deliver lines in the way he wants them delivered.

As soon as I sit in the chair next to him, he hands me one of the pages. It's not in the play format like last time. It's just lines of quoted dialogue between Undertaker and Mr. Bumble.

Callum, says, "Okay, here we go, doing what you all demanded. I'll read the undertaker's lines, and Mister John here will read the lines of a character known as Mr. Bumble. I can guarantee you won't like it, because unlike a stage play wherein the dialogue has to stand on its own, a writer like Dickens characterizes in writing how the lines are spoken. For example, 'Not a drop—not a drop, said Mr. Bumble, waving his right hand in a dignified, but still placid manner.'"

With that, Callum says, "Here we go. 'I have taken the measure of the two women that died last night.'"

I respond with the next line, that of Mr. Bumble: "You'll make your fortune."

Callum scratches his head, looking off into the distance. I guess he knows this story pretty well and is playing the part as Dickens wrote it. He looks at me and reads the next Undertaker line: "Think so? The prices allowed by the board are very small, Mr. Bumble."

Next, I think the Mr. Bumble character is about to make some kind of joke, so I say the line with a smile: "So are the coffins."

I must have guessed right because Callum is ready with the next Undertaker line: "Well, well, Mr. Bumble. There's no denying that, since the new system of feeding has come in, the coffins are something narrower and more shallow than they used to be. Well-seasoned timber is an expensive article, sir; and all the iron handles come by canal from Birmingham."

I continue smiling as I read, "Well, every trade has its drawbacks, and a fair profit is of course allowable."

"Of course, of course, and if I don't get a profit upon this or that particular article, why, I make it up in the long-run, you see." Callum laughs a bit. I think, it was meant to be a sarcastic laugh.

"Just so," I read.

"Though I must say, Mr. Bumble, that I have to contend against one very great disadvantage, which is, that all the stout people go off the quickest. I mean that the people who have been better off, and have paid rates for many years, are the first to sink when they come into the house. And let me tell you, Mr. Bumble, that three or four inches over one's calculation makes a great hole in one's profits, especially when one has a family to provide for, sir."

My next line seems to change the subject. "By the bye, you don't know anybody who wants a boy, do you? A porochial 'prentis, who is at present a dead-weight. A millstone, as I may say, round the porochial throat? Liberal terms. Uh, five pounds?"

Callum is grinning. I hope that means he likes what I'm doing.

He reads, "Gadso! That's just the very thing I wanted to speak to you about." He reaches out to tap my chest. "You know, dear me, what a very elegant button that is, Mr. Bumble; I never noticed it before."

I also look down at my chest. Even though I'm only wearing my thrift-store blue shirt with ordinary white buttons, I try to imagine I'm wearing some kind of fancy coat with fancy buttons. "Yes, I think it is rather pretty. The board presented it to me on New-year's morning. I put it on, I remember, for the first time, to attend the inquest on that reduced tradesman who died in a doorway at midnight."

Callum taps the side of his head. "I recollect. The jury brought in, Died from exposure to the cold, and want of the common necessaries of life, didn't they?"

"Yes, as I remember."

"And they made it a special verdict, I think, by adding some words to the effect, that if the relieving officer had—"

My next line starts with two words, followed by an exclamation point. That could mean it was loud, or angry. I'll go with angry. "Tush—foolery! If the board attended to all the nonsense that ignorant jurymen talk, they'd have enough to do."

Callum seems to be taking time to think before he responds: "Very true."

I quickly say, "Juries! Juries is ineddicated, vulgar, grovelling wretches." I'm sticking with angry. I hope that's what Dickens intended.

Callum nods. "So they are. So they are."

He repeated the undertaker's line twice, but I don't have time to wonder why. I'll try also combining my next two lines: "They haven't no more philosophy nor political economy about 'em. I despise 'em." I hope Callum didn't mind me modifying my lines. It just seemed like my character was feeling like what he had to say was urgent.

"No more they have. So do I."

I quickly respond with my next line: "I only wish we'd a jury of the independent sort in the house for a week or two. The rules and regulations of the board would soon bring their spirit down for them."

"Let 'em alone for that."

"Well, what about the boy?"

"Oh! Why, you know, Mr. Bumble, I pay a good deal towards the poor's rates."

"Hem! Well?"

"Well, I was thinking that if I pay so much towards 'em, I've a right to get as much out of 'em as I can, and so I think I'll take the boy."

With that line, we've reached he bottom of the page, and Callum turns to the class. "Well, what do you all think? Is dialogue in fiction as good as dialogue in a play?"

At first, none of the students seem to want to make a commitment. But then one guy sitting on the couch applauds, and that gets the others to join in.

As soon as they stop, Callum says, "Well, I guess that means you liked it. Or maybe you were applauding young Mister John here's acting job."

Nobody responds.

Callum says, "No? Well, if you could see the lines he was *supposed* to be reading, you'd see what a good acting job he was doing. Now, we could do more, but I expect you are all trying to resist looking at your wrist watches. Eager to get out of here to go on your dates? Or wanting to go see that latest movie you've all been hearing about? Well, whatever you oh-so-young folks like to do, I'll let you go do it. Now I know you didn't do what I told you to last time, read up on the Strindberg plays. So now, you have to do that, and also read up on Dickens, too. And don't just read the Cliffs Notes on Dickens. After you get out of that movie, no matter how exciting it was, go to the library and read some actual Dickens. Think about how different Dickens is from Strindberg, even though they were both writing about the human condition." He stands up and pulls me to my feet. "So, you all can go to your movie, me and John here are going go to get drunk."

He tows me to the front door, and on the way, he also manages to grab Cat's arm to also tow her along.

Once we're out on the sidewalk, he slows down and seems unsteady. As soon as he lets go of my arm, he sits down on the grass and seems to be having trouble remaining in a sitting position. Apparently, he was not just pulling me along by my arm, he was using his grip on my arm to steady himself. Now, he's completely lost it.

He looks up at me with glazed-over eyes. "Get me . . . get me to car. Quick. Other students. Not quite . . . feeling . . ."

I get ahold of his arm, and Cat grabs his other arm so we can pull him to his feet. We manage to get him to my car and try to get him into the front seat, but he resists and insists Cat get in first. He mumbles, "Only polite."

As soon as they're both in, I close the passenger door and go around to get into the driver's seat.

Callum sees a few of the students coming out of the house and yells, "Go, go! For Christ's sake, get me out of here."

I do as he said, but as soon as we're away from that neighborhood, I ask, "What's the matter, Callum?"

"Nothin'," he mumbles. "Nothin' tall."

Cat looks at me, but all I can do is shrug and keep on driving.

Callum slaps the car's dashboard and says, "Okay, I'm good. All things good. Just fine. Perfect. Matter fact, if anybody can handle speed, it's me. So what if it kills me? Nobody will mind. Nobody will miss ol' Callum."

Cat says, "That's not true, Callum. We would miss you. And your students would miss you."

Callum waves off her words. "No they won't. Already forgettin' me. Hey, there must be some brand new movie just out. Hell of a lot more important than anything I ever had to say."

I say, "What about your books, Callum? Your novels? I bet every one of those students wishes they could be as success-ful a writer as you."

He also waves that idea off. "Buncha nonsense. Crazy protagonists written by a crazy writer. Got published because I worked for a publisher who felt sorry for me. Successful? How do you define successful? By making money? No way to make money writing. Publisher always says they used up your advance on . . " He uses two fingers to make quote marks in the air "distruten spenses."

I'm not sure what that means, but he doesn't go on with it. He leans against Cat and seems to fall asleep.

He's all but lying on Cat's lap, but she doesn't push him off. She says, "Well, John, what're we gonna do with him?"

"I guess we'd better take him home. I know where he lives."

"Yeah. He's crashing and hard. I wonder how much he took."

"Took?"

"Yeah, didn't you hear him mention speed? Hard to say what kind of uppers he took, but I think maybe he needs speed to get himself through these classes. To get through life, probably."

"I don't know about that kind of thing, Cat. Not many drugs around that Illinois rock I came from."

"Really? I thought drugs were everywhere by now. I bet some of your Illinois housewives are getting uppers by prescription to get through their miserable days."

I glance at her. "Is that what you think? That their days are miserable?"

"Well. mine would be if I ever got stuck in that kind of situation."

"So, you don't ever plan to get married?"

"Is that a proposal?"

I do a sort of chuckle to show her I get her joke.

I park in front of Callum's apartment house, and we manage to get him out of the car. We get on both sides of him to walk him to his apartment. He is walking, sort of, so we finally manage to get him inside his apartment and aim him to the couch. He obliges by flopping down on it and immediately falling asleep.

I whisper to Cat, "Do you think he'll be all right if we just leave him here to sleep it off?"

"He will or he won't, she says, staring at him. I bet he's been in this state more than once, so we've done all we can. Let's get out of here."

Back in my car, as I pull away from the curb, Cat says, "I'm hungry. I've still got some of that food left. Let's go to my place."

As I drive to her apartment, she seems to be lost in thought, so I don't disturb her. When I pull up in front of her apartment building, she just sits there. Is she waiting for me to say something? I think about the first time I pulled up here and found her out by the pool telling others about the Gulf of Tonkin incident. Things sure seem to have advanced between us since then. Or am I making that up? I guess if we're being honest with each other now, I should just ask her. "Are you going to want me to stay with you tonight?"

She pretends to be open-mouthed surprised. "Why how presumptuous of you, Mister John. You think I'm so hard up I need to feed you in order to get you to sleep with me?"

"Very funny, Cat. What I was thinking was before I come in, I should go take care of Spud."

"Oh right, your supposed job. Forget that nonsense, John. A genius like you was not cut out to be a damn caretaker. Yes, stay with me tonight, and then stay with me from now on. My rich grandparents can afford our rent and food, so you don't need that frat house job anymore."

Is that what I want? I wasn't even sure she would want me to stay with her tonight, and now she says she wants me to move in.

"Uh oh, you're stalling. That means you're not inter-ested."

"No, Cat, I was just thinking."

"Well, don't think too long. How long do you think that kind of offer is going to last?"

Now she seems irritated. I reach over and take her hand. "Don't be like that, Cat. Your offer is a serious kind of thing, so I'm thinking about it seriously. I'd have to make some changes."

"Changes? Like what? Like resigning from your impor-tant duties over at the frat house? Or like resigning from your other job of ferrying those boys down to the Mexican whores?"

She jerks her hand away from me and stares out her side window.

I know what this is, it's her insecurity coming out again. She abruptly asked me to move in with her, and now, she's interpreting my hesitation to mean I don't want to. "Cat, listen to me. Yes, I do want to move in with you. I like you very much, so why wouldn't I? My duties over there at the frat house are no big deal. I wasn't thinking my staying at the frat house was any kind of permanent thing anyhow. That's not it. And I already told you I wouldn't be going back down to Mexico. I'm just taking your offer seriously, so I need to think through what it would mean."

She turns back to look at me, and I can see tears in her eyes. "You're afraid it would mean you'd have to put up with my . . . what would you call it, my changeability."

"No, Cat, I was thinking . . . well, I guess I was thinking that I've been a loner for so long, it would be a big change."

She starts to protest, but I hold up my hand to stop her. "Listen, Cat, there's no point in me going on about this. Yes, I do want to move in with you. Of course I do. Just let me go over to the frat house and get my stuff. Okay?"

Finally, she smiles. A little. And this time she grabs my hand and squeezes it. I hope that means all is well now.

She opens the car door and hops out. She leans back in and says, "Get over there and end that part of your life, and then come right back here and start this part. And hurry because I'm gonna fix you somethin' good to eat. We gotta do something about you always forgetting to eat." She closes the car door, and then leans down to wave at me through the window before turning away to go to her apartment.

Well, she was smiling, so I guess that means she's happy about this. I wonder how long she's been thinking about inviting me to stay with her. It's only been one day since I first set foot in her apartment, but maybe she was thinking about getting together with me before that.

As I drive to the frat house, I keep thinking about all the different houses I've lived in. I was one of many little kids crowded together in so many different temporary orphan homes I can't remember them all. But even then, I always found a way to stay alone, at least in my mind. But this is going to be different. Cat will expect me not only to be honest with her, but also to be "there" with her at all times.

Can I learn not to be the loner, at least when I'm with her? Well, I've agreed to do it, so I guess now I'll have to learn how to do it. I suppose, in this next new phase of my life, I'll learn about that, like I've learned about everything else. By doing it.

Chapter Twenty-Three

When I pull up in front of the frat house, I see guys unloading their cars. Looks like the frat guys are coming back from their summers away from the university.

When I get out to the backyard, I see a lot of guys have placed their cardboard boxes all along the sidewalk in front of the sleeping rooms. So far, it doesn't look like anybody wants my room, but that very well could happen at any time. So, Cat asking me to move in seems to have been exceptionally good timing for me. This whole trip has been like that, just going forward until something happens. So far, that something has always turned out to be good.

One of the guys notices me, and comes to shake my hand, saying "Hi there. Are you a new pledge?"

'No, I was hired this summer to kind of take care of the place. And to take care of the dog."

"Oh, good."

"But now, I've found a new place to live. Is Tin around? I should tell him."

"He's in the main building."

I find him in the dining hall, all by himself. He's eating a banana and reading a book.

I go sit next to him. "Hi, Tin, I'm glad I found you. I needed to tell you I'm leaving."

He seems surprised. "Oh, yeah? Back to Illinois?"

"No, no. I mean I can't be your groundskeeper any more. Or take care of Spud. I found another place to live."

"Oh yeah, a cheaper place than free?"

"Very funny. Actually, I met a girl. She wants me to move in with her."

"Wow! Very cool. Who is she?"

"I doubt if you know her. I met her on campus. She was leading an anti-war protest over at the fountain."

"Oh, yeah. I've seen her there. The war-protester girl."

"That's her."

"Good, good. She seems . . . uh, nice."

I smile at anybody thinking of Cat as "nice."

"Her name is Cat. A history major."

"History major, eh. Well, that figures. History major worrying about the next war."

I stand up. "Okay, I'd better go. She's fixing me something to eat"

"A place to live, and feeds you too. Looks like you fell into it, John, old boy."

I shake his hand and leave through the front door.

But then, I change my mind and go out back again to say goodbye to Spud.

I find him in his usual place, lying in the shade of the building, sound asleep. I don't need to wake him up. I just kneel down next to him and whisper, "So long, Spud. I'll come back to see you when I can.

He doesn't open his eyes, but it doesn't matter if he heard me; I will come back to see him sometimes.

I stand up and head for my car, but when I look back, I see he has one eye open. He's watching me walk away. Why that sly old dog. He knew I was leaving even before I said it. I wave goodbye, but he quickly closes his eye again.

Back at Cat's, I grab my few possessions and head for the apartment. I wonder if the neighbors are watching from behind their curtains. I guess that doesn't matter; they'll see me coming and going from now on.

I hesitate at her door. Should I knock? No, I guess I live here now too.

I go in and drop my bundle of stuff in a corner of the living room. I find Cat in the tiny kitchen fixing our lunch. I say, "Whatcha cooking?"

She partially turns to frown at me. "Not cooking anything up. I don't cook. Never did, never will, so don't expect it."

I do my appropriate chuckle. "That's the last thing I'd expect, Cat. I'm happy to get anything other than those dry bagels at the university cafeteria."

"Well, then I suspect you'll like what I'm fixing, something I bet they never gave under that rock back in Illinois. I figured since we got that good fresh bread, we should have something good to spread on it. Avocado."

"Avocado? What's that?"

Now it's her turn to chuckle. "Just as I expected. You've never heard of it, have you?"

"No. What is it?" I look over her shoulder. "Green food?"

She smiles. "An avocado is a fruit, but it doesn't taste sweet like a regular fruit. More like . . . well, you'll see. They don't grow in Arizona, but some of the bigger stores bring them in. From coastal California."

As before, we eat sitting in the living room as we watch TV. Cat was right, Avocado is nothing like any fruit I've eaten before. It's surprisingly good, even though, as she said, it's not sweet.

The only thing Cat wants to watch on TV is news, so she keeps on popping up to change the channel. There are only a few stations, and she keeps on having to adjust the double pointed metal antenna to try to get the Phoenix channels to come in clearer.

She finally gives up searching for news and says, "Come on, let's go to bed."

"Uh, it's still pretty early, Cat."

"Are you saying you don't want to come to bed with me?"

"No, if you're ready for bed, I am too."

She leads me into her bedroom, and when she takes off all her clothes, I do the same. But this time, since the daylight is still streaming through the window, I get the opportunity to look her over. She's been hiding her nice body in those loose-fitting clothes. Knowing her, that's probably quite intentional.

She hops into bed, but doesn't cover herself up, so I do the same. For several minutes, we just lie there next to each other. I stare up at the ceiling. She may be waiting for me to do something, but the last time I was in this bed with her, she pulled me close, and went right to sleep. This time, she's not doing anything.

Finally, she turns to me and says, "You, mister, are not a very romantic person."

"Well, the last time we were in this bed, you went right to sleep."

"Is that what you want to happen this time?"

"Uh, no, not really."

"Well, what do you want to happen?"

"Cat, this was your idea, so don't play this game with me. Of course, I'd like to make love to you, but I'm not sure what you want."

"So, here we are in bed together, both of us naked, and we're just talking."

"So we are."

She does a little sound, maybe a sort of chuckle, and rolls over on top of me. "Is this better?"

"Much better."

Chapter Twenty-Four

Last night confirmed my belief that Cat wanted to be in charge, even when it comes to love-making. Now, lying here with the first rays of dawn coming in the window, I'm realizing that although Cat comes on aggressively, I'm learning that she's really not all that sure of herself. She's always measuring herself, and is never quite sure she's as good as she wants to be. She accused me of being a genius, but hiding it. Now, I think she got focused on that because she wants to think of herself as a superior person and is always trying to measure up to anyone she's with.

She touches my shoulder. "You're awake. What're you thinking about"

"I was thinking about you, of course."

She turns onto her side to look at me. "Well, I would hope so. I was afraid you were just lying there wishing I would hurry up and wake up, because you're hungry. So, what were you thinking about me?"

"About what kind of person you are. I'm looking forward to getting to know you better."

"So, do you think making love helps you to get to know a person better?"

I smile and say, "Definitely. But mostly, just being with a person for a while is most of what's needed."

She nods.

I add, "Unless the person hides behind a facade, like uh, like Callum."

"Ha. Psychology again."

"Just pointing out the obvious."

"Obvious to you. What's obvious to me is that I'm hungry, and I don't have anything for breakfast. Or should I say, *we* don't have anything for breakfast since you live here now too."

"Do I?"

"You do. I'm not going to play landlord. I want you to accept that this is now your place too."

"Well, I wish I could help you pay the rent, but remember it was you that took away my ability to make money by driving frat guys down to Mexico."

"Aw, don't start thinking like that. I don't pay the rent on this place either. My rich grandparents off there in California insist on paying for everything. They even send me a monthly allowance. They really, really want their granddaughter to amount to something, to be a smart college graduate."

"Well, I hope I get the chance to thank them sometime."

"Ha! You'd better not hope for that. If they could actually see what I'm doing here with their money, they'd probably cut me off. They're so living in the past, they're probably going to vote for Goldwater."

"So, you don't think they'd approve of me?"

"Who knows? Being Republicans, maybe they wouldn't. Or maybe they'd see you as a clean-cut Midwestern fellow who might straighten me out."

"Do you think I will? Straighten you out, I mean."

"Not likely. I'm probably going to be the one trying to straighten you out, Illinois boy. Hang out with me for too long, and I'll have you wearing a beard and long hair to our anti-war demonstrations."

"Maybe."

"Right, maybe. But right now, we've got to think up something to eat for breakfast."

"I thought you only drank chocolate milkshakes. To keep from getting hungry."

"By damn, Johnny, you're right. Let's go get chocolate milkshakes, and then I'll take you to see the place we're going to rent downtown to be our draft counseling center.

We get into my car, and she guides me to a funny little booth just off of the main street that seems to sell only ice cream products. I can't imagine how they can compete with the new-era walk-up restaurants like McDonald's.

As soon as we get out of my car, and go to the window, the woman inside says, "Hi Cat, chocolate milkshake?"

Cat grins at her. "You bet. I'm hungry." She points at me. "And make him one too. We've gotta fatten him up."

We take our milkshakes to a beaten-up wooden picnic table that's next to the street.

Cat goes right to work on her milkshake, but waits until I've had a few drinks of my milkshake before asking, "Well?"

"Actually, not a bad breakfast."

"So, maybe I do have a few good ideas, eh?"

"Cat, we talked about that. You're the smartest person I've ever met, so knock off the defensive self-degradation talk."

"Defensive? Self-degradation? That's settles it, you're gonna be a psych major."

"Am I?"

"For sure. You've got me totally figured out."

"Figure you out? That'll be the day."

"Am I that complicated?"

"You know you are."

She frowns. "So, are you sure you want to move in with somebody so complicated? It could get . . . you know, complicated."

"It's one of the reasons I want to be with you."

"Is that right?"

"For sure."

She gets quiet as she drinks her milkshake, so I decide against taking that particular discussion any further. I think we're both aware that we have to just try living together, and time will make things a lot clearer. I get the feeling she's never had a live-in boyfriend, and I think I already made it clear to her that I haven't had that kind of relationship either.

"Well, Mister psychologist, was that our first psych discussion?"

With a smile, I say, "Could be. An interesting discussion over breakfast milkshakes."

"Maybe if you do become a psych major, you can do psych research on how milkshakes promote serious discussions."

I start to respond in kind, but hold back; I think I'm starting to learn she likes to have the last word.

She stands up. "Well, as much as I'd like to talk more about this, I know it's leading into a bad habit of mine, to over think things. Besides, I promised my friends I'd meet them downtown at our new draft counseling center. I want you to come too."

"Okay, but are you sure they'd want me there?"

"Regardless of what my girls might want, I know we have to get men involved. After all, as Callum once told me, it's men they want in the military, not us girls."

"Right. Callum said the same thing to me when we were watching you do anti-draft protest thing at the fountain. He said the Army doesn't want parents seeing their little girls getting their heads blown off."

"More likely they don't think girls would be quite so willing to go kill people in foreign lands."

I start to respond, but before I can say anything, she quickly says, "How about you, Mister Johnny, would you be willing to go kill people?"

Her question stops me. Being a soldier is something I've never thought about.

"Well?"

"I suppose I have to be honest and admit I haven't really thought about it."

"Haven't thought about it? Aren't you an American male, right at the likely draft age?"

"You're saying I should have been thinking about it. I guess you're right, but I just didn't."

She's quiet for a moment, and then reaches out to touch my cheek. "Well, John, you'd better start thinking about it. You know you *are* going to get drafted, sooner or later, don't you?"

"I suppose if that happens, I'll have to deal with it."

"Deal with it is right. That's why we have to get the draft counseling center started. You young males don't have a clue about how to deal with getting drafted. If I'm right, and there's about to be another foreign war, they're gonna need a hell of a lot of cannon fodder. You need to know what to do. Let's go downtown and get the others involved in this discussion. You can be a counselee."

Chapter Twenty-Five

Cat guides me to a storefront in downtown Tempe. The whole block looks pretty rundown, and the place they've rented had probably been designed to be a small shop of some kind. But if it had ever been rented for that purpose, it looks to have been abandoned long ago. Cat said one of her friends with money had rented the place. She probably got it cheap.

Inside, Cat's friends are busy cleaning the place up. It actually looks a little like a functioning operation. They've managed to find desks and chairs. A side table holds a coffee pot and paper cups, and they even have some donuts, labeled as free, but asking for a small donation.

After Cat talks for a few minutes with her friends, she sits me down in one of the chairs and sits opposite me. She leans forward and says, "Okay, Mister Draftee, how do you feel about war?"

I'm not sure where she's going with this, but I do want to play along, so I respond quickly, "Historically, or as a general concept?"

She frowns. "Now, don't try to frame it as a general issue. We're obviously going to have to start counseling draftees by finding out how badly they want to get out of being drafted and sent off to war. So, treat this as real. Now, Mister Draftee, when you get drafted, are you willing to go off to some foreign country and kill people, or maybe get killed yourself?"

"Okay, Cat, a young college-student counselee would probably say they hadn't really thought about it. Why would a young person think about getting killed in a war if there is no war going on?"

"But every young male had to go in and sign up for the draft."

"You're right, every young male had to do it, so it was just a normal thing, something to put off thinking about until later."

"Okay, let's change the scenario. Let's assume I'm right and the US is getting involved in another foreign war. How would you, as a young, draft-age male, will feel about it, then?"

She's got me thinking. That would be a whole different question, especially if the new war would be in a place nobody ever heard of. "Are you asking if, in that case, I would want to get out of the draft?"

"Yes. And don't forget, it will be a war of invasion, invading a primitive backwater country, using our unbelievably powerful and technologically-advanced weaponry to kill simple farmers who are just trying to get by."

"I agree that would be a different thing, Cat. In fact, so different it's hard to believe it could really happen."

"Well, take it from me, it really could. Throughout history, many very powerful countries have invaded smaller less powerful countries. It may not make sense to you, but it does make sense to the politicians and military planners. Don't forget what Goldwater said about the Commie hoards. He implied we have to stop them before they're on the beaches of California. It's how they all think. It justifies their little wars."

I'm still thinking about that when she says, "Okay, now what would you think about getting drafted and going off to kill such people in that kind of war of invasion?"

"Well, I guess that would be different. Not exactly like helping stop Hitler, or some other tyrant who's invading his neighboring countries.

"Right. We would be the invading tyrants."

"Okay, counselor, in that case, what would you advise?"

"That's what we're going to have to learn about. We've been hearing about how to immigrate to Canada, or how to use ailments, like back trouble or heel spurs to get out of it. But there must be other options. We have to learn about them all."

Suddenly, a man comes in through the front door and demands to see who is in charge.

Who the heck could this guy be? He's not tall, but hefty. He's probably still in his twenties, or maybe thirty. Why would he be demanding to know who is in charge? He's not wearing any kind of uniform, just a dark suit and black tie.

Cat goes to meet him, so I get up and go closer in case she needs my support.

The man says, "Are you in charge here?"

Cat says, "Who's asking?"

The man pulls out a black wallet with some kind of ID and says, "Campus security. Tell me, Miss, do you have a permit to run this place?"

Cat is obviously surprised, but from her slight smile I sus-pect she finds the overly confrontive manner of the man to be kind of humorous. I'm impressed with how confident she can be when she wants to be. Was she expecting something like this?

Cat makes a scoffing sound and says, "Now why would campus security be coming downtown here give us trouble? All we're doing is talking here."

Watching this scene play out, the whole thing seems totally absurd. Why would the university even need a campus security force, except maybe to give out parking tickets or some-thing over on campus?

The man says, "You have a sign out front that says this is a draft-counseling center."

Cat puts her shoulders back and looks him right in the eye. "And so it is? Is there a law against that?"

Good for her. This is the confident Cat I like to see.

The guy at first seems a bit taken back, but then he shakes his finger at Cat. "Counsel them to do what? Refuse to support their government?"

Cat gestures to the desks and says, "With the growing trouble in Asia, we know every young male now has a chance of getting drafted, so we—"

"So, you really are trying to get them break the law. Are you all students? I need to see some IDs"

That's it. I can't stand by any longer. I move up next to Cat and say, "Okay, mister, that's enough. Unless you have some specific legal reason to be here off-campus, I suggest you go back to giving out parking tickets over on campus."

"And who are you, young man?"

"Never mind who I am. You have no authority here. Let's go." I take his arm and try to lead him out the front door.

He resists and tries to pull his arm loose. I surprise myself by tightening my grip, and I'm surprised again by how weak he seems as he tries to pull away. Maybe I still have some strength left from all that construction work I did. Or maybe I'm just pissed off enough to get extra strong.

As I pull him to the door, he complains, "You'll be sorry you used force on an officer of the law."

"You're no officer of the law. You're just a pumped-up parking ticker writer trying to throw around authority you don't have. I suggest you stay over there in the university parking lots where you belong."

He pulls his arm loose and hurries out the door. I watch him get into an ordinary old white car and drive away. Undoubtedly his own car. They don't even give him any kind of patrol car. It proves I was right; he's just an ordinary campus ticker giver. He left, but he may not really have given up. He seemed upset about the idea of students starting a draft-counseling center. There may be others who feel the same way. I have the feeling Cat might have to expect more pushbacks, and the next time, the visitors could be real authorities.

When I turn back, everybody in the place starts clapping.

I'm surprised, but I just wave that off and head back for my chair.

Cat intercepts me before I can sit down. "Okay, Mister Hero. We need to talk." She leads me to the side. So, you thought the poor girl needed help against the big bad male."

I shake my head. "No, the guy just irritated me. It was obvious he was trying to puff up what little authority he had to tell you how he thought things should be."

"That was obvious, but you didn't think I could handle him."

"No, Cat, I didn't think that. Like I said, that type of person just irritates me. Sorry if I stepped on your toes."

"It isn't a matter of toes. It's just that I'm trying to hold together something here. In the future, let me be the boss."

"I think it's obvious to everybody that you are the boss. But there is another aspect to what happened. Now your troops know I'll support you, that we're a team. Assuming you do want to be a team with me."

"Of course, I want us to be a team. Aren't I the one that invited you to move in with me."

"Sure, but that's not all that's involved in being a team."

"Okay, mister psych major. Is that how relationships are supposed to work?"

"Seriously, Cat, when I was growing up in all those foster homes, I watched the married couples closely. Not many of them were in what I would call good relationships. They were married, but they didn't seem to be a team. They were living separate lives, having their own friends, and doing separate things. One woman had her women's club that she spent a lot of time with, while her husband had his job, and then went off with his friends every night."

"So, even back then, you were the observer. Amazing a kid in that kind of tough situation, could still be the observer, watching and analyzing. But I guess that's what geniuses do."

Maybe I do tend to over think things, but getting back to the main point. If you're going to be part of this draft-counseling center, I want to be a part of it in any way I can."

She looks me in the eyes. "But what if I'm like those people you saw in those foster homes? Maybe I don't really know how to . . . how to share. I guess the truth is, I haven't really ever done that. With anybody."

"As you know, I haven't either. But when we agreed to live together, didn't we sort of say we'd try it and see how it worked out? We have to work it out as we go along. And here we are, doing just that. We're working it out, aren't we?"

Finally, she smiles. "I guess we are." She pulls me close and kisses me, hard.

I guess that means now she doesn't care if her friends are watching. I take it as a non-verbal statement that she agrees we should at least try to have a full, honest relationship, as a team.

Chapter Twenty-Six

This morning, we're up early, as usual, and as we eat our breakfast cereal, Cat is studying an article in the Phoenix newspaper about the growing crisis in Vietnam. All I saw was the headline, something about the bombing of North Vietnam. I suspect the article is speculation about whether Johnson's bombing campaign in Vietnam is the way to win that war. There's a lot of that kind of speculation going on in the news, and Cat is predicting bombing will fail and lead to the need to send more and more US forces over there.

This morning, as usual, the moment she's done eating, she jumps up, gives me a kiss, and hurries out the door to the Center.

As for me, today, as usual, I have to decide if I want to go to the Center. I've been hanging around there, helping out when I can, but I don't really have a role there. Cat is so busy there, most days, I walk to the university library and spend my day reading. At first I was reading randomly, classic novels and various textbooks, but now I've moved, almost unconsciously, to the psychology section. Cat keeps suggesting I'll become a psychology major, so, I should do more reading about that field. I'm not sure what majoring in psychology would mean, but as Cat likes to point out, I am a habitual observer of people's behavior.

Today, I'm reading a book that describes the past history of psychology as mostly being about the practice and theory of how to treat patients with mental problems. The writings of Freud and Rogers are mentioned, but the book says they've moved out of favor, and now, psychological processes have been emerging as the main focus of psychology study. The book says "behaviorists" like John Watson and B.F. Skinner are getting a lot of attention as they promote a more scientific approach to understanding humans through the study of observable behaviors and how environmental factors can influence the development of those behaviors. I was surprised to read that the psychology department at Arizona State University is mentioned as one of the places that is very involved in that sort of study. Well, if I do decide to major in psychology, it seems that this university is a good place to do it.

I've just started reading a book by B.F Skinner when a young woman hurries up to me and says, "You have to come to the counseling center, right now!"

"Why? What's wrong?"

"Cat's in trouble. She said you spend your time here in the library, and I remember that other time you helped Cat when they tried to shut the center down. She needs that kind of help again."

She leads me out the library's front entrance and starts to run in the direction of downtown. She's a fast runner, but I must still have some of my high school cross country conditioning in me because I'm able to keep up with her.

As we approach the counseling center, there doesn't seem to be any trouble going on right now, but it's clear that something did happen: two young guys are out front replacing the missing big front window with a large piece of plywood.

I hurry inside and find Cat sweeping up the glass. I say, "What happened here, Cat?"

She just shakes her head and continues sweeping.

I touch her arm. "Cat, stop. Tell me what happened."

"No big deal. I can handle it."

"Handle it? What is there to handle? What happened to your front window?"

She continues sweeping as she says, "Bastards. Bastard cops. Used their damn Billy clubs to smash out our window.

"Cops? Really? The police smashed out your front window? Why would they do that?"

"Good question. Why?" She stops sweeping, and leans on her broom as she stares at the plywood that's becoming the new front window. Then, she throws the broom down and turns away.

She's obviously angry, but also maybe about ready to cry.

I take her in my arms, and that triggers the crying.

I don't say anything. I'll just hold her as long as she wants to be held.

But that isn't long. She pushes away and wipes her eyes with the backs of her hands. "They just showed up, John. With no warning. They walked right in and said we had no right to be doing 'this kind of thing.'" I tried to get them to tell me what they thought we were doing that was so wrong, but they ignored me and started yelling that everybody should get out. At first nobody moved. That was when they went to the front window and started smashing it with their clubs. Everybody got scared and ran for the door. My friends. My counselors. The boys that were only here looking for advice. They all got scared and ran away. Why would they run away, John? They left me here all alone."

"They didn't all run away, Cat. One of your counselors came and found me in the library. The others were probably were just scared. They'll be back."

"I grew up thinking the police were the good guys. Well those two cops were not good guys. They were . . . She points at the missing front window. "I don't know what they are, John. Bad. Mean."

"Cat, listen . . ." I stop mid-sentence. I'm pretty sure she won't want me to start what she calls my psychologist talk, but she did say I should always be honest with her, so I'd better do exactly that. "Cat, we talked about observing people to understand them. That means we have to try to understand that some people are going to see things differently than we do. In fact, some people are going to have strong negative feelings about what you're doing here, You know you're just trying to help the young male students, but those cops, and maybe a lot of others, might see you as being unpatriotic. Patriotism can elicit strong emotional feeling in people. You're right, I have been reading about it. When a person has strong beliefs about something is confronted with contrary evidence, they will try to reduce the cognitive discomfort that evidence creates. It's called cognitive dissonance. They may even try to get rid of what's creating that contrary evidence."

"So, you really are going to play psychologist with me

again. Why should I care what those kind of people think?"

"Well, all I'm saying is you may have to face the fact that this may not be the end of this kind of pushback."

"Pushback? Is that what you call what those bastards did? Illegally smashing private property and scaring my friends half to death."

"I guess they're so upset about what you're doing here, they felt like they needed to do something about it."

She turns away and picks up the broom again. She goes back to vigorously sweeping up the glass.

I follow her. "Listen, Cat, I'm not saying your thinking is wrong, I'm just saying to be better prepared, we need to understand how some people are going to react."

She ignores me and continues sweeping.

Maybe this is not the time for logic and reason. I suppose we can have this conversation later, at home. "Okay, Cat. Tell me what I can do. Do you have another broom?"

She doesn't stop sweeping, and without looking at me, she says, "No, we don't have another broom. I don't even know why we should have to be sweeping glass." She starts sweeping even harder.

I get ahold of her arm to try to stop her. Cat, stop sweeping and talk to me. Tell me what you're going to do. What do you need me to do? I agree that you and your friends are doing something important here, so we need to figure out how to keep going."

"Yeah, so important. As soon as my friends got a little bit of what you're calling 'pushback,' they all ran away. And just when we were learning enough about the draft process to really help."

Okay, then tell me about that. Let's go over and sit down in those chairs so you can tell me about that progress. You can counsel me. Tell me what I'm going to do if they really do get another war going, and I get drafted."

"Aw, what's the use. Nobody will pay any attention to me."

"Well, if a big war really does get going in Vietnam, the male students will wake up real quick and want to know what to do. They'll need you and your friends here to advise them."

"I know we can help them, John. We really can. One of my really sharp girls is writing a paper about the draft for her History of the Cold War class. She found out that when the Korean War got going, they drafted over one and half million boys. When more and more boys started getting killed in Korea, they lowered the induction age to eighteen and extended the duty commitment to two years."

"Didn't parents complain about that?"

"Are you kidding? With the usual rah rah for war, they were proud to have their sons go off to war for God and country. That is, until they started coming home in body bags."

"So, do you think it'll be the same if the war in Vietnam gets going? Will people really support another war?"

"Sure they will. And they may have to start drafting boys right out of the draft-registration process. And you can bet they'll make getting out of the draft a lot harder. They'll get rid of deferments, like deferring married men and college students."

"But for now, once I start college, will there still be a college deferment?"

"Yes, but you have to be a full-time student. As soon as their next war gets going, that particular deferment is not likely to last long. When they need more cannon fodder, they'll find a way to get it."

"So, what are you advising?"

"Number one, stay in college, but be ready when the college deferment goes away."

"Be ready to do what?"

"Be ready to run! To get out of this damn warmongering country."

"That's it? No other options?"

"Not really. We're trying to find out more, but so far we haven't been able to talk to anybody who really knows. We've been hearing about some medical conditions that can get you deferred, but those may just be rumors."

She turns toward the door, and I see what she's looking at. It's two of her counselors coming back. She's frowning. Maybe she's not quite ready to forgive them for running away.

While Cat greets them, or maybe berates them, I decide to back off and give her room to be the boss. I should head back to the library.

I say goodbye to Cat and leave.

But halfway back to the library, I'm starting to feel restless. It's a feeling I've been having lately, as if I should go back out into the desert and just wander around.

Now that I think about it, is this the kind of feeling that made me just start driving that day back in Illinois. After all, I still do have my good old Moby, my "wings" to fly away. Am I not sure I really do want to be a college student? Or is it just that I need to take some time to go out by myself and explore once in a while?

Walking and thinking, I find myself at the edge of the campus. Beyond is only the river bed. The river is dry this time of year, but I can smell the dampness the water left behind. It's not exactly the desert, but it is open space where nobody goes. There, I may be able to get away from humanity, at least for a little while.

Chapter Twenty-Seven

By the time I get back to the apartment, Cat is there, surprisingly early in the day for her to have left her draft-counseling center. She's sitting on the floor in front of her little TV set."

I ask, "What's going on?"

She doesn't look away from the TV as she says, "They're saying it's just been revealed that the US has been helping the French in Vietnam by sending helicopters over there, with US pilots to fly them."

"So, they're admitting what you already knew. What are the news people saying about it?"

"That's about all they're saying. I think the TV people are as shocked as anybody. But they have to be careful. They don't want to be seen as taking sides against the government. They did mention that the students at a couple of the big universities back east are starting on-campus protests and what they call teach-ins."

I say, "Teach-ins sound like a good idea. Universities are supposed to be places of learning, aren't they?"

"Supposedly."

"So, don't you think you and your history-major friends could do some of those teach-ins here?"

"Maybe. Don't forget, Arizona State University is a state school, and the right-wing politicians at the capital have control of the university's purse strings. The administrators of this campus may be worried about being seen as condoning anti-government activity."

"So?"

She stands up. "I've got to get back to the Center. I just came here to make sure you were all right. We need to get the word out. We know the US is getting ready to start up another big war, but the people need to know it too. We need to do some real protests. Maybe we should try to shut down the university."

I say, "Okay, I understand you have to go. Things are back

in operation at the Center now? Everybody came back?"

"Yeah, they did. And some of the boys they were counseling came back, too. Some of the draft-age boys are finally getting worried about another new war."

"I'm glad they came to your center. They need information."

"Well, they *sure* do need information, real information. They have no idea what's coming."

"And what is coming, Cat?"

"What is coming is a new war, a bigger war than Korea."

"Korea was pretty big, wasn't it?"

"Sure it was. Thirty-six thousand US soldiers were killed, and hell of a lot more were seriously injured. We got involved in Korea because that country was supposedly being threatened by the Commies from the north. But then, we were the invaders, and history shows invaders never win. A couple of thousand years ago, the Romans invaded the Middle East, and the British Isles, and other places. We now see what happened to them. The Ottoman Empire tried to invade their neighbors, and failed. The Mongols tried the same thing. All of them failed. Not to mention Germany's invasions in Europe and Japan's invasions in Asia that led to the total destruction of their countries."

"So, you're saying this time, we'll be the invaders. But I doubt the Vietnamese have any kind of military to do much against us."

"You wouldn't think so, but we have to go with the truth of history. In every case, the invaders somehow lost, even if they were more powerful. The reason is, people will always turn against invaders. Anyhow, like I said, I've got to get back to the Center. We need to make plans."

She hurries out the door without giving me the usual kiss. I know her well enough by now to know that although nobody can be happy about the prospect of another war, she is energized by the chance to try to do something about it.

And what does it mean for me? If there is a war, and I get drafted, how will I respond to that?

Chapter Twenty-Eight

This morning, after Cat goes to the Draft-Counseling Center, I do what has now become routine for me, reading at the library. On my way, I'm surprised to see Callum sitting on a bench next to the sidewalk. I stop and ask, "What are you doing here, Callum? People watching?"

He looks up at me and nods. "That's exactly what I'm doing, John. You'd be surprised what you can learn about people just by how they walk. What they wear. How their faces reveal what they're thinking about."

"Okay, on that subject, I'll be registering for my first classes here soon, and I'm thinking about taking psychology courses."

"Not creative writing?"

"Not me. I'm no writer."

"I bet you could be a great writer. Think about it."

"And what would I write about?"

"Write about your life. How you got where you are."

"Why would anybody want to read about that?"

"You think your life isn't interesting enough? Okay, you could write about me. I'm interesting."

I give him to required quick laugh, and add, "You're a really good teacher. I guess I could write about that."

"Ha! Let's talk about something real. "How it's going with Cat?"

"Cat? With regard to?"

"Don't play coy with me, John. Have the two of you shacked up yet?"

"I did move in with her, but she's so involved with her Draft Counseling Center, I don't get to spend much time with her."

"Yeah, I heard about that Counseling Center. How's that going? You know there are some people who're not going to take that kind of anti-patriotism lying down."

"They did have a visit from the cops. Broke out their front window. But Cat doesn't respond to that kind of pressure. She gets her back up, and it energizes her."

"I would expect anything else from her."

I have the feeling he's about to say more when two men in suits come down the sidewalk toward us. They move in close behind me, and one of them, the more heavy-set of the two, says, "Where you from, son?"

What are these two all about? They don't look like cops, not exactly, but I suspect that's what they want me to think. I say, "Why are you asking me that?"

"We're talking to all the out-of-state students. You have to come with us."

"Come with you? Why?"

"Are you an out-of-state student?"

This is getting weird. "I live here. In Tempe."

"Well, you'll have to prove that, son. We have evidence that out-of-state students are not responding to the order to report for induction." He gets ahold of my elbow.

I say, "I haven't received any such notice," and jerk my arm away.

That seems to really irritate him. Good.

The other guy moves back. Maybe he doesn't want to be any part of what this guy is doing.

He again tries to grab my arm, but I don't let him. What the hell is this guy up to thinking he can come onto this campus and go around grabbing students?

He says, "You'll have to prove it. Males of your age are now being drafted to help this country, so you'll have to come with us to the draft board office to verify your status."

I'm not about to go anywhere with this guy.

But before I can say that, Callum steps forward and says, "Okay, stop this. What authority do you have on this campus? We need to see some kind of credential."

The guy lets go of my arm and confronts Callum. He says, "Whoever you are, you should butt out of this. It's between me and this draft-dodger."

Callum surprises me by pushing his chest up against the much larger guy. He says, "I'm a professor at this university, and I'm asking you to prove you have the right to be on this campus accosting one of my students."

"The guy takes a step back and says, "Well, maybe you are a professor, but I have a right to be here. This campus is open to the public."

Callum says, "So you're nothing but a member of the public. In other words, you have no authority to be accosting students. I suggest you leave before I call the campus police."

"Oh, yeah? You must be one of the lily-livered liberals who approve of draft dodging."

Callum shakes his head and laughs at the guy. "A silly alliteration mouthful to describe exactly who I am. And what about you? You're nothing but a walking cliché. I heard there were nut cases like you that crawl out of the swamp sometimes. But now, I think it's time for you and your friend to get down on your knees and beg this young man's forgiveness."

The guy seems confused. Finally, he says, "Hell with that. We're just trying to do something about what we've been hearing is going on at this college. Our country is trying to do something about world-wide Communism, and we're not going to stand by and let these young punks tell us we can't do what needs to be done."

Callum has his right hand bunched into a fist. Is he going to punch the guy? Is this going to turn into a fist fight? I haven't been in a real fist fight since back in my days in the orphan homes, but I wouldn't mind throwing a few hard punches onto this guy's face.

But no, the guy's pal jumps forward and pulls him away. They turn and hurry away down the sidewalk.

Callum is laughing. He throws his arm around my shoulders and says, "Well, that was invigorating, eh what? Seems like we need to go get a drink to celebrate kicking those scumbags off of our campus, right?"

"You go without me, Callum. I think I'd better go to Cat's draft-counseling center to tell her this kind of thing is going on here on campus."

"Yeah, you're right, old buddy." He removes his arm from my shoulder, and shakes my hand. "Better let them know. I've got a feeling that in a conservative state like Arizona, this little incident may turn out to be a little tip of a big iceberg."

He hurries away in the direction of main street. This time, he's moving pretty fast, not doing his usual stopping to look at things. After just about getting himself into a fight with a much bigger guy, he probably really does need a drink. I wonder if when he gets too drunk he gets himself into fights. But no time to go see what he's up to right now. I'd better do what I said, go tell Cat what happened.

At the draft-counseling center, everybody has pulled their chairs together in the corner. I hear Cat's shrill voice saying, "They can't do that. It's got to be illegal."

Another young woman says, "We'll go to court if we have to. My lawyer father'll make them sorry they messed with us."

Most of the other young women chime in: "Right!"

They break up the meeting and go back to their individual desks where there are plenty of boys waiting to be counseled.

Cat sees me and hurries over. "The damn authorities are putting pressure on the building's landlord to evict us." She uses her thumb to point back over her shoulder. "But Allison says her father is some kind of big-time lawyer in Phoenix. We have a one-year lease on this place, and she says her father will prove they have no legitimate reason to break it."

She looks back at her friends, and I have the feeling she'd like to get back to them. I say, "Something happened over on campus you should know about. I was stopped by a couple of guys who demanded I prove I hadn't received a draft notice. Just because of my age."

"What? What did they say?"

"They said they were looking for out-of-state students who might be trying to avoid the draft."

"I knew it. Damn. Damn. Damn. It's going to be us against this whole right-wing state." She touches my arm. "Are you all right? Did they hurt you?"

"They tried to take me off campus with them, but Callum happened to be there. Believe it or not, he was ready to fight the biggest guy."

"Callum? Trying to fight? Wish I could've seen that."

"He seemed to be enjoying it. But you should know the guy called him a lily-livered liberal. Says a lot about how they think, doesn't it? You can imagine what they think about what you're doing here."

She looks back at her friends. "Right. I'd better warn everybody." She hurries away.

There's nothing else I can do here, so I might as well go back to the library.

But before I can get out the door, Cat comes running to stop me. She grabs my arm and says, "I almost forgot to tell you. We're doing a big protest. This afternoon."

"Really? What kind of protest?"

"A march to the administration building. A couple of the guys are out right now putting up posters about it. Meet us at the fountain at five. We'll start from there. Okay?"

"Sure. I'll be there."

At the library, instead of going to the psychology book section, as usual, I look around for other library resources and learn they have a complete set of Shakespeare plays on video tape. I go to that desk and ask if I can watch the two plays I've heard of, Hamlet and Macbeth. The young woman retrieves them, but when she asks for my student ID, I have to tell her I haven't yet signed up for my fall classes. She says that's all right and hands me the tapes. She directs me to a small cubicle that has a tape player and a screen to watch them.

I wonder why she decided she didn't need my student ID. Maybe she doesn't get much demand for Shakespeare plays on video, and she was just happy to have somebody requesting a resource she could provide.

I'm enjoying watching the plays, but the clock on the library wall says it's time to go meet Cat. Lucky that clock is there; I was so involved in watching the plays, I might have completely forgotten to go to the fountain to meet her.

I make it to the fountain in time to see Cat at her usual spot up on the concrete lip of the fountain, trying to organize the march. She's yelling through her trusty bullhorn to get everybody shaped up to do an orderly march to the university administration building.

There are a lot more protesters ready to march than I would have expected, given that the fall semester hasn't even started yet. There's quite a mix of male and female students, and even some older people that I suspect might be university employees. Maybe even faculty.

As soon as the march gets started, the students form up into a wide column, most of them chatting amongst themselves. They're obviously enjoying this march.

A couple of young campus security officers are keeping pace with the marchers. Are they expecting trouble?

I start to join Cat at the head of the line, but I notice two men in white short-sleeved shirts and khaki pants walking to the side of the marchers. They sure don't fit in. What are they doing here?

I drop back to keep my eye on them, and after about a block, they stop to talk to a group of four men who are dressed similarly. What are those guys up to? Are they here to make trouble? One of them, a big guy with a pot belly and the kind of string tie I've seen other men in Arizona wear, says something and points at the marchers. The group starts moving toward the front of the procession, where Cat is.

I hurry to intercept them; I get in front of the string-tie

guy and say, "Hi there. I haven't seen you guys on this campus before. Did you come onto this university campus to show how much you hate war?"

The guy lets out a short scoffing laugh and tries to push past me.

I move to stay in front of him and say, "Maybe I should call campus security over." I point. "He can explain to you the rules of conduct on this campus."

That stops the guy. He says, "Rules? What're you talkin' about, kid?"

"Yes, there are rules. This is a peaceful march conducted by students who are registered at this university. Are you men registered students are this university?"

My talk about campus security and rules has made his friends pull back a bit, but the string-tie guy seems determined to make a show of his bravery, or whatever it is he thinks he's doing. He again tries to push past me, but I can tell that now he's not quite as sure of himself as before, so I put my hand against his chest and push him back. I'm not really looking to spoil Cat's march by starting any kind of fight, but I have a feeling this guy will back off.

He raises his big fist and growls at me, actually growls like he thinks he's a bear or something.

But then he stops and stares at me. I was in enough fights as a kid to know when somebody is not quite ready to pull the trigger, so I laugh at him and say, "So now you're not just going to come onto this campus to disrupt a peaceful march, but attack a student?"

He doesn't seem to want to look bad by lowering his fist, but before he can do anything, one of his pals steps forward and pulls him away.

They all hurry away toward the campus exit, but I call after them, "Hey, you don't have to run away. Anybody has the right to march against war."

They keep going without looking back.

Odd how this little encounter was so much like the one

earlier, with self-described patriots coming onto this campus to cause trouble. The word must be getting out about Cat's antiwar activity.

Some of the marchers are clapping. I guess they noticed what was going on. I try to wave off their attention, but a few of the boys come to pat me on the back.

I quickly say, "C'mon, let's just keep marching."

The march makes it to the administration building without more interference, so I can just stay back and watch.

Despite the modernity of most of the buildings on this campus, the administration building is older, a rather plain two-story affair. Cat must believe the administrators that run this campus are on the second floor because that's where she's directing her bullhorn. She's demanding they come out and talk to "students who care."

Despite her yelling, no one comes out, so she leads the group in a chant: "No more war. No more war."

Surprisingly, given the fact that they're just chanting at the side of a building and getting no response, they keep it up for quite a while.

But as the day gets hotter, the crowd begins to disperse. Cat is the last to leave, and she's still shouting at the building. She's getting hoarse, so I go to join her. I say, "I don't think anybody's coming out."

She turns to me, panting, as if she'd been running. "They're scared to actually come out and talk like normal human beings. Hey, Goddam it, we're students. We pay their salary."

"I guess they don't look at it that way."

She tries to clear her throat, but she's still very hoarse. "Don't they realize what's going to happen? If they don't talk to us now, our movement is gonna get bigger and bigger. They can't just ignore us. The more this war gets going, the more upset the students are going to get."

I can't think of anything to say to her except to repeat, "They don't see it that way. Every human sees the world in a way that works for them."

That only gets a frown from her. "I can see you've been in the library again, reading those psychology books. Okay, mister psychologist, what *do* you think would get their attention? Trouble? What if our protest march would have led to men coming from off campus to beat us up? Don't you think that might have gotten their attention?"

"I guess you saw that almost happened."

"Yes, and I did see what you did. Couldn't resist playing the hero, could you?"

"I didn't want to see you or any of your friends get hurt."

"Didn't I tell you I don't need protecting?

I see where she's going with this. "What did you want me to do, Cat? Let them hurt you and your friends?"

"No, but you're also supposed to see the bigger picture. If they're going to reveal themselves, we should let them. That's why I just decided our next march is gonna go off campus. And I'm gonna try to get the press to show up."

"And you hope the troublemakers will show up."

"Why not? I'm gonna tell the local press and the campus newspaper there's gonna be trouble."

"Would you really want your friends to get hurt, just so your movement will get more attention?"

"You have a better idea?"

I know how she wants me to answer that. Does she want me to promise I won't try to defuse the situation. I'm not sure I can promise that, so I just say, "And where is this off-campus march going to be?"

"City Hall, where else? That oughta get their attention."

"I'm sure it will. But are your friends ready for that kind of confrontation?"

"So, you, the big strong male, thinks us poor little girls can't take care of ourselves?"

She's getting really fired up now. No matter what I say, it's probably going to be the wrong thing.

She pokes me in the chest and says, "Nothing to say?"

"Listen, Cat. You know I'm on your side. I'm only trying

to help you think it through. Somebody could get really hurt. Patriotism is a powerful motivator. To them, there's no two ways about it, you either support your country, or you don't. Haven't you noticed all the US flags sprouting up on front porches around here?"

"Patriotism? Is that what they call it? They're warmongers. That the real fact. They like wars."

"If there is a war, I suppose they think their country must need to do it. People learn things like patriotism when they're children. The pledge of allegiance to the flag, in God we trust, my country right or wrong."

"So? Are they still children? Do they wanna see a lot of young boys killed to justify their patriotism?"

"Listen, Cat, there's no reason for people to unlearn the lessons they learned early, especially if the politicians and their friends continue to reinforce those ideas."

"Ah, here we go again. Psychology."

"Yes, I have been reading psychology books. And that brings us back to where this discussion began. If you insist on taking your marchers off campus, I think their beliefs might very well lead to violence. Violence against you and your friends."

"And I'm going to repeat what I said, if they do that, it proves their dumb patriotic getting-in-line to follow warmonger politicians like Goldwater and Johnson is what leads to pointless wars. History has shown that over and over again."

I can see she's not going to back down. I made the false assumption she wouldn't want her friends to get hurt, but she seems willing to let that happen if it accomplishes her goals. She may even be willing to be a martyr herself. She could be getting herself into a kind of Joan of Arc complex.

"Well, that stopped you. Nothing to say?"

"Okay, Cat. I can see you want to go ahead with this march downtown, but let's do it in a way that makes it as safe as possible. I'm willing to march next to your group as a guard, and you may have some other male friends from college that will also help."

"No way! You haven't been listening, John. We have the right to do a peaceful march to the city hall. If they want to interfere with that right, want to attack girls, it'll show them for what they are."

I know I'm not going to convince her that marching off campus is a bad idea, so I'd better back off. I'll stay involved to see if I can protect her, despite her wishes. I say, "Okay, we're going to march off campus. To the city hall. Why there?"

"Have you seen that monstrosity of a city hall building? That big building, with those fat white columns, it looks like something out of a deep south plantation. It shrieks, look at us we are in command."

"Okay, Cat, when do you plan to do this off-campus march?"

"As soon as possible. As soon as we can plaster this town with flyers announcing it."

"Are you trying to let the townspeople know about it?"

"You bet. Our posters will say it's an anti-war march from campus, but anybody can join in."

"Do you really think anybody besides students will? As I understand it, Arizona is a very Republican state. Goldwater has been their senator for a lot of years now."

"Why not? Do they want another war? How about the local high school kids? Especially the boys. Do you think they'll want to go off to some foreign country to get killed?"

"Maybe they will. Patriotism, remember?"

"Well, we'll see, won't we? Like I said, we'll plaster the town with posters and see who shows up."

I have to bite my tongue to keep from saying that's exactly what I'm worried about, who might show up.

Twenty-Nine

It only takes Cat and her crew a few days to create posters about their march to city hall and start posting them all over town. The march is scheduled for Saturday, and the march is all Cat wants to talk about. I stay in a supporting role, but also keep my ears open about any potential trouble. The design of her poster, which makes some very inflammatory criticisms of the "warmongering" President and his lap dogs in Congress, including Goldwater, seems to be intentionally inviting trouble from the locals.

There must have been a lot of talk on campus about the march to city hall because on Saturday, when we gather at the fountain to get the march started, a surprising number of students show up. Maybe a lot of students have shown up for the fall semester, but until classes start, they've got nothing else to do. So why not join in for a nice walk downtown. If so, I can only hope their "nice walk" doesn't get them hurt.

Cat leads the group across campus, using her trusty bullhorn to yell at every student we pass to join in. And sure enough, some of them do cheerfully join in. I doubt they have any idea of what the march is all about.

Just before we exit campus, I see Callum ahead. He's sitting on a bench, watching the marchers go by. He's smiling and nodding. I wonder what he thinks of Cat's big march to city hall. I go up to him. "Hi Callum. Are you going to join us?"

His grin turns into a scowl. "Are you kidding? Anti-war marches on campus are one thing, but marching into this particular town at this particular time is quite another. All they'll see is a bunch of rich college students telling them their beliefs are wrong."

"As you might imagine, Callum, I did happen to mention that to Cat. I expect you know her response."

"Ah, so these off-campus marches are her latest thing, and she's doesn't care if she gets confrontations?"

"You might say that."

"And when Cat decides to do something, you need to stay loyal, right?"

"I am loyal, Callum. And as she would say, she's on the right side of history."

He chuckles at that. "Does history have a right side?"

"I don't have time to get into a philosophical debate about it right now, Callum. I need to keep up with the marchers."

"No you don't. You could just come with me. We could hit a bar and have a few drinks while we have a philosophical debate about it. Wouldn't you'd rather do that?"

"Or you could walk along with me. We could talk while we walk."

He shakes his head. "Sounds too much like exercise, something I avoid at all cost."

"A little exercise wouldn't hurt you."

"I know, I know, it might make me live longer, but who wants that?"

I reach out to shake his hand, and he shakes it vigorously as he says, "Go ahead. Keep up with your girl. She's worth it, even if she does have some crazy ideas."

I say goodbye to him and jog to catch up with the marchers. I stay a bit to the side so I can keep an eye on what onlookers might do. So far, all seems peaceful. The police are ready for the march, and they're holding back the cars at every intersection. Hopefully, the police presence will help keep troublemakers away.

The next intersection is more of a main street, and a man in a big black car is getting out. He doesn't seem happy that his way is being blocked. As I pass, I'm close enough to hear him begging the policeman to let him by so he can use his car to run over what he calls "them damn traitors." The cop says, "I wish I could."

I don't see how that kind of response from the police can help defuse the situation. But we do make it to the city hall without running into any trouble, other than a few people yelling insults at us.

I haven't seen the City Hall building before, but now that I do, I see Cat's point: it's old-fashioned facade with large white columns. It does seem out of place in this town.

Cat doesn't waste any time: she starts yelling through her squawky bullhorn, demanding that the "rulers' come out and talk about "the coming war."

Not surprisingly, nobody does come out. But as Cat leads the group in "No more war, no more war" chants, I notice a group of men moving closer to her, and sure enough, the big guy I confronted at the on-campus march, is with them.

As I move closer, the big guy seems to have picked out a young male marcher who has happily joined in with the chanting.

Luckily, by the time I get there, the big troublemaker hasn't struck down the young marcher; he just pushes him.

The young man turns around and demands to know why the man pushed him.

Not a good idea. For Cat's sake, I hope I can take care of the big guy like I did at the on-campus march.

As if the whole scene is playing out in slow motion, I make it to the big guy just as he's telegraphing his blow to the young man's face. I get ahold of the back of the big guy's collar and pull as hard as I can.

Caught off guard, he falls backward. But he's soon on his feet, red faced, and charging at me.

His wild charge actually seems funny, reminding me of the time when one of my fellow orphans, also a pretty big kid who was a known bully, came at me over some supposed slight. Back then, the kid was also red in the face, and he was swinging his fists wildly. It was easy enough to grab the front edges of that kid's coat and swing him down to the ground. So, when the big guy charges at me, I do the same thing to him: I grab the front edges of his jacket and throw him down. Unfortunately, this time,

I must have more adrenaline going, because I throw him down to the ground harder than I intended. He sits up, but he isn't trying to stand up. He just sits here, staring at blood on his hands. A lot of blood is coming out of his mouth. It's as if he can't quite figure out where all the blood is coming from. He must have bit his tongue, hard.

That's all I have time to look because two of his friends come charging at me, and before I know it, they've got me on the ground, punching my face. Luckily, some of the other male marchers immediately come to my aid. They push away my attackers and get me to my feet.

The attackers are picking up their big friend, and I'm ready for more trouble, but the group leads their leader away, probably to take him to a hospital for stitches. Damn, getting stitches in his tongue will undoubtedly be a lot more painful than the fight was.

A photographer runs up and starts taking pictures of me. I turn away. Had he also been taking pictures of the fight? If that's a newspaper photographer, I expect his photos will be just what Cat wanted. As brief as the fight was, it may not look so brief in newspaper photos.

I go to the front of the group where Cat is leading the chanting through her trusty bullhorn. I don't see any more troublemakers.

The chanting goes on for quite a while, but as with the march to the administration building on campus, nobody comes out of the building, and the marchers begin to drive away.

But that doesn't stop Cat: she's still shouting at the building, demanding that they come out and explain why they want a war that's going to kill all the young boys.

Eventually, it's only Cat and me, and Cat is still shouting at the building. I'm not sure why Cat's friends have abandoned her. Maybe they're embarrassed to be there any longer since nobody is coming out, and even the police have left.

Cat finally gets hoarse and gives up her shouting. She turns to me and says, "None of the warmongers will come out and face us."

Before I can say anything in response, she touches my face and says, "What the hell happened to you?"

"Oh, some guys wanted to make trouble, but they ran away."

"Not before they beat the shit out of you. You've got blood all over your face. Cuts."

"Oh, yeah. I did notice one of the guys that was hitting on me had big sharp-looking rings on every finger. He must have planned that."

"Sharp rings? Doesn't your face hurt?"

"I guess a little. It's no big deal."

She grabs my hand. "Come on. Let's find someplace where I can clean you up while you tell me exactly what happened."

We end up at a drinking fountain in the city park where she uses her handkerchief to wipe away some of the blood. As she does it, she demands to know every detail.

I try to summarize how the fight got started, but she stops me when I mention the photographer. "What? A photographer saw it? Do you think it might have been from the local paper?"

"Could be. He was taking pictures of my face. That could make it look a lot worse than it was."

"All right! That's great! Just what we needed. Shows what monsters these Arizona right-wing radicals are. Attacking peaceful marchers. I need to get to the campus newspaper. Right away so they can get the story into tomorrow's edition.

The news about the fight seems to have distracted her from the blood-cleanup task. She wants me to go with her to the campus newspaper to show them my face, but I'm not willing to be "the face" of her anti-war movement. Failing that, she says, "Okay, meet you at home," and she's off at a trot, heading back toward campus.

Now what? Should I go back to her apartment and get a look at my face in the bathroom mirror to see if any serious damage was done? It doesn't feel all that bad. Maybe I should just go to the library and continue my psychology studies.

Actually, I feel more like getting a drink . Maybe I can still find Callum at his favorite bar.

No, what I really feel like doing is going to the desert, the perfect place to think through things.

As I walk to my car, for some reason, I remember Deb advising me to go out to the Superstition Mountains that are in the desert east of here. Yes, that's where I should go. Out there, I can walk for a long time and put all this war talk and anti-war talk aside. Or at least put it into the background for a while.

Chapter Thirty

I don't get back to Cat's apartment until well after dark. I was looking forward to telling her about my amazing hike up into the Superstition Mountains, about the sheer cliffs that towered above me, about the infinite variety of tiny flowers on the desert floor, about the troublesome cactus plants that keep on trying to attach themselves to my pants, about the cautious coyote that stared at me, wondering what I was doing in his domain. But I don't get the chance because she ambushes me at the door. "Where the hell have you been? I've been worried sick."

All I can say is, "What's wrong? I thought you were busy at the campus newspaper."

"Right, I was. But then I went to the Counseling Center, and there was a guy there from Illinois. He said the draft boards back there are drafting every single male as soon as they hit twenty years of age. I thought maybe they'd come here and nabbed you."

"Calm down, Cat, there's no chance of that."

"No chance? They're drafting every single Illinois male as soon as they hit age twenty. Isn't that you?"

"Yes, but I never registered for the draft."

"What? How did you get out of that?"

"I just didn't. Remember, I was an orphan, and I didn't have any friends, so I never heard anybody talk about it. The truth is I just never thought about it."

"Jesus, John. One thing we've already researched at the Center is that if we tell our clients not to register it's a felony with a possible prison sentence."

"Okay, that means it's too late to register now. So what would your advice be for me to do?"

"You should go to Canada. Right now."

"I'm not going to Canada, Cat. It's almost time to register for the fall classes, and I've decided not to declare a major. I just want to take all kinds of classes. Psychology. History. Maybe even some creative writing classes."

"But as soon as you register, at your age, somebody is bound to start wondering if you have a student deferment. At the Center, we've learned that to get a student deferment, you have to be carrying a full load. And even then, as soon as they start sending troops to Vietnam, that deferment is for sure gonna go away."

Her words are making me feel roped in, and it's not a feeling I'm used to, especially now that I'm on the road going wherever I feel like going.

"Well, John, that certainly got you quiet. If you aren't going to run away to Canada, what are you gonna do?"

"I guess I'll do what I always do, think about it."

"Well, if nothing else, you can be an interesting case for our Draft Counseling Center. But if any twenty-year-old males come in and tell us that they've never had registered for the draft, I'm not sure what we could tell them. Except, like I said, to run away to Canada. But hey, what if all the eighteen-year-olds refused to register? Wouldn't that mean they couldn't have any more wars?"

"I didn't refuse to register, I just didn't."

"Yeah, but what if? Maybe we could get the ones that have registered to burn their draft cards."

"Now Cat, you know that might attract more attention than you really want."

"So? The more attention to these insane wars, the better."

"I think we saw your march to the city hall got plenty of attention. The wrong kind."

"Naw, that was only a start. A test run. Wait until we start putting together our really big marches. You just wait and see."

She heads for the phone, and from what I can hear, she's talking to somebody about a campaign to get boys to refuse to register for the draft. And maybe get them to burn their draft cards in public.

Chapter Thirty-One

The next morning, Cat heads out to her Draft Counseling Center even earlier than usual. I wonder what she's got planned now.

I take my time to eat some breakfast cereal while I think about what she heard about drafting in Illinois. Is it possible the Illinois draft boards really are drafting all the twenty-year-olds? Maybe I should at least try to stay out of sight until I hear more about that. Despite Cat's fears about what the US was going to do as soon as Congress passed Johnson's Gulf of Tonkin Resolution "blank check" for military operations in Vietnam, there hasn't been a mass invasion of that little country. Cat claims there's plenty going on over there in Vietnam, secret US military operations pretending to be advisors, but it doesn't seem like the press has done much with that information.

On my way to the library, I remember I promised and go back to see Spud. I could also ask Tin what he's been hearing about the draft. A quick trip over to the frat house to say hi to Spud before I go to the library will only take a few minutes.

When I pull up in front of the frat house, the place looks even busier than before. A lot of the members must all be arriving for the fall semester.

I'll just go see Spud in the back yard, and then head for the library.

But he's not in his usual spot in the shade. I ask one of the guys who's busy moving his stuff into a room if he knows where Spud it. I say, "I promised I come by to see him once in a while."

He looks me over. "You must be John, the guy who used to take care of him."

"Yeah."

"Well, Spud is just fine. He's in your room with the little girl. But that's not the problem. It's the woman. We know that sometimes a guy will sneak a girl in for a night or two, but you shouldn't be moving one in for longer. Especially not a Spanish speaker with a daughter."

"A Spanish-speaking woman and a little girl?"

"Are you gonna act like you didn't know her? She said she's waiting for you. If that's not true, she has to go."

What would Clara and Maria be doing here? I quickly say, "No, no, it's all right. I'll take care of it."

"See that you do."

He goes back to his task, and I head for my old room.

Inside, Clara is in my old bed, asleep. Maria is in the other bed with her arm around Spud, who seems perfectly content with the situation.

As soon as I walk in the door, Maria looks up and shouts, "John! You come." She seems really happy to see me.

I guess Clara remembered this room from when we stayed here while I waited for Tin to bring back my car. But why are they here? Is she afraid of something? Could the bosses from Canal Street have come all the way up to Mesa to track her down?

Clara turns over and looks at me, blinking.

I say, "Hi Clara. What are you doing here?"

She hesitates, and then points at Maria and says, "*Tu dice.*"

Maria says, "They come. Trouble."

"Who came? The men from Mexico?"

Clara says, "No. *they.*" She again points at Maria.

I go to sit down on the bed next to Maria. While I pet Spud, I ask her, "What's wrong, Maria? Who came?"

"Bad men. Police. They no want us here. Say not legal. They put all in bus. We hide in trees."

I think I'm getting it. It must be the immigration police. But they must have known for a long time there were undocumented people working in the orange orchards, so, why did they decide to come and round them up now? Could it be because of the upcoming presidential election?

Clara sits up. "Give *dinero*."

"Give money, Clara? To do what?"

"*México*. Go."

"You want me to take you back down to Mexico?"

"*Sí. Como antes.*"

I look at Maria, and she says, "Go in car. Please."

"Take you to Mexico? I don't know, Maria. I have things to do here. I'm about to register for college classes."

"Please, Mister John."

"But to where, Clara? Back to the border? I thought you didn't want to go to Nogales anymore."

"*No Nogales. Otro lugar.*"

So, they want to go back to Mexico, but not to the border. "How far, Maria? How far from the border? I need to know how long I'd be gone."

She points at Clara. "*Mamá tiene. Mapa.*"

Clara takes a folded piece of paper and hands it to me.

It's a hand-drawn map. I think I recognize the shape of Mexico, and the coast with the water indicated by squiggly lines. The word "Guadalajara" is on the map, an inch or so inland from the coast. Another word is on the map, Melaque, but this word is right next to the coast. Nearby is the word "Ejido" with a circle around it. I point to it and ask Maria, "Is this the place you want to go to?"

"*Sí. Por favor, señor* John.*"

"How far is it?"

She says, "*No lo sé, señor* John. Woman from there, Sofia, tell. Good place. She *vive* there. Come *aquí* pick oranges, summer come, go back . Gone back *México* before bad men come."

I point to the Ejido word on the map. "A woman from this place in Mexico? Does she have a place for you to stay down there?"

"*Si, si.* She nice."

So, they want to pay me to drive them down to this Ejido place, but they don't know how far it is. From Clara's drawing, it doesn't seem to be very close to Mexico's northern border, so it wouldn't be like the quick trips down to Canal Street.

Maria reaches out to me. "Please, *señor* John. Please."

"Let me think, Maria."

Am I thinking seriously about doing this? I would like to help them, but I'm very involved here now. It's not like when I first set out from Illinois, driving just to be driving, going anywhere I felt like, just to see what I ran across. Now I feel . . . what? Connected. I guess that's the word. But connected to what? To this place? No, more like to people. Somehow, I feel connected to everybody I've met here. Not just Cat, but also to Callum and Cat's friends at the Draft Counseling Center. And even to Deb, Tin, Mark, and the guys I met briefly here at the frat house. Even to Spud, as odd as that seems. For the first time in my life, it feels like I'm part of a . . . a community.

But I wouldn't be giving any of that up if I was to drive Clara and Maria down to Mexico. This time, I'd be going to a new place, see it, and come right back. I'd be back in time to register for classes. It can't be too far, but I need to get a real map of Mexico to be sure.

Clara abruptly stands up. "*Él no ayuda. Nos vamos.*"

Just like Clara: she wants what she wants, and if she doesn't get it, she'll leave. Such strong-willed impatience.

I hold up a hand to stop her. "Okay, Clara. I'll help you, but first I have to take care of some things here. You stay here in this room until I get back." I turn to Maria. "Understand? Stay here. It won't be long."

She smiles. "*Si, si*. Ww wait."

Outside the room, I go back to the guy who told me they were in my old room and say, "It's okay, they were just waiting for me to drive them to . . . where they're going. I'll be right back to get them, okay?"

He just shrugs, so I hurry out to my car. I guess I'd better go find Cat at the Draft Counseling Center. I wonder what she's going to say about this. Will she understand? Once before, when we were talking about Clara, she seemed to be a bit jealous.

At the Counseling Center, I park and go inside. The place is deserted except for Cat and a couple of her friends. Where is everybody? Did something happen?

Cat sees me and runs to grab my arm. She's out of breath. "You shouldn't be here, John. Didn't you hear what's been happening?"

"Slow down a minute, Cat. Just tell me what happened.

"We got raided, that's what happened. The police came in and started asking all of our male clients for proof that they were registered for the draft."

"What kind of proof?"

"They demanded to see their draft cards. But of course, that's not really what they wanted. It's all about intimidation. When boys protested they didn't have their draft cards with them, they started threatening to 'run them in.' I started shouting that they had no right to run anybody anywhere, and they said that I was under arrest. One of them grabbed my arm. I thought they were going to drag me out, but Allison saved me. Remember Allison, whose father is a big-time lawyer in Phoenix? She demanded the cops show a warrant. "

"So, did they back off?"

"Sort of. They made all the male students show identification, and they wrote down the names of any who were over age twenty. I'm sure they're gonna take those names to the local draft board, and find a way to get them drafted right away. You're lucky you weren't here."

"Don't some of the boys have student deferments?"

"I said that to the cops, and they said student deferments are about to end."

"Wouldn't ending deferments be up to Congress?"

"We've been researching it, and we found out to qualify for a 2-S deferment, the student had to be enrolled full-time in an accredited college or university and making satisfactory progress in their studies. You know what that 'satisfactory progress' phrase means, don't you? It means they can decide for themselves what it means. They'll just start grabbing male students and say they say their deferments are invalid because they weren't making satisfactory progress."

"Do you think it will come to that?"

"You should have seen their attitude. They were saying every single male in this room should be happy to be in the Army helping to defend our country from the Communists."

"Okay, Cat, I get it. But I've got something else to talk to you about."

"Can't it wait until we get home tonight?"

"No. It's something I need to do right away. I'll be gone for a few hours. Maybe longer. I'm not sure."

"You're gonna be gone, but you don't know for how long? What's going on, John?"

"It's Clara, and her little daughter, Maria. They want me to drive them back down to Mexico. Remember I took them over to Mesa to work in the orange orchards. Well, they can't stay there any longer because the immigration officials showed up and arrested anyone who couldn't prove they were US citizens."

"Really? Well, that makes sense, doesn't it? It's this right wing state we're in. All the war talk and patriotism has infiltrated everything. They think all the boys should be eager to join the Army and all girls should get married and just support their husbands."

"So, you think it's all related? Even immigration raids."

"Of course it's related. Don't you see it? Those in power are now seeing their chance to use that power to *get* us, the ones who won't go along."

"Okay, Cat. Well, anyhow I think I should help Clara and her daughter. They need help."

"Absolutely. Yes, go. Mexico works as well as Canada. You should get the hell out of this crazy country before they can draft you and send you off to Vietnam to get killed."

"Well, I wasn't planning to go for very long, just long enough to take them down there and come right back."

"But why not hang around down there long enough to see what happens here. I assume they have phones down there. We could talk on the phone, and I'll tell you when things calm down here."

"I don't know, Cat. How long do you think this war fever is going to last?"

"As long as this new war lasts. All I know is if you stay here, they're gonna grab you and either throw you in prison for failing to register for the draft, or throw you into the Army and send you off to get killed."

"Jeez, Cat, I hadn't thought about staying down there. Don't you need me here?"

"Sure, I would rather have you here, but right now, I don't think you should be anywhere in this war-crazed country. Just get out of here and wait to see what happens. I'll be here waiting for you when this all calms down."

Her friend Allison holds up the phone and yells "Cat! Come here."

Cat gives me a quick kiss and says, "I'd better take that phone call."

She hurries away.

I go out and sit in my car to think. Has the evolving war in Vietnam gotten everybody caught up in what my psychology books would call you-versus-me feelings? But maybe Cat is so involved in her anti-war movement that she sees everything as being about the war. It's understandable that this latest raid on her Center would make her feel like that. But maybe they won't actually send troops over there. It hardly makes sense to me that the US would want to get involved in yet another war in Asia after what happened in Korea. But Congress did quickly pass the so-called Gulf of Tonkin Resolution. Does that mean they're all eager for another war? They might think a war against such a small and undeveloped country would be a quick victory. Maybe they think it will make up for the drawn-out and bloody disappointment of Korea.

Whatever the truth is, my decision right now is whether to take Clara and Maria to where they want to go in Mexico. It's what they need, and also what Cat wants me to do. I might do it.

But as I reach to turn the key, I realize I'm having the same kind of feeling that I had back in Illinois, the feeling that got me to start my car and just start driving on Route 66. That feeling is what got me here. Am I thinking about doing something like that again?

No, this is a different feeling. I'm not ready to abandon my life here like I abandoned my life in Illinois. In a short time, I've carved out a new life here. I met Cat, and I'm about to register for college classes, something I've wanted to do for a long time. But then, Clara says she has money to pay me to drive them down to Mexico, and that would help assure I can keep going to college once I've started. And, like Cat said, once I'm down there, I can call her to see what's going on here.

I guess I'm deciding to do it. Well, I guess I'll see where this next driving trip takes me.

Chapter Thirty-Two

Once I pick up Clara and Maria and get some gas, I'm on the route to Mexico. Interesting how familiar this road has become.

For some reason, Clara has placed herself and Maria in the back seat, so as I zoom down the highway, without either of them saying a word, it almost feels like I'm driving alone. When I hit the road that day in Illinois, I was very much a loner. Quite a contrast with how involved I've been with people since I got to Arizona.

I take the route that goes through the small city of Casa Grande, and on the long straight stretches through the desert, I can really open up Moby's powerful engine. Interesting that no matter how fast I go, and no matter how many cars I pass, there's not a peep out of my passengers in the back seat. Maybe they're asleep.

But no, as I cross the border into Mexico, they both disappear out of my rearview mirror. They must be on the floor behind the front seat. I guess Clara is still afraid she might be recognized by people from Canal Street.

As I drive through the city, it occurs to me that I should fill Moby up with gas before we get out of the city. Not sure how many gas stations there will be outside of the city. That means I'll need to get some Mexican money, pesos.

I say to my passengers, "I need to stop somewhere to get some Mexican pesos."

Clara says, "No. *Tengo dinero.*"

She has money. I say, "Okay. I need to stop and get some gas."

From the look Clara gives me, I don't think she likes the idea of stopping in the town she used to live in, but I have no choice, so when I see a Pemex gas station, I pull in and ask Maria how to tell the attendant to fill my car up.

Clara rolls down the window and says, "Hasta el topo."

The attendant looks at her oddly, but he does start putting the gas in.

When he's finished, Clara pays him an amount he asks for.

I say, "I also need a map of Mexico."

Apparently, the attendant understood that, because he goes into a very dirty looking building, and soon comes back to give me a map.

I look at the map to see if anything compares with Clara's hand-drawn map. I see the city named Guadalajara, and not far away, on the coast, I see the city of Melaque. But there is no Ejido on the map. Maybe it's a local place name, not a city.

I pull back out onto the street and keep on heading south until I see a road sign that matches the route number shown on the map. I guess I'm on the right road, but I'm still not sure how far away Melaque is. From doesn't seem very close.

I'm mostly driving through desert landscapes, but sometimes the road takes me right through the middle of small towns.

The highway finally takes me closer to the coast, but the road is still the same, narrow and beat up, and there's often no shoulders to speak of. It means I can't really open Moby up.

The need to be constantly vigilant on the bad road makes the night seem to pass slowly, but when dawn finally comes, I see a sign that says I'm approaching a city named Puerto Vallarta. My map shows it right next to the coast.

As I slowly make my way through the narrow streets of the quaint city, it looks like it would be an interesting place to stop and look around. But Clara and Maria are apparently still asleep in the back seat, so I just drive on through.

After a few more hours, pushing Moby harder now, I drive into the city of Melaque. It's a smallish city, with what looks like only one main street. I sure don't see any signs pointing to a place named Ejido. I'll have to ask somebody.

Driving slowly through the town, looking for any sign of Ejido, I see what looks like a grocery store. Through the open front, I see aisles cluttered with packaged food and canned goods. It reminds me that once again, I've driven through the night and part of a second day, forgetting to eat or drink. I should stop and at least get a few Snickers bars.

When I stop, Clara pops up and says, "*¿Por qué te detienes?*"

I look to Maria, and she says, "Why stop?"

I say, "I need to get something to eat. Can I get you something?"

Clara says, "No," and sits back.

I say, "This town is called Melaque, like on your map, but I don't see any Ejido."

I start to get out, but then I remember I don't have any local money. I turn back to Clara. " Do you have any idea where I can exchange money?"

Without replying, she takes out some bills and hands them to me. It looks like a lot of Mexican money. I wonder how much that many bills will buy me.

I go into the store, and the first thing I notice is stacks of bottled water. Does it mean the local water is not safe to drink?

I take a bundle of the water to the cashier, and ask him, "Snickers bars?"

He says, "*Cuanto?*"

I hold up five fingers, and he leaves. But he's soon back with five Snickers bars. Either they're a universal food everywhere in the world, or this store caters to US visitors.

I take out one of the larger bills Clara gave me, and it must be enough because the man takes it without a word.

I start to pick up the water and the Snickers bars, but he says, "*Esperar*" and digs into a metal box. He hands me a few Mexican bills and some change. He says, " *Gracias señor.*"

I guess things are cheap here. If I did what Cat wants me to do and stay here for a while, it wouldn't cost very much.

Back in the car, I offer a couple of Snickers bars and some water to Clara.

She takes a bottle of water, but refuses the Snickers bar.

Maria does the same, but I force a Snickers bar into her hands and she quietly says, "*Gracias.*"

I drive on down the street.

Less than a block later, Clara says, "Stop!"

She's pointing to another store, and this one has a large amount of fruit and vegetables out front in wooden bins.

She gets out and doesn't go into the store, but instead waits for the proprietor to come out. She shows him the hand-drawn map. He puzzles over it, and then points to the north, back the way we came. She buys a fairly large bunch of bananas and brings it back to the car. She gets into the back seat with Maria and hands her a banana. She says, "*El hombre dice que podría estar en la costa. Quizás a veinte kilómetros.*" She points to the north.

I ask Maria what she said, and Maria says, "Man say maybe *Veinte.*" She points toward the same direction Clara did. Well, maybe we will find the Ejido place after all.

I drive north, watching for any road that turns off toward the coast, and after maybe half an hour, I see a dirt road. Could this Ejido place only be accessed by that narrow dirt road?

I pull off onto the road, and after a short drive, I see what looks like some kind of town ahead, close to the ocean. But I don't see any signs identifying it as Ejido.

One of the first things we come to is a kind of open-air store with a sign on an awning out front that says, "*Farmacia.*" Could be the local pharmacy. I slow down to look at it. There are a lot of shelves full of bottles. Medicine? Also a small amount of packaged foods. I wonder if this is the only store in town.

A heavy-set man is sitting in a kind of laid-back lawn chair next to a dial telephone that's on a small table. It has a sign on it, in Spanish, and some numbers. Is it the local version of a pay phone?

Clara says, "Stop."

As soon as I stop, she jumps out and goes to talk to the heavy-set man. He listens to her, and then points on down the street.

She hurries back to the car and tells Maria to get out.

Maria asks, "*¿Por qué?*"

Her mother answers, "*Él dice dónde está Sofía. Vamos.*"

I ask, "What's going on, Clara?"

She says, "We go. Gracias," and shoves five US twenty-dollar bills into my hand.

I watch them walk away on the dirt street. I heard her say the name Sofia. That was the name of her friend from the orange orchards. It means I've fulfilled my promise to bring them here, so now I guess I should head back. But looking at that phone, maybe I should first try to call Cat.

I go to the man in the lawn chair. "Can I use that phone?"

"*Si*. Tell number. I dial."

It seems like at this time of day, Cat should be at the Counseling Center. I tell the man the Center's phone number, and he says, "*Dinero?*"

I hold out the Mexican bills I got in change in Melaque, not sure if it will be enough.

But he hands me back two of the bills. An honest man.

He dials the number and hands me the phone.

I listen, but all I hear is static. I'm about to hand the phone back to the man, when Cat answers.

"Hello, Cat. It's me. I'm in Mexico. Pretty far down."

She says, "John, is that you? I can barely hear you."

I repeat, louder this time, "I'm in Mexico. I'm about to head back."

"No, no! Don't come back here. Not yet. We got raided again, and they're looking for you. They don't know your name, but they described you. They say they want the draft-dodger that interfered with a legitimate legal procedure."

"You want me to stay down here? For how long?"

"Not sure, but I'm glad you found a phone. Call me tomorrow. Maybe I'll know more by then."

"So, I'm just supposed to stay here? I don't know anybody in this place."

"Just for a while. Hey, I've got to go. Things are happening fast. We're organizing more demonstrations and marches. We may even do a march in Phoenix."

Before I can tell her marching in Phoenix is not such a good idea, she says, "Gotta go. Call me tomorrow." The line goes dead.

I hang up the phone and thank the man.

With nothing else to do, I leave my car next to the store and walk down the middle of the dirt street, thinking I should go back, no matter what Cat thinks. There just isn't anything for me to do in this sleepy little village.

But before I head back, I might as well look around a bit. After all, this is a brand new place, and new places was what I drove away from Illinois looking for.

As I walk, I can see this little village is really different from any place I've ever been. The few tiny houses I pass are made out of sticks laced together, and they're using palm fronds as roofs. Between the sticks, I can see inside, families going about their business. I try not to look. Must be a pretty mild climate here, so mild they can make houses out of sticks. And apparently, the people don't mind their neighbors looking into their homes.

But the next house I see ahead is a small house made out of bricks. It also has a roofs made out of palm fronds.

When I get closer, I can see that the house is not made out of what I would call normal red bricks; the bricks are brown. Made out of mud?

Walking on, I come to more houses made out of the brown bricks. The houses don't have any windows, so again, I can see inside. A very friendly town.

Well, at least this place I've ended up in is interesting. When I drove away from Illinois, I sure never imagined I'd end up in a place like this.

Interesting that all of the mud brick houses are close to what seems to be a pretty nice beach. But there are no swimmers or sun bathers, only wooden boats, lined up, with ropes leading up to the houses.

And there are no houses on the other side of the street. This Ejido place must strictly be a village of fishermen. All they need is access to the ocean.

When I come to the end of the houses, I walk down to the beach. It's a nice sandy beach, so I sit down to watch the waves come in. They're not big waves, just gentle waves that lap at the shore. I can see that this place is in a narrow bay. If I ever did decide to stay here for a while, the gentle ocean bay seems like a perfect place for swimming. During the summers, back in Illinois, I used to swim in the pond at the park. If I stayed here, I could probably get back into swimming. In fact, it seems kind of surprising tourists haven't discovered this place . But there are no hotels, or restaurants, and no stores, except for that one that identifies itself as a *farmacia.*

After sitting in the sand for a while, watching the waves and the sea birds, I'm getting restless. There's still plenty of light left in the day, so I might as well walk back to my car and head back for Arizona, no matter what Cat says.

I get up, but before I get very far, a guy with pretty long blonde hair comes out of one of the mud brick houses. He's wearing a pair of ragged shorts and no shirt. He waves at me and says, "Hey, you American?"

"Yeah, you?"

"Sure am. You must be new here. Draft-dodger, right?"

"Is that why Americans show up here?"

He gives me a short laugh. "Sure. Why else would a draft-age *gringo* show up in this Ejido."

"No, I brought a friend here. From Arizona. So, this village is called Ejido?"

Naw, an Ejido isn't a place, it's the name for a government thing. Coastal land set aside for the people. Not for foreigners."

"But you're here."

"Not for long, I hope. Only until the US realizes what folly it is to go gallivanting off here and there to start new wars." He partly turns to point back at the house. "Us draft dodgers are camped out in this house. We made it by stamping around bare-foot in the mud to make bricks. There's a good mud place back in the forest. Hey, you could join us. We can always use another pair of feet."

"You want my feet?"

He laughs again. "Right. We've gotten so good at making mud bricks and roasting them over a campfire, that the locals are buying them from us. Some of them have replaced their stick houses with our bricks. Hey, it pays us enough for our food. What else does a person need, actually?" He again points back at the house, this time using his thumb. "It's only one room with a dirt floor, but it keeps the rain off of us. You could join us, if you've got a sleeping bag."

"Actually, if I stay for a while, I can sleep in my car. It's got a big back seat."

"That's cool. But where you gonna find a bathroom in this town? We dug a pit toilet. It works. Not only that, there's water from their water tower. Comes twice a day."

"Well—"

"Hey, how about this? You can park your car in our back yard. Pay us back by helping us stomp out bricks, and sometimes giving me a ride into Melaque. For shopping. Go on. Get your car. I'll show you where to park it."

He goes back inside, leaving me to walk to my car. But do I want to park my car in their back yard? That would mean I'm going to stay for a while. That's what Cat would want me to do, but is it what I want to do?

Well, Cat did want me to stay and call her back tomorrow. I could stay until then. I guess this is sort of what I wanted when I left Illinois. Change. Seeing new places. Doing new not-ordinary things. I guess I could at least stay here overnight. After I call Cat tomorrow, I'll decide what to do next.

Chapter Thirty-Three

Somebody is pounding on my car door. I sit up and roll down the window. It's the blond-headed guy, still without a shirt on.

He says, "Glad you decided to stay. Hey, my name's Ralph, by the way, but nobody calls me that. Call me Trace."

"Why Trace?"

"Long story. Doesn't matter."

"Okay. My name's John."

"John? That's no name for a cool dude like you. Hey, how about we call you . . . uh, how about Slick. No, not Slick. Or, how about Slim? You really are damn skinny. Don't you ever eat?"

"I eat. When I think of it."

"Hey, there's a lady in this town that'll make you a stack of tortillas for a couple of pesos. Add beans, and that'll fatten you up. You got any money?"

"A little."

"All it takes here is a little. But now, we gotta go stomp around in the mud. You up for that?"

Well, stomping around in the mud to make bricks is about as not-ordinary as you can get. I might as well check that out. I say, "Sure. Why not?"

"Great. Come in the house. We'll feed you some tortillas, and then we'll go to work."

I follow him into the house. Two young guys that look very much alike, both with very long light-brown hair, are sitting on what looks like straw mats, eating what looks like tortillas . There is no furniture.

Trace points at them and says, "That's the twins. Twin daft dodgers from California."

They both nod to me and go back to their eating.

Trace puts some tortillas into my hand, and after one bite

I can tell they're really good. I guess I have again been forgetting to eat.

But Trace doesn't let me sit down to eat them. He says, "Okay, everybody, let's go stamp mud."

I guess he's the supervisor of the brick making process.

I follow the three of them on down the dirt road for maybe a half mile. Then, Trace leads us off the main road onto a narrow trail through the forest. We soon come to a swampy area, and I'm instantly surrounded by mosquitoes. I try to slap them away, but it's hopeless. The others are not bothering to slap at them. Are they just so used to being stung by mosquitoes that they don't notice anymore?

We come to their mud brick-making place. It's obvious that over time, their stomping has created a wide pit full of mud. There are wooden frames stacked close by. They've even created a dirt dike to control how much swampy water they let into their pit.

Trace goes off into the jungle, but the twins sit down to take off their shoes. They wade right into the mud pit and start doing a kind of rhythmic stomping, a repeated kind of back and forth dance.

I watch them for a few moments Do I want to join them? Well, barefoot stomping around in the mud is definitely not ordinary. It might even be fun. I take off my shoes and join the stomping dance. After a few minutes, I get into the rhythm of it. It really is kind of fun.

While I continue to stomp, I notice Trace has come back out of the forest. He's carrying an armload of sticks.

I see what he's doing; he's getting ready to build a fire.

The two stompers stop stomping and begin pressing the mud into the wooden forms. Trace joins them.

I stop stomping and stand aside to watch them. They must have been doing this for some time, because they're very good at it. Quick and efficient. They're packing mud into the wooden forms and setting them aside in rows to dry.

When they've filled all the wooden forms with mud, the

twins go to the swampy water to rinse off their hands and feet.

I do the same.

Once we have our shoes back on, Trace says, "Good work, guys. Let's go home and get somethin' to eat."

I say, "You're not ready to start your fire?"

"Nope, the bricks need to dry for a while. Then we bury them in hot coals. Took us quite a few tries to work out the timing. But hey, thanks for helping us stomp in the mud. You picked it up right away."

"Yeah, it's kind of fun."

He reaches his hand out.

I assume he wants to shake my hand, but when I put my hand out, he just slaps it and grins at me.

I think that means he's accepting me into their circle of draft-dodging, mud-stomping gringos.

Back at the village, Trace goes into their house, but comes right back out with four thin towels. He heads them out to us.

I ask, "What do I do with this?"

He gives me his usual quick laugh, and says, "Aren't you hungry?"

"Actually, I am."

"Well, then, let's go get some tortillas."

He leads us between two of the mud brick houses. I'm hearing a kind of metallic clanking. Some kind of machine?

We go around back of the house, and I see where the clanking sound is coming from: it's a sort of machine. A little dried-up man is using a bicycle to pull along a chain that has a metal screen with tortillas on it. The tortillas pass over an open flame and then to the end where they are flipped onto the towels of the waiting customers. A little girl collects their coins, and does a little curtsy to each customer to thank them.

We get in line, and when it's my turn, I catch a few tortillas on my towel and pay the girl. She thanks me, and I thank her back. Then, I mimic the others by folding my towel over to keep the tortillas hot.

And they are hot! I can feel the heat through my towel.

The other customers don't seem to notice, but they're so hot, I have to keep the towel moving back and forth between my hands until they cool down a little.

Before we can get back to the house, the odor of my tortillas smells so good I fold back the towel and take one out. I stuff it into my mouth. It's good. Damn good. I think I've had tortillas before, but only store-bought tortillas. They sure never tasted this good. Maybe this is not such a bad place to end up after all.

When we get back to the house, Trace goes into the backyard and builds a small fire. He puts a skillet on the fire and dumps in some beans from a can.

I've already eaten most of my tortillas, but luckily I do have one left for the beans. Like the twins, I hold it out, and Trace dollops a scoop of bean onto it.

I'm not especially a fan of beans, but on these homemade tortillas, they taste pretty damn good.

Before the twins are even finished eating, Trace hurries us back to the mud brick-making place where he gets a big fire going.

As we sit down on the ground to wait for the fire to die down, Trace says, "You know, John, this wouldn't be a bad place for you to hide out. A paradise, actually. If you just go about your business, the locals will pretty much ignore you. They know you're a *gringo*, but unlike other coastal places, they don't especially seem to want to build up any kind of tourist trade here. They're fishermen, and that's it. Their wives cook for them and take care of the kids. We got to know some of them when they liked our mud brick house and asked us to build them one."

I ask, "How many houses have you built?"

"Hey, we don't build houses. No way. We just sold them bricks, so they could make their own."

"But you did build your own house, so you do know how to do it. You could make money building houses here. You could even hire the locals to work for you."

Trace is frowning, but the other two seem interested, so I

add, "As this little village grows, you could get a pretty good house-building business going here."

Trace says, "You volunteering to run this supposed new business?"

I smile and shake my head to show him that's not what I meant. "No, I don't plan on being here that long."

"Hey, Johnny boy, you should at least stay here until this nonsense about a new war dies down."

"What do you think about this Vietnam thing, Trace? My girlfriend thinks it'll turn into a big war."

"Well, that's the question, isn't it? A lot of people think a war with big powerful US against dinky little Vietnam won't last long, but who knows. Another gringo draft-dodger came through here last week, and he said he'd been to that part of the world. Said it's all jungles and bugs. Not the place a big army like the US is used to fighting in."

I nod and say, "Yeah, my girlfriend thinks it might last longer than anybody thinks, because the US will be the invader. She's a college history major and says history shows invaders never win."

"You got a girlfriend? What does she think about you being a draft-dodger down here in Mexico?"

His question makes me wonder why I haven't been thinking of myself as a draft-dodger. Am I here to avoid the draft? I guess it depends on why the US is drafting young guys like me. To send them to Vietnam to kill the local people? Would I be willing to do that? It's odd that I haven't asked myself that question before. Thinking about it now, I know for sure I wouldn't much like the idea of going to a faraway little Asian country to kill the people that live there.

Trace is smiling at me. He says, "Well John, that got you thinking, didn't it? Maybe you haven't been thinking about being a draft-dodger. But at your age, with all the callups they're doing now, you must have gotten a draft notice."

"I'm from Illinois, and nobody back there knows where I am."

"Well, I bet you did get drafted, whether you know it or not."

"Maybe. At Arizona State University, where I was, some people are suspecting the out-of-state male students are trying to avoid the draft back in their home state."

"I can testify about that, John. They're not just going after out-of-state students. I was a college student in California, but they canceled my college deferment, saying I wasn't making sufficient progress. And then, it wasn't long before I got the letter saying I was drafted. I didn't respond to that letter, just kept on going to class. But I soon I got another letter saying I was a draft-dodger. The letter didn't use those words. It said because I didn't respond to my draft notice, I was in violation of some military statute or other. It said I had to go to a downtown place where a military bus would pick me up to take me to a military prison. It told me to pack only one extra pair of underwear and socks. Well, I did pack a change of underwear, and my socks, and a few other things, but not to report to any bus to go to prison; I took a different bus, one that came down here. I ended up in Guadalajara. I'd taken Spanish in high school, so I did all right there, and I eventually worked my way down here before my money ran out. But the villagers here were kind to me. Fed me some of those great tortillas and let me sleep on the beach. They even gave me some blankets."

"So, eventually you figured out how to make mud bricks. And you built your house."

"Well, it wasn't that easy. An old guy pointed out this little vacant piece of land. Told me I could make a house here out of sticks if I wanted to. I was doing that when a French traveler came by. He spoke in French, but I figured out he was trying to tell me I'd be better off making my house out of mud bricks. Said he'd seen them doing that in Africa. Seemed like a good idea to me. I found the mud in the forest and started making mud bricks. It wasn't long before the twins came, and they helped me start making a house out of the dried mud bricks. We got two walls built before the whole thing collapsed. We didn't realize the bricks needed to be fire-hardened. But eventually, we got it right, and here we are."

"So, now you've got a little draft dodgers community going here. And a way to make money, so you can stay."

"I guess you could call us that, a community of draft dodgers. I like the sound of that. And you make four. I bet once you get to know this place, you'll become a permanent member. You'll find hiding out in paradise ain't so bad."

Is he right? When I got in my car in Illinois to start driving on Route 66, it this where that road was actually taking me?

Chapter Thirty-Four

At first, I called Cat every day, but she always told me the same story, a rapidly evolving US war in Vietnam, elimination of most draft exemptions, and frequent police raids on her Draft Counseling Center. She says the aggressive way they do it is very intimidating, that they're obviously trying to scare them into shutting down. She also says she's heard they're increasing immigration agent raids out at the orange orchards. At the end of every breathless phone call, she always says she misses me, but in no way should I even think about coming back yet.

So, I'm stuck here, sometimes making mud bricks with the other draft dodgers, but more often just aimlessly exploring trails through the jungle.

This morning, I'm up early, sitting on the beach, watching the sea birds circle out there over the bay. It's something I often do these days, bored, waiting for something to change. But nothing ever does change in this little village: Trace and his draft-dodger friends make mud bricks, the fishermen gather at dawn to push their wooden boats out to sea, and the rest of the locals just go about their business, pretty much ignoring me. Life here is mostly about ocean fishing. A few also raise chickens. The kids that are too young to go fishing, play in the street, hike the trails, sometimes climb the palm trees to throw down coconuts.

The sun is bright, coming in my car's front window. As I wake up, the brightness combines with the weird dream I was having. I think it was about mountain climbing, not cliff climbing with ropes and climbing gear, but just endlessly walking up a steep slope that never seemed to end.

Staring up at my car's cloth ceiling, I wonder what that dream was supposed to mean. Getting stuck in repetition and routine, I expect, something I hate. I don't normally dream at all—or more accurately, don't remember much about my dreams other than vague images and feelings. But for some reason, that dream is very clear. Does it mean I should shake myself out of this situation and do something completely different?

Well, after a dream like that, there's no way I'm going to get back to sleep, so I get out of my car and look around. There doesn't seem to be anybody stirring in the house, and the town's fisherman will have already left for their day out on the water. Nothing for me to do, as usual.

I notice Trace's fishing setup that's leaning up against the back of the house. He showed me how to use it, but for some reason, I haven't tried it yet. It's only a few lures attached to a piece of wood that has a lot of fishing line wrapped around it. You're supposed to let the line out by unwrapping it from the board, and if you catch something, you bring the fish in by re-wrapping it back around the board.

Why not try it out. Noting else to do.

I take the fishing setup down to the deserted beach. I attach a lure, unwrap some line, and throw it out.

So, this is fishing. What am I supposed to do, just sit here all day staring at the fishing line leading out into the water? I'm already deciding fishing is not my thing

"Catch anything?"

I turn my head. It's a stranger, a really tall *Gringo*. I say, "Nope. I don't think there are any fish in this ocean."

He does an appropriate chuckle and sits down next to me.

I ask him, "New here? Met Trace yet?"

"Yeah. Just hitched in last night. Heard about this place up in Puerto Vallarta. Draft dodgers on a beach making mud bricks." He does his little chuckle again.

"Oh? Are you a draft dodger."

He shrugs and says, "Thinking about it."

"Just thinking about it?"

"Well, I did get drafted, but didn't want to go to that Vietnam place to kill people, so I've been thinking about staying down here until this new war is over and done with."

"I wouldn't count on that. Remember Korea."

"Yeah. If it lasts that long, I might sign up to be a medic. They word is they'll train you."

"But you said you've already been drafted, and you didn't go."

"I hear if they can get you to sign up to be a medic, that all gets washed away. In a real war, they'll need medics. Bad."

"Really? Washed away?"

"That's what I heard." He stands up. "Well, good luck with your fishing." He walks away.

So, a guy who doesn't want to be a soldier, doesn't want to kill people, but says he might join up to be a medic. An interesting concept, joining the military to help people.

I think maybe I should talk to him some more. I wrap up my fish line and go back to the house. Trace and his mud stompers are eating, probably just about to go stomp mud bricks.

But I don't see the new guy. I ask Trace where he is.

"The tall guy? He rolled into town last night and slept on our floor. But this morning, he said he didn't want to help us make mud bricks. Just now, he came back by and said he was gonna hitchhike back up to Tucson and join the Army. Weird guy."

"Okay, Well, Trace, I'm ready to shove off, too. Thanks for letting me stay for a while."

"I didn't do anything but let you park your car in the backyard."

"Well, thanks for that. And for teaching me how to make mud bricks."

He gives me his usual little laugh, shakes my hand, and tells his draft dodgers it's time to go make mud bricks.

With his little group of draft-dodgers, he really is becoming an industrious brick-making businessman and leader. Good for him.

I head for the *farmacia* phone. This time of the morning, Cat should be at her Center.

Sure enough, it's Cat that answers the phone. I tell her

right off, that I'm coming back.

"No! Listen John, you can't imagine what it's like here now. We did another anti-war march, this time to the ROTC building, so they've cracked down on us even more. The only way we're staying open is with the help of Allison' lawyer father. And even though we're still open, we often have to meet our clients on campus because they're afraid to come downtown here to the Center."

"There's nothing for me down here in Mexico, Cat. I've got to come back there and make some decisions."

"Decisions about what? Classes at the university have already started, so you can't do that, and like I told you before, they're looking for you. For you specifically."

"Do they know my name?"

"Not yet, but they described you as the person who attacked an official of the government during our march on city hall."

"You know I didn't do that."

"Doesn't matter if you did or not. They make up things. They'll make up a crime that could get you drafted, or thrown in jail."

"I'm sorry to hear that things have gotten so tough for you, Cat, but I'm coming—"

"It's not tough for me. I'm a girl, remember? They think I don't matter. What they want is boys, draft-age boys. This war in Vietnam has got them all fired up. Of course, they're too old to get drafted, too old to be in any danger, so they see themselves as helping the war effort by helping the Army get fresh cannon fodder."

"Listen, Cat. I'll be at your place by tomorrow. You can tell me more then."

There's a long silence, before she says, "I don't know what you're up to, John, but if you really are coming back, go straight to the apartment. Don't even stop for food or gas in this college town. And look around before you go in. I'm sure I saw some guy watching my place."

"Okay. Well, I'm looking forward to seeing you, Cat."

"Of course, I'm looking forward to seeing you too, John, but I still wish you weren't coming."

After I said one more goodbye, and she said her one more warning, we hung up.

Okay, one more thing before I leave town. I should find Clara and Maria to tell them goodbye. I know they're living in one of the mud-brick house, but I've only seen them once on the street, together. That time, I said hi to them, and Maria said hello back to me, in English. But Clara grabbed her and hurried them away. I got the feeling Clara still wants Maria to be in hiding.

I go to that house, and say, "Hello" through the open door.

It's Maria that comes to the door. She smiles and says, "Oh, hi. Mister John."

She says the greeting with confidence. Has she found somebody in this little village to help her with her English? I hope so.

"I'm leaving, Maria. Heading back to the US. I came to say goodbye."

"Oh, no. Never see."

"I was around, Maria, but I never saw you or your mother out on the street."

She glances back into the house. "*Mamá asustada.* How you say, not . . . brave?"

"Afraid?"

"Yes, afraid. Not want me go out." She again glances back into the house.

"I understand, Maria. She's very protective of you."

Maria abruptly steps out of the house and hugs me.

I'm about to tell her I'll try to come back someday to see her, but I hear Clara call, which causes Maria to bolt back inside the house.

Clara must have forbidden her to talk to me, maybe forbid her to talk to any male.

Back at my car, I think about what I need to get going. Food? I still have a few of the great local tortillas. I guess that will have to do.

And I don't have anything else to retrieve, because I don't have much with me. My sleeping bag is in the back seat, and that's about it. I remember thinking about not having any of my stuff when I drove away from Illinois. But that time I didn't really know I was leaving for good. As it turned out, I didn't need any of that stuff, and still don't now. I wonder how many people in this country think they could walk away from their home without bringing anything with them, and despite that, do fine. I think they'd be surprised at how little they really need.

Chapter Thirty-Five

The drive back to the States seems easier than the drive down, probably because I know the route. I have money, and I know to tell the gas station attendants to fill my gas tank: "*Hasta arriba.*"

When I arrive at Cat's apartment, it's dark, but as she advised, I do park a ways away and look around to see if anybody is watching her place. There's nobody around, so I hurry inside and find her sleeping on the couch. I wonder how long she's been sleeping there in anticipation of me arriving. I'm kind of tired from the long non-stop drive, so I think about not waking her. I could go into the bedroom to get a little sleep before we talk.

But no, as soon as I move across the room, she wakes up. She quickly sits up and says, "So, you're here already. Did anybody see you come in?"

"I don't think so. And I'm really glad to see you."

"Well, I'm glad to see you too, but I'm not glad you're here. Why did you come back? I told you not to. You can't imagine how bad things are here. They've all but shut down our Draft Counseling Center, and they're trying to scare people away from our anti-war demonstrations."

I hurry to sit next to her. "Slow down, Cat. You've got time to tell me what's been going on, but can't we just be happy to see each other first?"

She falls into my arms.

We both just hold each other, and I'm happy for that, but then, she pushes back and says, "Okay, so tell me, why did you come back? Your girlfriend Clara kick you out down there?"

"I never saw Clara. She and her daughter got there and hid away.

But you'll be interested in who I did meet down there. There's a group of draft dodgers in a little village by the ocean, and they're doing well. Your draft counselors need to know about that place."

"So, why didn't you stay with them?"

"Well, I got to thinking about how long this new war is going to go on and—"

"It'll go on a lot longer than they think."

"That's what I got to thinking. Did I want to just stay down there and make mud bricks while all that is going on, maybe for years?"

"Mud bricks?"

"Yeah, that's what those draft dodger guys do down there to make a living. The point is, I kept thinking that there was no real reason for me to be there."

"Except to avoid getting drafted and turned into a killer of innocent people. If you stay here, they'll get you. I guarantee it."

"Yeah. Listen, Cat, what if I join up before they can draft me? I'd still be able to be with you at least for a while."

She's staring at me. "You've gone crazy."

"No listen, I don't want to kill innocent people, but what if I could learn how to help people?"

"What're you talking about?"

"I was talking to a guy down there who said the Army is always looking for medics."

"So now you're switching from psychology to medicine? What do you know about being a medic?"

"The guy said they'll train you. He said they really need medics."

"Who knows if that's true. You need to turn around and go right back down there. That place sounds a hell of a lot better than this crazy warmongering country. Please. At least get away until we see how big this Vietnam thing is going to get."

'There's no place for me down there, Cat. But I can't be sure if that guy knew what he was talking about until I do some investigating. I need to find out if it really is true that they'll train me, and not just turn me into a soldier."

"Of course they'll turn you into a soldier. They need cannon fodder"

"Well, I need to at least check into it. Find somebody who knows about becoming an Army medic. There's an Army building on campus."

"There sure is. Guess who we've been protesting. The building that houses the campus ROTC office."

"Okay, I'll go talk to them. Maybe somebody there will know about how to be a medic."

"More likely they're in with the local draft board. We talked about this before, John. You may have already gotten drafted back there in Illinois."

"I need to find out about that too."

"Okay, stop. I need some sleep, and knowing you, you may not have slept since forever. Let's go to bed. Just to sleep. Okay? I was already worn out, and now you've worn me down even more with all this talk about joining the enemy."

As soon as we get into her bed, she grabs me. But soon, she's sound asleep and breathing softly.

As I lie there staring up into the darkness, I can't help but remember the first time I was in this bed with her. A lot has happened since then. I've changed, and she's changed too. She's now a full-on anti-war leader and draft counseling manager. Now, she thinks about little else.

And me? How much have I changed? Although my leaving Illinois wasn't actually all that long ago, it seems like another lifetime. For sure, I'm nothing like the naive kid who drove away from Illinois, not having any idea where I was going. I've been in a lot of different situations since then, so many I'm not actually sure how it all happened so fast. Amazing how much inserting yourself into different environments and situations can change who you are. But what about my next step. Am I really going into the Army? Talk about a big change. I could end up in a dramatically different situation in an almost unimaginably different environment. Is Cat right? Will I end up a soldier in a far away place called Vietnam? Who knows who I'd become if that happens.

Chapter Thirty-Six

Cat is up before me, and I'm still getting dressed when she rushes into the bedroom chewing some kind of breakfast bar. She gives me a quick kiss and says, "Got to rush. Don't do anything until I get back. Stay inside."

And then she's gone. I peek out between the curtains and watch her hurry away. She must be heading for the Draft Counseling Center. She probably spends all of her days there now.

Interesting that when I first saw her, she was pretty much by herself, shouting anti-war slogans through a megaphone. Now look at what she's built. She's absolutely sure she's on the side of good and right.

Well, good for her, but I need to do what's right for me. And what is that? This emerging war might well be going to change the lives of every draft-age boy. Will it also change my life?

I guess I'd better go to that on-campus ROTC building and see what I can find out. I hurry to campus and head for the north end, an area I haven't visited much. Sure enough, I see a few young male students in military uniforms going into an older two-story building. That must be the place.

Inside, the building has a really old feel to it: an aging, but still polished, hardwood floor, ornate door frames, a high ceiling. Some of the doors are open, and I can see unformed male students listening to lectures from older men who are also in uniform.

I go up the wide stairs to the second floor where there are only offices. The office at the top of the stairs has a brass plate next to the door labeled "Lieutenant Colonel Richards." The door to that office is open, and there's a desk inside, but nobody is manning it. I go in and there's another office with an open door. The man inside is sitting behind a large desk. He's dressed in a white shirt and a black tie, but there's a dark military uniform coat hanging on a coat rack. He must be the guy in charge.

I tap on his door sill and he looks up from his papers. He hesitates and then waves me in. He says, "What can I do for you son?"

"Sorry to bother you, sir, but I need some information, and I didn't see anybody else to ask."

"Are you a student?"

"I was planning to register this term, but I had to go out of town. But what I wanted to ask about was an Army matter."

"An Army matter. Okay, what is it?"

"Maybe it's too small a matter to bother you with, sir."

"No Army matter is too small a matter for me, son."

"Well, I was thinking about joining up. But I wondered how to become a medic."

"A medic? That's a noble ambition. "You'd better sit down." He gestures to the chair in front of his desk.

"Maybe I shouldn't bother you with something like that."

He leans back in his chair. "What is it you don't want to say, son?"

"Well, I think I might have gotten drafted, but I don't want to shoot people. I'd rather be a medic. Help people."

He smiles what I think could be a wry smile.

"Might have gotten drafted?"

"Well, I came here from Illinois. To go to college. But I'm twenty years old, so I might have already gotten drafted back in Illinois."

He nods, staring at me.

I think I've said too much. This older Army officer with graying hair is probably a long-time military man, and he might think I'm putting down what he's been doing his whole life. "I'm sorry, sir, I'm not saying there's anything wrong with being a soldier. It's just that—"

"It's all right. I appreciate your honesty. Not everyone is cut out to carry a weapon. To want to become a medic is a noble aspiration. But you should know, regarding the draft, you are not in the military until you receive a conscription letter, and you act on it. If you are a student, you might be deferred."

"I thought student deferments were going away."

"There's a lot of rumor and speculation about that. Too much, in my opinion. I teach classes here, classes on aerospace studies, and a lot of my students have already received deferments."

"Oh, okay. So, maybe I could get a deferment."

"You just have to be a full-time student."

"Oh. But my girlfriend told me they're eliminating deferments."

"Your girlfriend knows about such things?"

"Yes. She's involved with the Draft Counseling Center. Downtown."

He smiles. "Oh, yes, I'm familiar with that group. Students. They've been picketing this building."

"Oh, I'm sorry."

"No, it's all right. They have a right to speak their minds. Free speech is an important element of our democracy. But let's get back to your goal of becoming a medic. Have you thought about joining the Army Reserves?"

"I don't know anything about that."

"The Reserves give you the chance to serve and go to school at the same time. You can earn meaningful benefits while serving part-time. They encourage enlistees to develop new skills, like you wanting to learn medical skills. They want to train leaders. Hopefully, after you receive your degree, you'll stay in the Army and serve as an officer."

"I hadn't thought about anything like that. So, enlisting in the Army Reserves could be a way for me to become a medic?"

"Certainly. There's an Army Reserve Enlistment office in Phoenix. You should go talk to them. I'll write down the address."

"Oh, thank you, sir,"

"Fine. If you enlist, come back here, and we'll see about getting you signed up for some of our classes here on this campus. And I think I also know a way to get you involved in some early medical training."

Chapter Thirty-Seven

As soon as I'm out of the building, I head straight for my car back at Cat's apartment. Once there, I hesitate. Before I drive to that Reserve Enlistment office in phoenix, maybe I should go tell Cat the good news. I sure hope she agrees it is good news.

No, I should first go find out how it all works.

Driving away from Tempe toward Phoenix, strangely, it feels very much like that day I drove away from Illinois, as if I'm heading in a new direction, with a new purpose.

Epilogue

I am now a lowly private in the Army Reserves. Cat was not happy that I drove into Phoenix and signed on the dotted line without talking to her about it, but she is happy that, after I finish my initial training, I'll still be able to live with her while I study. I only have to serve one weekend a month, plus two weeks a year of readiness training.

The only possible hitch in that plan is the growing US involvement in Vietnam. More and more US "advisers" are being sent over there to help the South Vietnamese government fight the North Vietnamese Communists. There are now pictures showing up in the news of US military aircraft there, being piloted by American pilots. It's becoming pretty obvious that Cat was right, we *are* very involved in the war that's going on in Vietnam, and we're getting more and more deeply involved every day. It seems like it's only a matter of time before US troops start being sent over there.

And that may include me. At our last meeting, the commander of my unit announced, "If the war really gets going over there in Vietnam, you all should expect that at some point this unit may very well be called up to go there, at least in a support role. That's why we're being kept "combat ready.""

www.ingramcontent.com/pod-product-compliance
Lightning Source LLC
Chambersburg PA
CBHW072216170626
46813CB00003B/958